The Invader

The Invader

A Novel

Margaret L. Woods

MINT EDITIONS

The Invader: A Novel was first published in 1907.

This edition published by Mint Editions 2020.

ISBN 9781513279954 | E-ISBN 9781513284972

Published by Mint Editions®

 MINT
EDITIONS

minteditionbooks.com

Publishing Director: Jennifer Newens
Design & Production: Rachel Lopez Metzger
Project Manager: Micaela Clark
Typesetting: Westchester Publishing Services

CONTENTS

I

Dinner was over and the ladies had just risen, when the Professor had begged to introduce them to the new-comer on his walls. The Invader, it might almost have been called, this full-length, life-size portrait, which, in the illumination of a lamp turned full upon it, seemed to take possession of the small room, to dominate at the end of the polished-oak table, where the light of shaded candles fell on old blue plates, old Venetian glass, a bit of old Italian brocade, and chrysanthemums in a china bowl coveted by collectors. Every detail spoke of the connoisseurship, the refined and personal taste characteristic of Oxford in the eighties. The authority on art put up his eye-glasses and fingered his tiny forked beard uneasily.

"There's no doubt it's a good thing, Fletcher," he said, presently—"really quite good. But it's too like Romney to be Raeburn, and too like Raeburn to be Romney. You ought to be able to find out the painter, if, as you say, it's a portrait of your own great-grandmother—"

"He did say so!" broke in Sanderson, exultantly. "He said it was an ancestress. Fletcher, you're a vulgar fraud. You've got no ancestress. You bought her. There's a sale-ticket still on the frame under the projection at the right-hand lower corner. I saw it."

Sanderson was a small man and walked about perpetually, except when taking food: sometimes then. He was a licensed insulter of his friends, and now stood before the picture in a belligerent attitude. The Professor stroked his amber beard and smiled down on Sanderson.

"True, O Sanderson; and at the same time untrue. I did buy the picture, and the lady was my great-grandmother once, but she did not like the position and soon gave it up. This picture must have been done after she had given it up."

"Is this a conundrum or blather, invented to hide your ignominy in a cloud of words?" asked Sanderson.

"It's a *hors d'oeuvre* before the story," interposed Ian Stewart, throwing back his tall dark head and looking up at the picture through his eye-glasses, his handsome face alive with interest. "'Tak' awa' the kickshaws,' Fletcher, 'and bring us the cauf.'"

The Professor gathered his full beard in one hand and smiled deprecatingly.

"I don't know how the ladies will like my ex-great-grandmother's story. It was a bit of a scandal at the time."

"Never mind, Mr. Fletcher," cried a young married woman, with a face like a seraph, "we're all educated now, and scandal about a lady with her waist under her arms becomes simply classical."

"Not so bad as that, Mrs. Shaw, I assure you," returned the Professor; "but I dare say you all know as much as I do about my great-grandmother, for she was the well-known Lady Hammerton."

There were sounds of interest and surprise, for most of the party knew her name, and were curious to learn how she came to be Professor Fletcher's great-grandmother. Mr. Fletcher explained:

"My great-grandfather was a distinguished professor in Edinburgh a hundred years ago. When he was a widower of forty with a family, he was silly enough to fall in love with a little miss of sixteen. He taught her Latin and Greek—which was all very well—and married her, which was distinctly unwise. She had one son—my grandfather—and then ran away with an actor from London. After that she made a certain sensation on the stage, but I suspect she was clever enough to see that her real successes were personal ones; at all events, she made a good marriage as soon as ever she got the chance. The Hammerton family naturally objected. You'll find all about it in those papers which have come out lately. I believe, ladies, they were almost as much scandalized by her learning as by her morals."

"She told Sydney Smith years after, I think," observed Stewart, "that she had to be a wit lest people should find out she was a blue. There's a good deal about her in the Englefield *Memoirs*. She travelled extraordinarily for a woman in those days, and most of the real treasures at Hammerton House come from her collections."

"I thought they were nearly all burned in a great fire, and she was burned trying to save them," said Mrs. Shaw.

"A good many were saved," returned Fletcher; "she had rushed back to fetch a favorite bronze, was seen hurling it out of the window—and was never seen again."

"She must have been a very remarkable woman," commented Stewart, meditatively, his eyes still fixed on the picture.

"Know nothing about her myself," remarked Sanderson; "Stewart knows something about everybody. It's sickening the way he spends his time reading gossip and calling it history."

"Gossip's like many common things, interesting when fossilized," squeaked a little, white-haired, pink-faced old gentleman, like an elderly cherub in dress-clothes. He had remained at the other end of the room because he did not care for pictures. Now he toddled a little nearer and every one made way for him with a peculiar respect, for he was the Master of Durham, whose name was great in Oxford and also in the world outside it. He looked up first at the pictured face and then at Milly Flaxman, a young cousin of Fletcher's and a scholar of Ascham Hall, who had taken her First in Mods, and was hoping to get one in Greats. The Master liked young girls, but they had to be clever as well as pleasing in appearance to attract his attention.

"It's very like Miss Flaxman," he squeaked.

Every one turned their eyes from the picture to Milly, whose pale cheeks blushed a bright pink. The blush emphasized her resemblance to her ancestress, whose brilliant complexion, however, hinted at rouge. Milly's soft hair was amber-colored, like that of the lady in the picture, but it was strained back from her face and twisted in a minute knot on the nape of her neck. That was the way in which her aunt Lady Thomson, whose example she desired to follow in all things, did her hair. The long, clearly drawn eyebrows, dark in comparison with the amber hair, the turquoise blue eyes, the mouth of the pictured lady were curiously reproduced in Milly Flaxman. Possibly her figure may have been designed by nature to be as slight and supple, yet rounded, as that of the white-robed, gray-scarfed lady above there. But something or some one had intervened, and Milly looked stiff and shapeless in a green velveteen frock, scooped out vaguely around her white young throat and gathered in clumsy folds under a liberty silk sash.

Mrs. Shaw cried out enraptured at the interesting resemblance which had escaped them all, to be instantly caught by the elderly cherub in the background, who did not care about art, while the Professor explained that both Milly's parents were, like himself, great-grandchildren of Lady Hammerton. The seraph now fell upon Milly, too shy to resist, had out her hair-pins in a trice and fingered the fluffy hair till it made an aureole around her face. Then by some conjuring trick producing a gauzy white scarf, Mrs. Shaw twisted it about the girl's head, in imitation of the lady on the wall, who had just such a scarf, but with a tiny embroidered border of scarlet, twisted turban-wise and floating behind.

"There!" she cried, pushing the feebly protesting Milly into the full light of the lamp the Professor was holding, "allow me to present to you the new Lady Hammerton!"

There was a moment of wondering silence. Milly's pulses beat, for she felt Ian Stewart's eyes upon her. Neither he nor any one else there had ever quite realized before what capacities for beauty lay hid in the subdued young face of Milly Flaxman. She had nothing indeed of the charm, at once subtle and challenging, of the lady above there. She, with one hand on the gold head of a tall cane, looking back, seemed to dare unseen adorers to follow her into a magic, perhaps a fatal fairyland of mountain and waterfall and cloud; a land whose dim mists and silver gleams seemed to echo the gray and the white of her floating garments, its autumn leaves to catch a faint reflection from her hair, while far off its sky showed a thin line of sunset, red like the border of her veil. Milly's soft cheeks and lips were flushed, her eyes bright with a mixture of very innocent emotions, as she stood with every one's eyes, including Ian Stewart's, upon her.

But in a minute the Master took up Mrs. Shaw's remark.

"No," he said, emphatically; "not a new Lady Hammerton; only a rather new Miss Flaxman; and that, I assure you, is something very preferable."

"I'm quite sure the Master knows something dreadful about your great-grandmother, Mr. Fletcher," laughed Mrs. Shaw.

"I think we'd better go before he tells it," interposed Mrs. Fletcher, who saw that Milly was feeling shy.

When the ladies had left, the men reseated themselves at the table and there was a pause. Everyone waited for the Master, who seemed meditating speech.

"My mother," he said—and somehow they all felt startled to learn the fact that the Master had had a mother—"my mother knew Lady Hammerton in the twenties. She was often at Bath."

The thin, staccato voice broke off abruptly, and three out of the five other men present being the Master's pupils, remained silent, knowing he had not finished. But Mr. Toovey, a young don overflowing with mild intelligence, exclaimed, deferentially:

"Really, Master! Really! How extremely interesting! Now do please tell us a great deal about Lady Hammerton."

The Master took no notice whatever of Toovey. He sat about a minute longer in his familiar posture, looking before him, his little round hands on his little round knees. Then he said:

"She was a raddled woman."

And his pupils knew he had finished speaking. What he had said was disappointingly little, but uttered in that strange high voice of his, it contained an infinite deal more than appeared on the face of it. A whole discreditable past seemed to emerge from that one word "raddled." Ian Stewart, to whose imagination the woman in the picture made a strange appeal, now broke a lance with the Master on her account.

"She may have been raddled, Master," he said, "but she must have been very remarkable and charming too. Hammerton himself was no fool, yet he adored her to the last."

The Master seemed to hope some one else would speak; but finding that no one did, he uttered again:

"Men often adore bad wives. That does not make them good ones."

Stewart tossed a rebel lock of raven black hair back from his forehead.

"Pardon me, Master, it does make them good wives for those men."

"Oh, surely not good for their higher natures!" protested Toovey, fervently.

The Master took three deliberate sips of port wine.

"I think, Stewart, we are discussing matters we know very little about," he said, in a particularly high, dry voice; and every one felt that the discussion was closed. Then he turned to Sanderson and made some remark about a house which Sanderson's College, of which he was junior bursar, was selling to Durham.

Fletcher, the only married man present, mourned inwardly over his own masculine stupidity. He felt sure that if his wife had been there she would have gently led Stewart's mind through these paradoxical matrimonial fancies, to dwell on another picture; a picture of marriage with a nice girl almost as pretty as Lady Hammerton, a good girl who shared his tastes, and, above all, who adored him. David Fletcher felt himself pitiably unequal to the task, although he was as anxious as his wife was that Stewart should marry Milly. Did not all their friends wish it? It seemed to them that there could not be a more suitable couple. If Milly was working so terribly hard to get her First in Greats, it was largely because Mr. Stewart was one of her tutors and she knew he thought a good deal of success in the Schools.

There could be no doubt about Milly Flaxman's goodness; in fact, some of the girls at Ascham complained that it "slopped over." Her clothes were made on hygienic principles which she treated as a branch of morals, and she often refused to offer the small change of polite society because it weighed somewhat light in the scales of truth. But these were foibles that the young people's friends were sure Ian Stewart would never notice. As to him, although only four and thirty, he was already a distinguished man. A scholar, a philosopher, and an archæologist, he had also imagination and a sense of style. He had written a brilliant book on Greek life at a particular period, which had brought him a reputation among the learned and also found readers in the educated public. His disposition was sweet, his character unusually high, judged even by the standard of the academic world, which has a higher standard than most. Obviously he would make an excellent husband; and equally obviously, as he had no near relations and his health was delicate, it would be a capital thing for him to have a home of his own and a devoted wife to look after him. Their income would be small, but not smaller than that of most young couples in Oxford, who contrived, nevertheless, to live refined and pleasant lives and to be well-considered in a society where money positively did not count.

But if Fletcher did not succeed in forwarding this matrimonial scheme in the dining-room, his wife succeeded no better when the gentlemen came into the drawing-room. She rose from a sofa in the corner, leaving Milly seated there; but Mr. Toovey made his way straight to Miss Flaxman, without a glance to right or left, and bending over her before he seated himself at her side, fixed upon her a patronizing, a possessive smile which would have made some girls long for a barbarous freedom in the matter of face-slapping. But Milly Flaxman was meek. She took Archibald Toovey's seriousness for depth, and as his attentions had become unmistakable, had several times lain awake at night tormenting herself as to whether her behavior towards him was or was not right. Accordingly she submitted to being monopolized by Mr. Toovey, while Ian Stewart turned away and made himself pleasant to an unattractive lady-visitor of the Fletchers', who looked shy and left-alone. When Mrs. Fletcher tried to effect a change of partners, Ian explained that he found himself unexpectedly obliged to attend a College meeting at ten o'clock. In a place where there are no offices to close and business engagements are liable to crop up at any time in the evening, there was no need for extravagance of apology for this early departure.

He changed his shoes in the narrow hall and put on his seedy-looking dark overcoat, quite unconscious that Mrs. Fletcher had had the collar mended since he had taken it off. Then he went out into the damp November night, unlit by moon or star. But to Stewart the darkness of night, on whatever corner of earth he might chance to find it descended, remained always a romantic, mysterious thing, setting his imagination free among visionary possibilities, without form, but not for that void. The road between the railing of the parks and the row of old lopped elms, was ill-lighted by the meagre flame of a few gas-lamps and hardly cheered by the smothered glow of the small prison-like windows of Keble, glimmering through the bare trees. There was not a sound near, except the occasional drip of slow-collecting dews from the branches of the old elms. Afar, too, many would have said there was not a sound; but there was, and Ian's ear was attuned to catch it. The immense inarticulate whisper of night came to him. It came to him from the deserted parks, from the distant Cherwell flowing through its willow-roots and osier-islands, from the flat meadow-country beyond, stretching away to the coppices of the low boundary hills. It was a voice made up of many whispers, each imperceptible, or almost imperceptible in itself; whisper of water and dry reeds, of broken twigs and dry leaves fluttering to the ground, of heaped dead leaves or coarse winter grass, stirring in some slight movement of the air. It seemed to his imagination as though under the darkness, in the loneliness of night, the man-mastered world must be secretly transformed, returned to its primal freedom; and that could he go forth into it alone, he would find it quite different from anything familiar to him, and might meet with something, he knew not what, secret, strange, and perhaps terrible.

Such fancies, though less crystallized than they must needs be by words, floated in the penumbra of his mind, coming to him perhaps with the blood of remote Highland ancestors, children of mountains and mist. His reasonable self was perfectly aware that should he go, he would find nothing in the open fields at that hour except a sleeping cow or two, and would return wet as to the legs, and developing a severe cold for the morning. But he heard these far-off whisperings of the night playing, as it were, a mysterious "ground" to his thoughts of Milly Flaxman. The least fatuous of men, he had yet been obliged to see that his friends in general and the Fletchers in particular, wished him to marry Milly, and that the girl herself hung upon his words with a tremulous sensitivity even greater than the enthusiastic female student usually exhibits towards those of her lecturer. In the abstract he intended to marry; for he did not desire to be left an old bachelor in college. He had been waiting for the great experience of falling in love, and somehow it had never come to him. There were probably numbers of people to whom it never did come. Should he now give up all hope of it, and make a marriage of reason and of obligingness, such as his marriage with Miss Flaxman would assuredly be? Thank Heaven! as her tutor he could not possibly propose to her till she had got through the Schools, so there were more than six months in which to consider the question.

And while he communed thus with himself, the mysterious whispers of the night came nearer to him, in the blackness of garden trees, ancient trees of College gardens brooding alone, whispering alone through the dark hours, of that current of young life which is still flowing past them; how for hundreds of years it has always been flowing, and always passing, passing, passing so quickly to the great silent sea of death and oblivion, to the dark night whose silence is only sometimes stirred by vague whispers, anxious yet faint, dying upon the ear before the sense can seize them.

II

Parties in Oxford always break up early, and Milly had a good excuse for carrying her aching, disappointed heart back to Ascham at ten o'clock, for every one knew she was working hard. Too hard, Mr. Fletcher said, looking concernedly at her heavy eyes, mottled complexion, and the little crumples which were beginning to come in her low white forehead. Her cousins, however, had more than a suspicion that these marks of care and woe were not altogether due to her work, but that Ian Stewart was accountable for most of them.

The Professor escorted her to the gates of the Ladies' College; but she walked down the dark drive alone, mindful of familiar puddles, and hearing nothing of those mysterious whispers of night which in Ian Stewart's ears had breathed a "ground" to his troubled thoughts of her.

She mounted the stairs to her room at the top of the house. It was an extremely neat room, and by day, when the bed was disguised as a sofa, and the washstand closed, there was nothing to reveal that it served as a bedroom, although a tarnished old mirror hung in a dark corner. The oak table and pair of brass candlesticks upon it were kept in shining order by Milly's own zealous hands.

Milly found her books open at the right place and her writing materials ready to hand. In a very few minutes her outer garments and simple ornaments were put away, and clothed in a clean but shrunk and faded blue dressing-gown, she sat down to work. The work was Aristotle's *Ethics*, and she was going through it for the second time, amplifying her notes. But this second time the Greek seemed more difficult, the philosophic argument more intricate than ever. She had had very little sleep for weeks, and her head ached in a queer way as though something inside it were strained very tight. It was plain that she had come to the end of her powers of work for the present—and she had calculated that only by not wasting a day, except for a week's holiday at Easter, could she get through all that had to be done before the Schools!

She put Aristotle away and opened Mommsen, but even to that she could not give her attention. Her thoughts returned to the bitter disappointment which the evening had brought. Ian Stewart had been next her at dinner, but even then he had talked to her rather less than to Mrs. Shaw. Afterwards—well, perhaps it was only what she deserved for not making it plain to poor Mr. Toovey that she could never return his feelings. And now the First, which she had looked to as a thing that would set her nearer the level of her idol, was dropping below the horizon of the possible. Aunt Beatrice always said—and she was right—that tears were not, as people pretended, a help and solace in trouble. They merely took the starch out of you and left you a poor soaked, limp creature, unfit to face the hard facts of life. But sometimes tears will lie heavy and scalding as molten lead in the brain, until at length they force their way through to the light. And Milly after blowing her nose a good deal, as she mechanically turned the pages of Mommsen, at length laid her arms on the book and transferred her handkerchief to her eyes. But she tried to look as though she were reading when Flora Timson came in.

"At it again, M.! You know you're simply working yourself stupid."

Thus speaking, Miss Timson, known to her intimates at Ascham as "Tims," wagged sagely her very peculiar head. A crimson silk handkerchief was tied around it, turban-wise, and no vestige of hair escaped from beneath. There was in fact none to escape. Tims's sallow, comic little face had neither eyebrows nor eyelashes on it, and her small figure was not of a quality to triumph over the obvious disadvantages of a tight black cloth dress with bright buttons, reminiscent of a page's suit.

Milly pushed the candles farther away and looked up.

"I was wanting to see you, Tims. Do tell me whether you managed to get out of Miss Walker what Mr. Stewart said about my chances of a First."

Tims pushed her silk turban still higher up on her forehead.

"I can always humbug Miss Walker and make her say lots of indiscreet things," Tims returned, with labored diplomacy. "But I don't repeat them—at least, not invariably."

There was a further argument on the point, which ended by Milly shedding tears and imploring to be told the worst.

Tims yielded.

"Stewart said your scholarship was A 1, but he was afraid you wouldn't get your First in Greats. He said you had a lot of difficulty in expressing yourself and didn't seem to get the lead of their philosophy and stuff—and—and generally wanted cleverness."

"He said that?" asked Milly, in a low, sombre voice, speaking as though to herself. "Well, I suppose it's better for me to know—not to go on hoping, and hoping, and hoping. It means less misery in the end, no doubt."

There was such a depth of despair in her face and voice that Tims was appalled at the consequence of her own revelation. She paced the room in agitation, alternately uttering incoherent abuse of her friend's folly and suggesting that she should at once abandon the ungrateful School of *Literæ Humaniores* and devote herself like Tims, to the joys of experimental chemistry and the pleasures of practical anatomy.

Meantime, Milly sat silent, one hand supporting her chin, the other playing with a pencil.

At length Tims, taking hold of Milly under the arms, advised her to "go to bed and sleep it off."

Milly rose dully and sat on the edge of her bed, while Tims awkwardly removed the hair-pins which Mrs. Shaw had so deftly put in. But as she was laying them on the little dressing-table, Milly suddenly flung herself down on the bed and lay there a twisted heap of blue flannel, her face buried in the pillows, her whole body shaken by a paroxysm of sobs. Tims supposed that this might be a good thing for Milly; but for herself it created an awkward situation. Her soothing remarks fell flat, while to go away and leave her friend in this condition would seem brutal. She sat down to "wait till the clouds rolled by," as she phrased it. But twenty minutes passed and still the clouds did not roll by.

"Look here, M." she said, argumentatively, standing by the bed. "You're in hysterics. That's what's the matter with you."

"I know I am," came in tones of muffled despair from the pillow.

"Well!" Tims was very stern and accented her words heavily, "then—pull—yourself—together—dear girl. Sit up!"

Milly sat up, pressed her handkerchief over her face, and held her breath. For a minute all was quiet; then another violent sob forced a passage.

"It's no use, Tims," she gasped. "I cannot—cannot—stop. Oh, what would—!" She was going to say, "What would Aunt Beatrice think of me if she knew how I was giving way!" but a fresh flood of tears suppressed her speech. "My head's so bad! Such a splitting headache!"

Tims tried scolding, slapping, a cold sponge, every remedy inexperience could suggest, but the hysterical weeping could not be checked.

"Look here, old girl," she said at length, "I know how I can stop you, but I don't believe you'll let me do it."

"No, not that, Tims! You know Miss Burt doesn't—"

"Doesn't approve. Of course not. Perhaps you think old B. would approve of the way you're going on now. Ha! Would she!"

The sarcasm caused a new and alarming outburst. But finally, past all respect for Miss Burt, and even for Lady Thomson herself, Milly consented to submit to any remedy that Tims might choose to try.

She was assisted hurriedly to undress and put to bed. Tims knew the whereabouts of the prize-medal which Milly had won at school, and placing the bright silver disk in her hand, directed her to fix her eyes upon it. Seated on her heels on the patient's bed, her crimson turban low on her forehead, her face screwed into intent wrinkles, Tims began passing her slight hands slowly before Milly's face.

The long slender fingers played about the girl's fair head, sometimes pressed lightly upon her forehead, sometimes passed through her fluffy hair, as it lay spread on the pillow about her like an amber cloud.

"Don't cry, M.," Tims began repeating in a soft, monotonous voice. "You've got nothing to cry about; your head doesn't ache now. Don't cry."

At first it was only by a strong effort that Milly could keep her tear-blinded eyes fixed on the bright medal before her; but soon they became chained to it, as by some attractive force. The shining disk seemed to grow smaller, brighter, to recede imperceptibly till it was a point of light somewhere a long way off, and with it all the sorrows and agitations of her mind seemed also to recede into a dim distance, where she was still aware of them, yet as though they were some one else's sorrows and agitations, hardly at all concerning her. The aching tension of her brain was relaxed and she felt as though she were drowning without pain or struggle, gently floating down, down through a green abyss of water, always seeing that distant light, showing as the sun might show, seen from the depths of the sea.

Before a quarter of an hour had passed, her sobs ceased in sighing breaths, the breaths became regular and normal, the whole face slackened and smoothed itself out. Tims changed the burden of her song.

"Go to sleep, Milly. What you want is a good long sleep. Go to sleep, Milly."

Milly was sinking down upon the pillow, breathing the calm breath of deep, refreshing slumber. Tims still crouched upon the bed, chanting her monotonous song and contemplating her work. At length she slipped off, conscious of pins-and-needles in her legs, and as she withdrew, Milly with a sudden motion stretched her body out in the white bed, as straight and still almost as that of the dead. The movement was mechanical, but it gave a momentary check to Tims's triumph. She leaned over her patient and began once more the crooning song.

"Go to sleep, M.! What you want is a good long sleep. Go to sleep, Milly!"

But presently she ceased her song, for it was evident that Milly Flaxman had indeed gone very sound asleep.

III

Tims was proud of the combined style and economy of her dress. She was constantly discovering and revealing to an unappreciative world the existence of superb tailors who made amazingly cheap dresses. For two years she had been vainly advising her friends to go to the man who had made her the frock she still wore for morning; a skirt and coat of tweed with a large green check in it, a green waistcoat with gilt buttons, and green gaiters to match. In this costume and coiffed with a man's wig, of the vague color peculiar to such articles, Tims came down at her usual hour, prepared to ask Milly what she thought of hypnotism now. But there was no Milly over whom to enjoy this petty triumph. She climbed to the top story as soon as breakfast was over, and entering Milly's room, found her patient still sleeping soundly, low and straight in the bed, just as she had been the preceding night. She was breathing regularly and her face looked peaceful, although her eyes were still stained with tears. The servant came in as Tims was looking at her.

"I've tried to wake Miss Flaxman, miss," she said. "She's always very particular as I should wake her, but she was that sound asleep this morning, I 'adn't the 'eart to go on talking. Poor young lady! I expect she's pretty well wore out, working away at her books, early and late, the way she does."

"Better leave her alone, Emma," agreed Tims. "I'll let Miss Burt know about it."

Miss Burt was glad to hear Milly Flaxman was oversleeping herself. She had not been satisfied with the girl's appearance of late, and feared Milly worked too hard and had bad nights.

Tims had to go out at ten o'clock and did not return until luncheon-time. She went up to Milly's room and knocked at the door. As before, there was no answer. She went in and saw the girl still sound asleep, straight and motionless in the bed. Her appearance was so healthy and natural that it was absurd to feel uneasy at the length of her slumber, yet remembering the triumph of hypnotism, Tims did feel a little uneasy. She spoke to Miss Burt again about Milly's prolonged sleep, but Miss Burt was not inclined to be anxious. She had strictly forbidden Tims to hypnotize—or as she called it, mesmerize—any one in the house, so that Tims said no more on the subject. She was working at the Museum in the early part of the afternoon, only leaving it when the light began to fail. But after work she went straight back to Ascham. Milly was still asleep, but she had slightly shifted her position, and altogether there was something about her aspect which suggested a slumber less profound than before. Tims leaned over her and spoke softly:

"Wake up, M., wake up! You've been asleep quite long enough."

Milly's body twitched a little. A responsive flicker which was almost a convulsion, passed over her face; but she did not awake. It was evident, however, that her spirit was gradually floating up to the surface from the depths of oblivion in which it had been submerged. Tims took off her Tam-o'-Shanter and ulster, and revealed in the simple elegance of the tweed frock with green waistcoat and gaiters, put the kettle on the fire. Then she went down-stairs to fetch some bread and butter and an egg, wherewith to feed the patient when she awoke.

She had not long left the room when the slumberer's eyes opened gradually and stared with the fixity of semi-consciousness at a stem of blossoming jessamine in the wall-paper. Then she slowly stretched her arms above her head until some inches of wrist, slight and round and white, emerged from the strictly plain night-gown sleeve. So she lay, till suddenly, almost with a start, she pulled herself up and looked about her. The gaze of her wide-open eyes travelled questioningly around the quiet-toned room which two windows at right angles to each other still kept light with the reflection of a yellow winter sunset. She pushed the bedclothes down, dropped first one bare white foot, then the other to the ground and looked doubtfully at a pair of worn felt slippers which were placed beside the bed, before slipping her feet into them. With the same air as of one assuming garments which do not belong to her, she put on the faded blue flannel dressing-gown. Then she walked to the southern window. None of the glories of Oxford were visible from it; only the bare branches of trees through which appeared a huddle of somewhat sordid looking roofs and the unimposing spire of St. Aloysius. With the same air, questioning yet as in a dream, she turned to the western window, which was open. Below, in its wintry dulness, lay the garden of the College, bounded by an old gray wall which divided it from the straggling street; beyond that, a mass of slate roofs. But a certain glory was on the slate roofs and all the garden that was not in shadow. For away over Wytham, where the blue vapor floated in the folds of the hills, blending imperceptibly with the deep brown of the leafless woods, sunset had lifted a wide curtain of cloud and showed between the gloom of heaven and earth, a long straight pool of yellow light.

She leaned out of the window. A mild fresh air which seemed to be pouring over the earth through that rift in heaven which the sunset had made, breathed freshly on her face and the yellow light shone on her amber hair, which lay on her shoulders about the length of the hair of an angel in some old Florentine picture.

Miss Burt in galoshes and with a wrap over her head was coming up the garden. She caught sight of that vision of gold and pale blue in the window and smiled and waved her hand to Milly Flaxman. The vision withdrew, trembling slightly as though with cold, and closed the window.

Tims came in, carrying a boiled egg and a plate of bread and butter. Tims put down the egg-cup and the plate on the table before she relaxed the wrinkle of carefulness and grinned triumphantly at her patient.

"Well, old girl," she asked; "what do you say to hypnotism now? Put *you* to sleep, right enough, anyhow. Know what time it is?"

The awakened sleeper made a few steps forward, leaned her hands on the table, on the other side of which Tims stood, and gazed upon her with startling intentness. Then she began to speak in a rapid, urgent voice. Her words were in themselves ordinary and distinct, yet what she said was entirely incomprehensible, a nightmare of speech, as though some talking-machine had gone wrong and was pouring out a miscellaneous stock of verbs, nouns, adjectives and the rest without meaning or cohesion. Certain words reappeared with frequency, but Tims had a feeling that the speaker did not attach their usual meaning to them. This travesty of language went on for what appeared to the transfixed and terrified listener quite a long time. At length the serious, almost tragic, babbler, meeting with no response save the staring horror of Tims's too expressive countenance, ended with a supplicating smile and a glance which contrived to be charged at once with pathos and coquetry. This smile, this look, were so totally unlike any expression which Tims had ever seen on Milly's countenance that they heightened her feeling of nightmare. But she pulled herself together and determined to show presence of mind. She had already placed a basket-chair by the fire ready for her patient, and now gently but firmly led Milly to it.

"Sit down, Milly," she said—and the use of her friend's proper name showed that she felt the occasion to be serious—"and don't speak again till you've had some tea. Your head will be clearer presently, it's a bit confused now, you know."

The stranger Milly, still so unlike the Milly of Tims's intimacy, far from exerting the unnatural strength of a maniac, passively permitted herself to be placed in the chair and listened to what Tims was saying with the puzzled intentness of a child or a foreigner, trying to understand. She laid her head back in its little cloud of amber hair, and looked up at Tims, who, frowning portentously, once more with lifted finger enjoined silence. Tims then concealing her agitation behind a cupboard-door, reached down the tea-things. By some strange accident the methodical Milly's teapot was absent from its place; a phenomenon for which Tims was thankful, as it imposed upon her the necessity of leaving her patient for a few minutes. Shaking her finger again at Milly still more emphatically, she went out, and locked the door behind her. After a moment's thought, she reluctantly decided to report the matter to Miss Burt. But Miss Burt was closeted with the treasurer and an architect from London, and was on no account to be disturbed. So Tims went up to her own room and rapidly revolved the situation. She was certain that Milly was not physically ill; on the contrary, she looked much better than she had looked on the previous day. This curious affection of the speech-memory might be hysterical, as her sobbing the night before had been, or it might be connected with some little failure of circulation in the brain; an explanation, perhaps, pointed to by the extraordinary length of her sleep. Anyhow, Tims felt sceptical as to a doctor being of any use.

She went to her cupboard to take out her own teapot, and her eye fell upon a small medicine bottle marked "Brandy." Milly was a convinced teetotaller; all the more reason, thought Tims, why a dose of alcohol should give her nerves and circulation a fillip, only she must not know of it, or she would certainly refuse the remedy.

Pocketing the bottle and flourishing the teapot, Tims mounted again to Milly's room. Her patient, who had spent the time wandering about the room and examining everything in it, as well as she could in the fast-falling twilight, resumed her position in the chair as soon as she heard a step in the passage, and greeted her returning keeper with an attractive smile. Tims uttering words of commendation, slyly poured some brandy into one of the large teacups before lighting the candles.

"Now, my girl," she said, when she had made the tea, "drink this, and you'll feel better."

Milly leaned forward, her round chin on her hand, and looked intently at the tea-service and at the proffered cup. Then she suddenly raised her head, clapped her hands softly, and cried in a tone of delighted discovery, "Tea!"

"Excuse me," she added, taking the cup with a little bow; and in two seconds had helped herself to three lumps of sugar. Tims was surprised, for Milly never took sugar in her tea.

"That's right, M., you're going along well!" cried Tims, standing on the hearth-rug, with one hand under her short coat-tails, while she gulped her own tea, and ate two pieces of bread and butter put together. Milly ate hers and drank her tea daintily, looking meanwhile at her companion with wonder which gradually gave way to amusement. At length leaning forward with a dimpling smile, she interrogated very politely and quite lucidly.

"Pardon me, sir, you are—? Ah, the doctor, no doubt! My poor head, you see!" and she drew her fingers across her forehead.

Tims started, and grabbed her wig, as was her wont in moments of agitation. She stood transfixed, the teacup at a dangerous angle in her extended hand.

"Good God!" she exclaimed. "You are mad and no mistake, my poor old girl."

The "old girl" made a supreme effort to contain herself, and then burst into a pretty, rippling laugh in which there was nothing familiar to Tims's ear. She rose from her chair vivaciously and took the cup from Tims's hand, to deposit it in safety on the chimney piece.

"How silly I was!" she cried, regarding Tims sparklingly. "Do you know I was not quite sure whether you were a man or a woman. Of course I see now, and I'm so glad. I do like men, you know, so much better than women."

"Milly," retorted Tims, sternly, settling her wig. "You are mad, you need not be bad as well. But it's my own fault for giving you that brandy. You know as well as I do that I hate men—nasty, selfish, guzzling, conceited, guffawing brutes! I never wanted to speak to a man in my life, except in the way of business."

Milly waved her amber head gracefully for a moment as though at a loss, then returned playfully, "That must be because the women spoil you so."

Tims smiled sardonically; but regaining her sense of the situation, out of which she had been momentarily shocked, applied herself to the problem of calling back poor Milly's wandering mind.

"Sit down, my girl," she said, abruptly, putting her arm around Milly's body, so soft and slender in the scanty folds of the blue dressing-gown. Milly obeyed precipitately. Then drawing a small chair close to her, Tims said in gentle tones which could hardly have been recognized as hers:

"M., darling, do you know where you are?"

Milly turned on her a face from which the unnatural vivacity had fallen like a mask; the appealing face of a poor lost child.

"Am I—am I—in a *maison de santé*?" she asked tremulously, fixing her blue eyes on Tims, full of piteous anxiety.

"A lunatic asylum? Certainly not," replied Tims. "Now don't begin crying again, old girl. That's how the trouble began."

"Was it?" asked Milly, dreamily. "I thought it was—" she paused, frowning before her in the air, as though trying to pursue with her bodily vision some recollection which had flickered across her consciousness only to disappear.

"Well, never mind that now," said Tims, hastily; "get your bearings right first. You're in Ascham College."

"A College!" repeated Milly vaguely, but in a moment her face brightened, "I know. A place of learning where they have professors and things. Are you a professor?"

"No, I'm a student. So are you."

Milly looked fixedly at Tims, then smiled a melancholy smile. "I see," she said, "we're both studying—medicine—medicine for the mind." She stood up, locked her hands behind her head in her soft hair and wailed miserably. "Oh, why won't some kind person come and tell me where I am, and what I was before I came here?"

Tears of wounded feelings sprang to Tims's eyes. "Milly, my beauty!" she cried despairingly, "I'm trying to be kind to you and tell you everything you want to know. Your name is Mildred Flaxman and you used to live in Oxford here, but now all your people have gone to Australia because your father's got a deanery there."

"Have they left me here, mad and by myself?" asked Milly; "have I no one to look after me, no one to give me a home?"

"I suppose Lady Thomson or the Fletchers would," returned Tims, "but you haven't wanted one. You've been quite happy at Ascham. Do try and remember. Can't you remember getting your First in Mods. and how you've been working to get one in Greats? Your brain's been right enough until to-day, old girl, and it will be again. I expect it's a case of collapse of memory from overwork. Things will come back to you soon and I'll help you all I can. Do try and recollect me—Tims." There was an unmistakable choke in Tims's voice. "We have been such chums. The others are all pretty nasty to me sometimes—they seem to think I'm a grinning, wooden Aunt Sally, stuck up for them to shy jokes at. But you've never once been nasty to me, M., and there's precious few things I wouldn't do to help you. So don't go talking to me as though there weren't any one in the world who cared a brass farthing about you."

"I'm sure I'm most thankful to find I have got some one here who cares about me," returned Milly, meekly, passing her hand across her eyes for lack of a handkerchief. "You see, it's dreadful for me to be like this. I seem to know what things are, and yet I don't know. A little while ago it seemed to me I was just going to remember something— something different from what you've told me. But now it's all gone again. Oh, please give me a handkerchief!"

Tims opened one of Milly's tidy drawers and sought for a handkerchief. When she had found it, Milly was standing before the high chimney-piece, over which hung a long, low mirror about a foot wide and divided into three parts by miniature pilasters of tarnished gilt. The mirror, too, was tarnished here and there, but it had been a good glass and showed undistorted the blue Delft jars on the mantel-shelf, glimpses of flickering firelight in the room, amber hair and the tear-bedewed roses of a flushed young face. Suddenly Milly thrust the jars aside, seized the candle from the table, and, holding it near her face, looked intently, anxiously in the glass. The anxiety vanished in a moment, but not the intentness. She went on looking. Tims had always perceived Milly's beauty—which had an odd way of slipping through the world unobserved—but had never seen her look so lovely as now, her eyes wide and brilliant, and her upper lip curved rosily over a shining glimpse of her white teeth.

Beauty had an extraordinary fascination for Tims, poor step-child of nature! Now she stood looking at the reflection of Milly without noticing how in the background her own strange, wizened face peered dim and grotesque from the tarnished mirror, like the picture of a witch or a goblin behind the fair semblance of some princess in a fairy tale.

　　　MARGARET L. WOODS

"I do remember myself partly," said Milly, doubtfully; "and yet—somehow not quite. I suppose I shall remember you and this queer place soon, if they don't put me into a mad-house at once."

"They sha'n't," said Tims, decisively. "Trust to me, M., and I'll see you through. But I'm afraid you'll have to give up all thought of your First."

"My what," asked Milly, turning round inquiringly.

"Your First Class, your place, you know, in the Final Honors School, Lit. Hum., the biggest examination of the lot."

"Do I want it very much, my First?"

"Want it? I should just think you do want it!"

Milly stared at the fire for a minute, warming one foot before she spoke again. Then:

"How funny of me!" she observed, meditatively.

IV

Tims's programme happened to be full on the following day, so that it was half-past twelve before she knocked at Milly's door and was admitted. Milly stood in the middle of the room in an attitude of energy, with her small wardrobe lying about her on the floor in ignominious heaps.

"Tell me, Tims," said Milly, after the first inquiries, "are those positively all the clothes I possess?"

"Of course they are, M. What do you want with more?"

"Are they in the fashion?" asked Milly, anxiously.

Tims stared.

"Fashion! Good Lord, M.! What does it matter whether you look the same as every fool in the street or not?"

"Oh, Tims!" cried Milly, laughing that pretty rippling laugh so strange in Tims's ears. "I was quite right when I made a mistake, you're just like a man. All the better. But you can't expect me not to care a bit about my clothes like you, you really can't."

Tims drew herself up.

"You're wrong, my girl, I'm a deal fonder of frocks than you are. I always think," she added, looking before her dreamily, "that I was meant to be a very good dresser, only I was brought up too economical." Generally speaking, when Tims had uttered one of her deepest and truest feelings, she would glance around, suddenly alert and suspicious to surprise the twinkle in her auditor's eye. But in the clear blue of Milly Flaxman's quiet eyes, she had ceased to look for that tormenting twinkle, that spark which seemed destined to dance about her from the cradle to the grave.

Presently she found herself hanging up Milly's clothes while Milly paid no attention; for she alternately stood before the glass in the dark corner, and kneeled on the hearth-rug, curling-tongs in hand. And the hair, the silky soft amber hair, which could be twisted into a tiny ball or fluffed into a golden fleece at will, was being tossed up and pulled down, combed here and brushed there, altogether handled with a zeal and patience to which it had been a stranger since the days when it had been the pride of the nursery. Tims the untidy, as one in a dream, went on tidying the room she was accustomed to see so immaculate.

"There!" cried Milly, turning, "that's how I wear it, isn't it?"

"Good Lord, no!" exclaimed Tims, contemplating the transformed Milly. "It suits you, M., in a way, but it looks queer too. The others will all be hooting if you go down-stairs like that."

Milly plumped into a chair irritably.

"How ever am I to know how I did my hair if I can't remember? Please do it for me."

Tims smiled sardonically.

"I'll lend you my hair," she said; "the second best. But *do* your hair! You really are as mad as a hatter."

Milly shrugged her shoulders.

"You can't? Then I keep it like this," she said.

An argument ensued. Tims left the room to try and find a photograph of Milly as she had been.

When she returned she found her friend standing in absorbed contemplation of a book in her hand.

"This is Greek, isn't it?" she asked, holding it up. Her face wore a little frown as of strained attention.

"Right you are," shrieked Tims in accents of relief. "Greek it is. Can you read it?"

"Not yet," replied Milly, flushing with excitement, "but I shall soon, I know I shall. Last night I couldn't make head or tail of the books. Now I understand right enough what they are, and I know some are in Greek and some in English. I can't read either yet, but it's all coming back gradually, like the daylight coming in at the window this morning."

"Hooray! Hooray!" shouted Tims. "You'll be reading as hard as ever in a week if I don't look after you. But see here, my girl, you've given me a nasty jar, and I'm not going to let you break your heart or crack your brain in a wild-goose chase. You can't get that First, you know; you're on a fairly good Second Class level, and you'd better make up your mind to stay there."

"A fairly good Second Class level!" repeated Milly, still turning the leaves of the book. "That doesn't sound very exhilarating—and I rather think I shall do as I like about staying there."

Tims began to heat.

"Well, that's what Stewart said about you. I don't believe I told you half plain enough what Stewart did say, for fear of hurting your feelings. He said you are a good scholar, but barring that, you weren't at all clever."

Milly looked up from her book; but she was not tearful. There was a curl in her lip and the light of battle in her eye.

"Stewart said that, did he? Now if I were a gentleman I should say—'damn his impudence'—and 'who the devil is Stewart'; but then I'm not. You can say it."

Tims stared. "Oh, come, I say!" she exclaimed. "I don't swear, I only quote. But my goodness, when you remember who Stewart is, you'll be—well, pained to think of the language you're using about him."

"Why?" asked Milly, her head riding disdainfully on her slender neck.

"Because he's your tutor and lecturer—and a regular tiptop man at Greek and all that—and you—you respect him most awfully."

"Do I?" cried Milly—"did perhaps in my salad days. I've no respect whatever for professors now, my good Tims. I know what they're like. Here's Stewart for you."

She took up a pen and a scrap of paper and dashed off a clever ludicrous sketch of a man with long hair, an immense brow, and spectacles.

"Nonsense!" said Tims; "that's not a bit like him."

She held the paper in her hand and looked fixedly at it. Milly had been wont seriously to grieve over her hopeless lack of artistic talent and she had never attempted to caricature. Tims was thinking of a young fellow of a college who had lately died of brain disease. In the earlier stages of his insanity, it had been remarked that he had an originality which had not been his when in a normal state. What if her friend were developing the same terrible disease? If it were so, it was no use fussing, since there was no remedy. Still, she felt a desperate need to take some sort of precaution.

"If I were you, M.," she said, "I'd go to bed and keep very quiet for a day or two. You're so—so odd, and excited, they'd notice it if you went down-stairs."

"Would they?" asked Milly, suddenly sobered. "Would they say I was mad?" An expression of fear came into her face, and its strangely luminous eyes travelled around the room with a look as of some trapped creature seeking escape.

There was an awkward pause.

"I'm not mad," affirmed Milly, swallowing with a dry throat. "I'm perfectly sensible, but any one would be odd and excited too who was—was as I am—with a number of words and ideas floating in my mind without my having the least idea where they spring from. Please, Tims dear, tell me how I am to behave. I should so hate to be thought queer, wanting in any way."

Tims considered.

"For one thing, you mustn't talk such a lot. You never have been one for chattering; and lately, of course, with your overwork, you've been particularly quiet. Don't talk, M., that's my advice."

"Very well," replied Milly, gloomily.

Tims hesitated and went on:

"But I don't see how you're going to hide up this business about your memory. I wish you'd let me tell old B., anyhow."

"I won't have any one told," cried Milly. "Not a creature. If only you'll help me, dear, dear Tims—you will help me, won't you?—I shall soon be all right, and no one except you will ever know. No one will be able to shrug their shoulders and say, whatever I do, 'Of course she's crazy.' I should hate it so! I know I can get on if I try. I'm much cleverer than you and that silly old Stewart think. Promise me, promise me, darling Tims, you won't betray me!"

Tims was not weak-minded, but she was very tender-hearted and exceedingly susceptible to personal charms. She ought not, she knew she ought not, to have yielded, but she did. She promised. Yet in her friend's own interest, she contended that Milly must confess to a certain failure of memory from over-fatigue, if only as a pretext for dropping her work for a while. It was agreed that Milly should remain in bed for several days, and she did so; less bored than might have been expected, because she had the constant excitement of this or that bit of knowledge filtering back into her mind. But this knowledge was purely intellectual. With Tims's help she had recovered her reading powers, and although she felt at first only a vague recognition of something familiar in the sense of what she read, it was evident that she was fast regaining the use of the treasures stored in her brain by years of dogged and methodical work. But the facts and personalities which had made her own life seemed to have vanished, leaving "not a wrack behind."

Tims, having primed her well beforehand, brought in the more important girls to see her, and by dint of a cautious reserve she passed very well with them, as with Miss Burt and Miss Walker. Tims seemed to feel much more nervous than Milly herself did when she joined the other students as usual.

There were moments when Tims gasped with the certainty that the revelation of her friend's blank ignorance of the place and people was about to be made. Then Mildred—for so, despising the soft diminutive, she now desired to be called—by some extraordinary exertion of tact and ingenuity, would evade the inevitable and appear on the other side of it, a little elated, but otherwise serene. It was generally marked that Miss Flaxman was a different creature since she had given up worrying about her Schools, and that no one would have believed how much prettier she could make herself by doing her hair a different way.

Miss Burt, however, was somewhat puzzled and uneasy. Although Milly was looking unusually well, it was evident that all was not quite right with her, for she complained of a failure of memory, a mental fatigue which made it impossible for her to go to lectures, and she seemed to have lost all interest in the Schools, which had so lately been for her the "be-all" as well as the "end-all here." Miss Burt knew Milly's only near relation in England, Lady Thomson, intimately; and for that reason hesitated to write to her. She knew that Beatrice Thomson had no patience with the talk—often silly enough—about girls overworking their brains. She herself had never been laid up in her life, except when her leg was broken, and her views on the subject of ill-health were marked. She regarded the catching of scarlet-fever or influenza as an act of cowardice, consumption or any organic disease as scarcely, if at all, less disgraceful than drunkenness or fraud, while the countless little ailments to which feminine flesh seems more particularly heir she condemned as the most deplorable of female failings, except the love of dress.

Eventually Miss Burt did write to Lady Thomson, cautiously. Lady Thomson replied that she was coming up to town on Thursday, and could so arrange her journey as to have an hour and a half in Oxford. She would be at Ascham at three-thirty. Mildred rushed to Tims with the agitating news and both were greatly upset by it. However, Aunt Beatrice had got to be faced sometime or other and Mildred's spirit rose to the encounter.

She had by this time provided herself with another dress, encouraged to do so by the money in hand left by the frugal Milly the First. She had got a plain tailor-made coat and skirt, in a becoming shade of brown; and with the unbecoming hard collar *de rigueur* in those days, she wore a turquoise blue tie, which seemed to reflect the color of her eyes. And in spite of Tims's dissuasions, she put on the new dress on Thursday, and declined to screw her hair up in the old way, as advised.

Accordingly on Thursday at twenty-five minutes to four, Mildred appeared, in answer to a summons, in the quiet-colored, pleasant drawing-room at Ascham, with its French windows giving on to the lawn, where some of the girls were playing hockey, not without cries.

Her first view of Aunt Beatrice was a pleasant surprise. A tall, upstanding figure, draped in a long, soft cloak trimmed with fur, a handsome face with marked features, marked eyebrows, a fine complexion and bright brown eyes under a wide-brimmed felt hat.

Having exchanged the customary peck, she waited in silence till Mildred had seated herself. Then surveying her niece with satisfaction:

"Come, Milly," said she, in a full, pleasant voice; "I don't see much signs of the nervous invalid about you. Really, Polly," turning to Miss Burt, "she has not looked so well for a long time."

"She's been much better since she dropped her work," replied Miss Burt.

"Taking plenty of fresh air and exercise, I suppose"—Aunt Beatrice smiled kindly on her niece—"I'm afraid I've kept you from your hockey this afternoon, Milly."

"Oh no, Aunt Beatrice, certainly not," replied Milly, with the extreme courtesy of nervousness. "I never play hockey now."

Lady Thomson turned to the Head with a shade of triumph in her satisfaction.

"There, Polly! What did I tell you? I was sure there was something else at the bottom of it. Steady work, methodically done, never hurt anybody. But of course if she's given up exercise, her liver or something was bound to get out of order."

"No, really, I take lots of exercise," interposed Milly; "only I don't care for hockey, it's such a horrid, rough, dirty game; don't you think so? And Miss Walker got a front tooth broken last winter."

Lady Thomson looked at her in a surprised way.

"Well, if you've not been playing hockey, what exercise have you been taking?"

"Walks," replied Milly, feebly, feeling herself on the wrong track; "I go walks with Ti—with Flora Timson when she has time."

Aunt Beatrice looked at the matter judicially.

"Of course, games are best for the physique. Look at men. Still, walking will do, if one takes proper walks. I hope Flora Timson takes you good long walks."

"Indeed she does!" cried Milly. "Immense! She walks a dreadful pace, and we get over stiles and things."

"Immense is a little vague. How far do you go on an average?"

Mildred's notions of distance were vague. "Quite two miles, I'm sure," she responded, cheerfully.

Aunt Beatrice made no comment. She looked steadily and scrutinizingly at her niece, and in a kind but deepened voice told her to go up to her room, whither she, Lady Thomson, would follow in a few minutes, just to see how the Mantegnas looked now they were framed.

As soon as the door had closed behind Mildred, she turned to Miss Burt. "You're right, in a way, Polly, after all. There is something odd about Milly, but I think it's affectation. Did you hear her answer? Two miles! When to my knowledge she can easily walk ten."

Meantime, Mildred mounted slowly to her room. She had tidied it under Tims's instructions and had nothing to do but to sit down and think until Lady Thomson's masculine step was heard outside her door.

Aunt Beatrice came in and laid aside her hat and cloak, showing a dress of rough gray tweed, and short—so far a tribute to the practical—but otherwise made on some awkward artistic or hygienic principle. Her glossy brown hair was brushed back and twisted tight, as Milly's used to be, but with different effect, because of its heaviness and length.

"Why have you crammed up one of your windows with a dressing-glass?" asked Aunt Beatrice, putting a picture straight.

"Because I can't see myself in that dark corner," returned Mildred, demurely meek, but waiting her opportunity.

"See yourself! My dear child, you hardly ever want to see yourself, if you are habitually neat and dressed sensibly. I see you've adopted the mannish style. That's a phase of vanity. You'll come back to the beautiful and natural before long."

Mildred leaned back in her chair and clasped her hands behind her head.

"I don't think so, Aunt Beatrice. I've settled the dress question once and for all. I've found a clean, tidy, convenient style of dress and I can't waste time thinking about altering it again."

"You don't seem to mind wasting it on doing your hair," returned Aunt Beatrice, smiling, but not grimly, for she enjoyed logical fencing, even to her opponent's fair hits.

"If I had beautiful hair like yours, I shouldn't need to," replied Mildred. "But you know how endy and untidy mine always was."

Aunt Beatrice, embarrassed by the compliment, looked at her watch. "It seems as if we women can't escape our fate," she said. "Here we are gabbling about dress when we've plenty of important things to talk over. Miss Burt wrote to me that you were overworked, run down, nerves out of order, and all the usual nonsense. I'm thankful to find you looking remarkably well. I should like to know what this humbug about not being able to work means."

"It means that—well, I simply can't," returned Mildred, earnestly this time. "I can't remember things."

"You must be able to remember; unless your brain's diseased, which is most improbable. But I ought to take you to a brain specialist, I suppose."

Milly changed color. "Please, oh please, Aunt Beatrice, don't do that!"

Lady Thomson, in fact, hardly meant it; for her niece's appearance was unmistakably healthy. However, the threat told.

"I shall if you don't improve. I can't understand you. Either you're hysterical or you've got one of those abominable fits of frivolity which come on women like drink on men, and destroy their careers. I thought we had both set our hearts on your getting another First."

"But, Aunt Beatrice, they say I can't. They say I'm not clever enough."

"Oh, that's what they say, is it?" Lady Thomson smiled in calm but deep contempt. "How do they explain the idiots who have got Firsts? Archibald Toovey, for instance?" Her eyes met her niece's, and both smiled.

"Ah, yes! Mr. Toovey," returned Milly, who had met Archibald Toovey at the Fletchers', and converted his patronizing courtship into imbecile raptures.

"But that quite explains your losing an interest in your work. Just for once, I should like to take you away before the end of term. We would go straight to Rome next Monday. We shall meet the Breretons there, and go fully over the new excavations and discoveries, besides the old things, which will be new, of course, to you. Then we will go on to Naples, do the galleries and Pompeii, and come back by Florence and Paris before Christmas. By that time you will be ready to settle down to your work steadily again and forget all this nonsense."

Mildred's face had lighted up momentarily at the word "Rome." Then she sucked her under lip and looked at the fire. When Lady Thomson's programme was ended, she made a pause before she said, slowly:

"Thank you so much, dear Aunt Beatrice. I should love to go, but—I don't think—no, I don't think I'd better. You see, there's the expense."

"Of course I don't expect you to pay for yourself. I take you."

"How very kind and sweet of you! But—well, do you know, you've encouraged me so about that. First, I feel now as though I could sit down and get it straight away. I will get it, Aunt Beatrice, if only to make that old Professor look foolish."

Lady Thomson, though disappointed in a way, felt that Milly Flaxman was doing credit to her principles, showing a spirit worthy of her family. She did not urge the Roman plan; but content with a victory over "nerves and the usual nonsense," withdrew triumphant to the railway station.

Tims came in when she was gone and heard about the Roman offer.

"You refused, when Aunt Beatrice was going to plank down the dollars? M., you are a fool!"

"No, Tims," Mildred answered, deliberately; "you see, I don't feel sure yet whether I can manage Aunt Beatrice."

V

Oxford is beautiful at all times, beautiful even now, in spite of the cruel disfigurement inflicted upon her by the march of modern vulgarity, but she has three high festivals which clothe her with a special glory and crown her with their several crowns. One is the Festival of May, when her hoary walls and ancient enclosures overflow with emerald and white, rose-color and purple and gold, a foam of leafage and blossom, breaking spray-like over edges of stone, gray as sea-worn rocks. And all about the city the green meadows and groves burn with many tones of color, brilliant as enamels or as precious stones, yet of a texture softer and richer, more full of delicate shadows than any velvet mantle that ever was woven for a queen.

Another Festival comes with that strayed bacchanal October, who hangs her scarlet and wine-colored garlands on cloister and pinnacle, on wall and tower. And gradually the foliage of grove and garden, turns through shade of bluish metallic green, to the mingled splendor of pale gold and beaten bronze and deepest copper, half glowing and half drowned in the low, mellow sunlight, and purple mist of autumn.

Last comes the Festival of Mid-winter, the Festival of the Frost. The rime comes, or the snow, and the long lines of the buildings, the fretwork of stone, the battlements, carved pinnacles and images of saints or devils, stand up with clear glittering outlines, or clustered about and overhung with fantasies of ice and snow. Behind, the deep-blue sky itself seems to glitter too. The frozen floods glitter in the meadows, and every little twig on the bare trees. There is no color in the earth, but the atmosphere of the river valley clothes distant hills and trees and hedges with ultramarine vapor. Towards evening the mist climbs, faintly veiling the tall groves of elms and the piled masses of the city itself. The sunset begins to burn red behind Magdalen Tower, all the towers and aery pinnacles rise blue yet distinct against it. And this festival is not only one of nature. The glittering ice is spread over the meadows, and, everywhere from morning till moonlight, the rhythmical ring of the skate and the sound of voices sonorous with the joy of living, travel far on the frosty air. Sometimes the very rivers are frozen, and the broad, bare highway of the Thames and the tree-sheltered path of the Cherwell are alive with black figures, heel-winged like Mercury, flying swiftly on no errand, but for the mere delight of flying.

It was early on such a shining festival morning that Mildred, a willowy, brown-clad figure, came down to a piece of ice in an outlying meadow. Her shadow moved beside her in the sunshine, blue on the whiteness of the snow, which crunched crisp and thin under her feet. She carried a black bag in her hand—sign of the serious skater, and her face was serious, even apprehensive. She saw with relief that except the sweepers there was no one on the ice. A row of shivering men, buttoned up to the chin in seedy coats, rose from the chairs where they awaited their appointed prey, and all yelled to her at once. She crowned the hopes of one by occupying his seat, but the important task of putting on the bladed boots she could depute to none. Tims, whom no appeal of friendship could induce to shiver on the ice, had told her that Milly was an expert skater. She was, in fact, correct and accomplished, but there was a stiffness and sense of effort about her style, a want of that appearance of free and daring abandonment to the stroke of the blade once launched, that makes the beauty of skating. Mildred knew only that she had to live up to the reputation of a mighty skater, and was not sure whether she could even stand on these knifelike edges. She laced one boot, happy in the belief that at any rate there would be no witness to her voyage of discovery. But a renewed yelling among the men made her lift her head, and there, striding swiftly over the crisp snow, came a tall, handsome young man, with a pointed, silky black beard and fine, short-sighted black eyes, aglow with the pleasure of the frosty sun.

It was Ian Stewart. The young lady whom he discovered to be Miss Flaxman just as he reached the chairs, was much more annoyed than he at the encounter. Here was an acquaintance, it seemed, and one provided with the bag and orange which Tims had warned her was the mark of the serious skater. They exchanged remarks on the weather and she went on lacing her other boot in great trepidation. The moment was come. She did not recoil from the insult of being seized under her elbows by two men and carefully planted on her feet as though she were most likely to tumble down. So far as she knew, she was likely to. But, lo! no sooner was she up than muscles and nerves, recking nothing of the brain's blind denial, asserted their own acquaintance with the art of balance and motion. Wondering, and for a few minutes still apprehensive, but presently lost in the pleasure of the thing, Mildred began to fly over the ice. And the dark, handsome man who had taken off his cap to her became supremely unimportant. Unluckily the piece of flood-ice was not endless and she had to come back. He was circling around an orange, and she, throwing herself instinctively on to the outside edge, came down towards him in great, sweeping curves, absorbed in the delight of this motion, so new yet so perfectly under her control. Ian Stewart, perceiving that the girl was absolutely unconscious of his presence, blushed in his soul to think that he had been induced to believe himself to be of importance in her eyes.

"Miss Flaxman," he said, skating up to her, "I see you have no orange. Can't we skate a figure together around mine?"

"I've forgotten all about figures," replied Mildred, with truth.

"Try some simple turns," he urged. "There are plenty here," and he held up a book in his hand like the one she had found in her own black bag. But it had "Ian Stewart, Durham College," written clearly on the outside.

"So that's Stewart!" thought Milly; and she could not help laughing at her own thoughts, which had created him in a different image.

Stewart did not know why she laughed, but he found the sound and sight of the laugh new and charming.

"It's awfully kind of you to undertake my education in another branch, Mr. Stewart," she answered, pouting, "in spite of having found out that I'm not at all clever."

She smiled at him mutinously, sweeping towards the orange with head thrown back over her left shoulder. Momentarily the poise of her head recalled the attitude of the portrait of Lady Hammerton, beckoning her unseen companions to that far-off mysterious mountain country, where the torrents shine so whitely through the mist and the red line of sunset speaks of coming night.

Stewart colored, slightly confused. This brutal statement did not seem to him to represent the just and candid account he had given Miss Walker of Miss Flaxman's abilities.

"Some one's been misreporting me, I see," he returned. "But anyhow, on the ice, Miss Flaxman, it's you who are the Professor; I who am the pupil. So I offer you a fair revenge."

Accordingly, Mildred soon found herself placed at a due distance from the orange, with Stewart equally distant from it on the other side. After a few minutes of extreme uneasiness, she discovered that although she had to halt at each fresh call, she had a kind of mechanical familiarity with the simple figures which he gave her.

Stewart, though learned, was human; and to sweep now at the opposite pole to his companion, now with a swing of clasping hands at the centre of their delightful dance, his eyes always perforce on his charming partner, and her eyes on him, undeniably raised the pleasure of skating to a higher power than if he had circled the orange in company with mere man.

So they fleeted the too-short time in the sparkling blue and white world, drinking the air like celestial wine.

The Festival of the Frost had fallen in the Christmas Vacation, and Oxford society in vacation is essentially different from that of Term-time, when it is overflowed by men who are but birds of passage, coming no one inquires whence, and flitting few know whither. The party that picnicked, played hockey, danced and figured on their skates through the weeks of the frost, was in those days almost like a family party. So it happened that Ian Stewart met the new Miss Flaxman in an atmosphere of friendly ease that years of term-time society would not have afforded him. How new she was he did not guess, but supposed the change to be in his own eyes. Other people, however, saw it. Her very skating was different. It had gained in grace and vigor, but she was seldom seen wooing the serious and lonely orange around which Milly had acquired the skill that Mildred now enjoyed. On the contrary, she initiated an epidemic of frivolity on the ice in the shape of waltzing and hand-in-hand figures in general.

Ian Stewart, too, neglected the orange and went in for hand-in-hand figures that season. Other things, too, he neglected; work, which he had never before allowed to suffer measurably from causes within his control; and far from blushing for his idleness, he rejoiced in it, as the surest sign of all that for him the Festival of Spring had come in the time of nature's frost.

It was not only the crisp air, the frequent sun, the joyous flights over the ringing ice that made his blood run faster through his veins and laughter come more easily to his lips; that aroused him in the morning with a strange sense of delight, as though some spirit had awakened him with a glad reveille at the window of his soul. He, too, was in Arcady. That in itself should be sufficient joy; he knew he must restrain his impatience for more. Not till the summer, when the lady of his heart had ceased to be also his pupil, must he make avowal of his love.

Mildred on her part found Stewart the most attractive of the men with whom she was acquainted. As yet in this new existence of hers, she had not moved outside the Oxford circle—a circle exceptional in England, because in it intellectual eminence, not always recognized, when recognized receives as much honor as is accorded to a great fortune or a great name in ordinary society. Stewart's abilities were of a kind to be recognized by the Academic world. He was already known in the Universities of the Continent and America. Oxford was proud of him; and although Mildred had no desire to marry as yet, it gratified her taste and her vanity to win him for a lover.

VI

Mildred had had no desire to spend her vacations with Lady Thomson, and on the ground of her reading for the Schools, had been allowed to spend them in Oxford. Tims, who had no relations, remained with her. She had for Mildred a sentiment almost like that of a parent, besides an admiration for which she was slightly ashamed, feeling it to be something of a slur on the memory of Milly, her first and kindest friend.

Mildred had recovered her memory for most things, but the facts of her former life were still a blank to her. She had begun to work for her First in order to evade Aunt Beatrice; but the fever of it grew upon her, either from the ambient air of the University or from a native passion to excel in all she did. Her teachers were bewildered by the mental change in Miss Flaxman. The qualities of intellectual swiftness, vigor, pliancy, whose absence they had once noted in her, became, on the contrary, conspicuously hers. Once initiated into the tricks of the "Great Essay" style, she could use it with a dexterity strangely in contrast with the flat and fumbling manner in which poor Milly had been wont to express her ideas. But in the region of actual knowledge, she now and again perpetrated some immense and childish blunder, which made the teachers, who nursed and trained her like a jockey or a race-horse, tremble for the results of the Greats Examination.

All too swiftly the date of the Schools loomed on the horizon; drew near; was come. The June weather was glorious on the river, but in the town, above all in the Examination Schools, it was very hot. The sun glared pitilessly in through the great windows of the big T-shaped room, till the temperature was that of a greenhouse. The young men in their black coats and white ties looked enviously at the girl candidate, the only one, in her white waist and light skirt. They envied her, too, her apparent indifference to a crisis that paled the masculine cheek. In fact, Mildred was nervous, but her nerves were strung up to so high a pitch that she was sensitive neither to temperature nor to fatigue, nor to want of sleep. And at the service of her quick intelligence and ready pen lay all the stored knowledge of Milly the First.

On the last day, when the last paper was over, Tims came and found her in the big hall, planting the pins in her hat with an almost feverish energy. Although it was five o'clock, she said she wanted air, not tea.

The last men had trooped listlessly down the steps of the Schools and the two girls stood there while Mildred drew on her gloves. The sun wearing to the northwest, shone down that curve of the High Street which all Europe cannot match. The slanting gold illumined the gray face of the University and the wide pavement, where the black-gowned victims of the Schools threaded their sombre way through groups of joyous youths in flannels and ladies in summer attire. On the opposite side cool shadows were beginning to invade the sunshine, to slant across the old houses, straight-roofed or gabled, the paladian pile of Queen's, the mediæval front of All Souls, with its single and perfect green tree, leading up to the consummation of the great spire of St. Mary's.

Already, from the tall bulk of the nave, a shadow fell broad across the pavement. But still the heat of the day reverberated from the stones about them. They turned down to the Botanical Gardens and paced that gray enclosure, full of the pride of branches and the glory of flowers and overhung by the soaring vision of Magdalen Tower. Mildred was walking fast and talking volubly about the Examination and everything else.

"Look here, old girl," said Tims at last, when they reached for the second time the seat under the willow trellis, "I'm going to sit down here, unless you'll come to tea at Boffin's."

"I don't want to sit down," returned Mildred, seating herself; "or to have tea or anything. I want to be just going, going, going. I feel as though if I stop for a minute something horrid will happen."

Tims wrinkled her whole face anxiously.

"Don't do that, Tims," cried Mildred, sharply. "You look hideous."

Tims colored, rose and walked away. She suddenly thought, with tears in her eyes, of the old Milly who would never have spoken to her like that. By the time she had reached the little basin in the middle of the garden, where the irises grew, Mildred had caught her up.

"Tims, dear old Tims! What a wretch I am! I couldn't help letting off steam on something—you don't know what I feel like."

Tims allowed herself to be pacified, but in her heart there remained a yearning for her earlier and gentler friend—that Milly Flaxman who was certainly not dead, yet as certainly gone out of existence.

It was towards the end of the last week of Term, and the gayeties of Commemoration had already begun. Mildred threw herself into them with feverish enjoyment. She seemed to grudge even the hours that must be lost in the unconsciousness of sleep. The Iretons, cousins from

India, who had never known the former Milly, took a house in Oxford for a week. She went with them to three College balls and a Masonic, and spent the days in a carnival of luncheon and boating-parties. She attracted plenty of admiration, and enjoyed herself wildly, yet also purposefully; because she was trying to get rid of that haunting feeling that if she stopped a minute "something horrid would happen."

Stewart meantime was finding love not so entirely beautiful and delightful a thing as he had at first imagined it. In his dreamy way he had overlooked the fact of Commemoration, and planned when Term was over to find Mildred constantly at the Fletchers' and to be able to arrange quiet days on the river. But if he found her there, she was always in company, and though she made herself as charming to him as usual, she showed no disposition to forsake all others and cleave only to him. He was not a dancing man, and suffered cruelly on the evenings when he knew her to be at balls, and fancied all her partners in love with her.

But on the Thursday after Commemoration, the Fletchers gave a strawberry tea at Wytham, as a farewell festivity to their cousins. And Ian Stewart was there. With Mrs. Fletcher's connivance, he took Mildred home alone in a canoe, by the deep and devious stream which runs under Wytham woods. She went on talking with a vivacious gayety which was almost foolish. He saw that it was unreal and that her nerves were at high tension. His own were also. He did not intend to propose to her that day; but he could no longer restrain himself, and he began to speak to her of his love.

"Hush!" she cried, with a vehement gesture. "Not to-day! oh, not to-day! I can't bear it!" She put her head on her knee and moaned again, "Not to-day, I'm too tired, I really am. I can't bear it."

This was all the answer he could get, and her manner left him in complete uncertainty as to whether she meant to accept or to refuse him.

Tims had been at the strawberry tea too, and came into Mildred's room in the evening, curious to know what had happened. She found Mildred without a light, sitting, or rather lying in a wicker chair. When the candle was lighted she saw that Mildred was very pale and shivering.

"You're overtired, my girl," she said. "That's what's the matter with you."

"Oh, Tims," moaned Mildred. "I feel so ill and so frightened. I know something horrid's going to happen—I know it is."

"Don't be a donkey," returned Tims. "I'll help you undress and then you turn in. You'll be as jolly as a sandboy to-morrow."

But Mildred was crying tremulously. "Oh, Tims, how dreadful it would be to die!"

"Idiot!" cried Tims, and shook Mildred with all her might. Mildred's tiny sobs turned into a shriek of laughter.

"My goodness!" exclaimed Tims; "you're in hysterics!"

"I know I am," gasped Mildred. "I was laughing to think of what Aunt Beatrice would say." And she giggled amid her tears.

Tims insisted on her rising from the chair, undressing, and getting into bed. Then she sat by her in the half-dark, waiting for the miserable tears to leave off.

"Don't cry, old girl, don't cry. Go to sleep and forget all about it," she kept repeating, almost mechanically.

At length leaning over the bed she saw that Mildred was asleep, lying straight on her bed with her feet crossed and her hands laid on her bosom.

VII

About noon on Friday Milly Flaxman awoke. She lay very quiet, sleepy and comfortable, her eyes fixed idly on a curve in the jessamine-pattern paper opposite her bed. The windows were wide open, the blinds down and every now and again flapping softly, as a capricious little breeze went by, whispering through the leafy trees outside. There seemed nothing unusual in that; she always slept with her windows open. But as her senses emerged from those mists which lie on the surface of the river of sleep, she was conscious of a balmy warmth in the room, of an impression of bright sunshine behind the dark blinds, and of noises from the streets reaching her with a kind of sharpness associated with sunshine. She sat up, looked at her watch, and was shocked to find how late she had slept. She must have missed a lecture. Then the recollection of the dinner-party at the Fletchers', the verdict of Mr. Stewart on her chance of a First, and her own hysterical outburst returned to her, overpowering all outward impressions. She felt calm and well now, but unhappy and ashamed of herself. She put her feet out of bed and looked round mechanically for her dressing-gown and slippers. Their absence was unimportant, for no sense of chill struck through her thin night-gown to her warm body, and going to the window, she drew up the blind.

The high June sun struck full upon her, hot and dazzling, but not so dazzling that she could not see the row of garden trees through whose bare branches she had yesterday descried the squalid roofs of the town. They were spreading now in a thick screen of fresh green leaves. She leaned out, as though further investigation might explain the phenomenon, and saw a red standard rose in full flower under her window. The thing was exactly like a dream, and she tried to wake up but could not. She was panic-stricken and trembling. Had she been very, very ill? Was it possible to be unconscious for six months? She looked at herself in a dressing-glass near the window, which she had never placed there, and saw that she was pale and had dark marks under her eyes, but not more so than had been the case in that yesterday so strangely and mysteriously removed in time. Her slender white arms and throat were as rounded as usual. And if she had been ill, why was she left alone like this? She found a dressing-gown not her own, and went on a voyage of discovery. But the other rooms on her floor were dismantled and tenantless. The girls were gone and the servants were "cleaning" in a distant part of the College. She felt incapable of getting into bed again and waiting for some one to come, so she began dressing herself with trembling hands. Every detail increased the sense of strangeness. There were a number of strange clothes, ball-dresses and others, hanging in her cupboard, strange odds and ends thrust confusedly into her bureau. She found at length a blue cotton frock of her own, which seemed just home from the wash. She had twisted up her hair and was putting on the blue frock, when she heard a step on the stairs, and paused with beating heart. Who was coming? How would the mystery be resolved? The door opened and Tims came in—the old Tims, wrinkled face, wig, and old straw hat on one side as usual.

"Tims!" cried Milly, flying towards her and speaking with pale lips. "Please, please tell me—what has happened? Have I been very ill?" And she stared in Tims's face with a tragic mask of terror and anxiety.

"Now take it easy—take it easy, M., my girl!" cried Tims, giving her a great squeeze and a clap on the shoulder. "I'm jolly glad to see you back. But don't let's have any more of your hysterics. No, never no more!"

"Have I been away?" asked Milly, her lips still trembling.

"I should think you had!" exclaimed Tims. "But nobody knows it except me. Don't forget that. Here's a note for you from old B. Read it first or we shall both forget all about it. She had to go away early this morning."

Milly opened the note and read:

DEAR MILLY,

I am sorry not to say good-bye, but glad you are sleeping off your fatigue. I want to tell you, between ourselves, not to go on worrying about the results of the Schools, as I think you are doing, in spite of your pretences to the contrary. I hear you have done at least one brilliant paper, and although I, of course, know nothing certain, I believe you and the College will have reason to rejoice when the list comes out.

Yours affectionately,
MARY BURT

"What does it mean?—oh, what can it mean?" faltered Milly, holding out the missive to Tims.

"It means you've been in for Greats, my girl, and done first-rate. But the strain's been a bit too much for you, and you've had another collapse of memory. You had one in the end of November. You've been uncommonly well ever since, and worked like a Trojan, but you've not been quite your usual self, and I'm glad you've come right again, old girl. Let me tell you the whole business."

Tims did so. She wanted social tact, but she had the tact of the heart which made her hide from Milly how very different, how much more brilliant and attractive Milly the Second had been than her normal self. She only made her friend feel that the curious episode had entailed no disgrace, but that somehow in her abnormal condition she had done well in the Schools, and probably touched the top of her ambition.

"But I don't feel as though it had been quite straightforward to hide it up so," said Milly. "I shall write and tell Miss Burt and Aunt Beatrice, and tell the Fletchers when I go to them."

"You'll do nothing of the kind, you stupid," snapped Tims. "You'll be simply giving me away if you do. What is the good? It won't happen again unless you're idiot enough to overwork yourself again. Very likely not then; for, as an open-minded, scientific woman, I believe it to have been a case of hypnotism, and in France and the United States they'd have thought it a very interesting one. But in England people are so prejudiced they'd say you'd simply been out of your mind; although that wouldn't prevent them from blaming me for hypnotizing you."

While Tims spoke thus, there was a knocking without, and a maid delivered a note for Miss Flaxman. Milly held it in her hands and studied it musingly before opening the envelope. Her pale, troubled face colored and grew more serious. Tims had not mentioned Ian Stewart, but Milly had not forgotten him or his handwriting. Tims knew it too. She restrained her excitement while Milly turned her back and stood by the window reading the note. She must have read them several times over, the two sides of the sheet inscribed with Stewart's small, scholarly handwriting, before she turned her transfigured face towards the anxiously expectant Tims.

"Tims, dear," she said at length, smiling tremulously, and laying tremulous hands on Tims's two thin shoulders—"dear old Tims, why didn't you tell me?"

"Tell you what?" asked Tims, grinning delightedly. Milly threw her arms round her friend's neck and hid her happy tears and blushes between Tims's ear and shoulder.

"Mr. Stewart—it seems too good to be true—he loves me, he really does. He wants me to be his wife."

Most girls would have hugged and kissed Milly, and Tims did hug her, but instead of kissing her, she banged and slapped her back and shoulders hard all over, shaking the while with deep internal chuckles. It hurt, but Milly did not mind, for it was sympathy. Presently she drew herself away, and wiping her damp eyes, said, smiling shyly:

"He's never guessed how much I care about him. I'm so glad. He says he doesn't wonder at my hesitation and talks about others more worthy to love me. But you know there isn't any one except Mr. Toovey. Poor Mr. Toovey! I do hope I haven't behaved very badly to him."

"Never mind Toovey," chuckled Tims. "Anyhow, Milly, I've got a good load off my mind. I didn't half like having put that other girl into your boots. However, you've come back, and everything's going to be all right."

"All right!" breathed Milly. "Why, Tims, darling, I never thought any one in the world could be half so happy as I am."

And Tims left Milly to write the answer for which Ian Stewart was so anxiously waiting.

The engagement proceeded after the manner of engagements. No one was surprised at it and every one was pleased. The little whirlpool of talk that it created prevented Milly's ignorance of the events of the past six or seven months from coming to the surface. She lay awake at night, devising means of telling Ian about this strange blank in her life. But she shrank from saying things that might make him suspect her of an unsound mind. She had plainly been sane enough in her abnormal state, and there was no doubt of her sanity now. She told him she had had since the autumn, and still had, strange collapses of memory; and he said that quite explained some peculiarities of her work. She tried to talk to him about French experiments in hypnotism, and how it was said sometimes to bring to light unsuspected sides of a personality. But he laughed at hypnotism as a mixture of fraud and hysteria. So with many searchings of heart, she dropped the subject.

She was staying at the Fletchers' and saw Ian every day. He was all that she could wish as a lover, and it never occurred to her to ask whether he felt all that he himself could have wished as such. He was very fond of Milly and quite content with her, but not perfectly content with himself. He supposed he must at bottom be one of those ordinary and rather contemptible men who care more for the excitement of the chase than for the object of it. But he felt sure he was really a very lucky fellow, and determined not to give way to the self-analysis which is always said to be the worst enemy of happiness.

Miss Flaxman had been the only woman in for Greats, and as a favor she was taken first in *viva voce*. The questions were directed to probing her actual knowledge in places where she had made one or two amazing blunders. But she emerged triumphant, and went in good spirits to Clewes, Aunt Beatrice's country home in the North, whither Ian Stewart shortly followed her. Beyond the fact that she wore perforce and with shame, not having money to buy others, frocks which Lady Thomson disapproved, she was once more the adoring niece to whom her aunt was accustomed. And Lady Thomson liked Ian. She never expected men to share her fads.

In due time came the announcement of the First, bringing almost as many congratulatory letters as the engagement. And on August 2nd Milly sailed for Australia, where she was to spend two or three months with her family.

In October the newspapers announced that the marriage of Miss Mildred Beatrice Flaxman, eldest daughter of the Dean of Stirling, South Australia, with Mr. Ian Stewart, Fellow of Durham College, Oxford, would take place at Oxford in the second week in December.

VIII

"M adame dort toujours!" The dark-eyed, cherry cheeked, white-capped chamber-maid of the Hôtel du Chalet made the statement to the manager, who occupied a glass case in the hall. "She must have been very tired yesterday, pauvre petite!"

The manager answered phlegmatically in French with a German accent:

"So much the better if she sleeps. She does not eat. When the gentleman went out he wanted sanveeches to put in his pocket. One does not want sanveeches when one sleeps."

"All the same, I wish she would wake up. It's so odd to see her sleeping like that," returned the cherry-cheeked one; and passed about her duties.

The *déjeuner* was over, and those guests who had not already gone out for the day, were tramping about the bare, wooden passages and staircase, putting on knitted gloves and shouting for their companions and toboggans. But it was not till all had gone out and their voices had died away on the clear, cold air, that the sleeper in No. 19 awoke. For a while she lay with open eyes as still as though she were yet sleeping. But suddenly she started up in bed and looked around her with frowning, startled attention. She was in a rather large, bare bedroom with varnished green wood-work and furniture and a green pottery stove. There was an odd, thick paper on the wall, of no particular color, and a painted geometrical pattern in the centre of the ceiling. It was a neat room, on the whole, but on the bed beside her own a man's waistcoat had been thrown, and in the middle of the floor a pair of long, shabby slippers lay a yard apart from each other and upside down. There were other little signs of masculine occupation. A startled movement brought her sitting up on the bedside.

"Married!" she whispered to herself. "How perfectly awful!"

A fiery wave of anger that was almost hate swept through her veins, anger against the unknown husband and against that other one who had the power thus to dispose of her destiny, while she lay helpless in some unfathomed deep between life and death. Swifter than light her thoughts flew back to the last hours of consciousness which had preceded that strange and terrible engulfment of her being. She remembered that Mr. Stewart had tried to propose to her on the river and that she had not allowed him to do so. Probably he had taken this as a refusal. She knew nothing of any love of Milly's for him; only was sure that he had not been in love with her, Mildred, when she first knew him; therefore had not cared for her other personality. Who else was possible? With an audible cry she sprang to her feet.

"Toovey! Archibald Toovey!"

The idea was monstrous, it was also grotesque; and even while she plunged despairing fingers in her hair, she laughed so loud that she might have been heard in the corridor.

"Mrs. Archibald Toovey! Good Heavens! But that girl was perfectly capable of it."

Then she became more than serious and buried her face in her hands, thinking.

"If it is Mr. Toovey," she thought, "I must go away at once, wherever I am. I can't have been married long. I am sure to have some money somewhere. I'll go to Tims. Oh, that brute! That idiot!"—she was thinking of Milly—"How I should like to strangle her!"

She clinched her hands till the nails hurt her palms. Two photographs, propped up on the top of a chest of drawers, caught her eye. She snatched them. One was a wedding group, but there was no bridegroom; only six bridesmaids. It was as bad as such things always are, and it was evident that the dresses were ill-fitting, the hats absurd. Tims was prominent among the bridesmaids, looking particularly ugly. The other photograph might have seemed pretty to a less prejudiced eye. It was that of a slight, innocent-looking girl in a white satin gown, "ungirt from throat to hem," and holding a sheaf of lilies in her hand. Her hair was loose upon her shoulders, crowned with a fragile garland and covered with a veil of fine lace.

"What a Judy!" commented Mildred, throwing the photograph fiercely away from her. "Fancy my being married in a dressing-gown and having Tims for a bridesmaid! Sickening!"

But her anxiety with regard to the bridegroom dominated even this just indignation. Somehow, after seeing the photographs, she was convinced he must be Archibald Toovey. She determined to fly at once. The question was, where was she? Not in England, she fancied. The stove had been thrice-heated by the benevolent cherry-cheeked one, and the atmosphere of the room was stifling. This, together with the cold outside, had combined to throw a gray veil across the window-panes. She hastily put on a blue Pyrenean wool dressing-gown, flung open a casement and leaned out into the wide sunshine, the iced-champagne air. The window was only on the first floor, and she saw just beneath a narrow, snowy strip of ground, on either side and below it snow-sprinkled pinewoods falling, falling steeply, as it were, into space. But far below the blue air deepened into a sapphire that must be a lake, and beyond that gray cliffs, remote yet fairly clear in the sunshine, rose streaked with the blue shadows of their own buttresses. Above the cliffs, white and sharp and fantastic in their outline, snowy mountain summits showed clear against the deep blue sky. Between them, imperceptibly moving on its secular way, hung the glacier, a track of vivid ultramarine and green, looking like a giant pathway to the stars. Mildred guessed she was in Switzerland. She knew that it should be easy to get back to England, yet for her with her peculiar inexperience of life, it would not be easy. At any rate, she would dash herself down some gray-precipice into that lake below rather than remain here as the bride of Archibald Toovey. Just as she was registering a desperate vow to that effect a man came climbing up the woodland way to the left, a long-legged man in a knickerbocker suit and gaiters. He stepped briskly out of the pinewood on to the snowy platform below, and seeing her at the window, looked up, smiling, and waved his cap, with a cry of "Hullo, Milly!" And it was not Archibald Toovey.

Mildred, relieved from the worst of fears, leaned from the window towards him. A slanting ray caught the floating cloud of her amber hair, her face glowed rosily, her eyes beamed on the new-comer, and she broke into such an enchanting ripple of laughter as he had never heard from those soft lips since it had been his privilege to kiss them. Then something happened within him. Upon his lonely walk he had been overcome by a depression against which he had every day been struggling. He had been disappointed in his marriage, now some weeks old—disappointed, that is, with himself, because of his own incapacity for rapturous happiness. Yet a year ago on the ice at Oxford, six months ago in the falling summer twilight on the river, under Wytham Woods, he had thought himself as capable as any man of feeling the joys and pains of love. In the sequel it had seemed that he was not; and just as he had lost all hope of finding once again that buried treasure of his heart, it had returned to him in one delightful moment, when he stood as it were on the top of the world in the crisp, joyous Alpine air, and his eyes met the eyes of his young wife, who leaned towards him into the sunshine and laughed. He could not possibly have told how long the golden vision endured; only that suddenly, precipitately, it withdrew. A "spirit in his feet" sent him bounding up the bare, shallow hotel stairs, two steps at a time, dropping on every step a cake of snow from his boots, to melt and make pools on the polished wood. The manager, who respected none of his guests except those who bullied him, called out a reprimand, but received no apology.

Stewart strode with echoing tread down the corridor towards No. 19, eager to hold that slender, girlish wife of his in his arms and to press kisses on the lips that had laughed at him so sweetly from above. The walls of the hotel were thin, and as he approached the door he heard a quick, soft scurry across the room on the other side, and in his swift thought saw Milly flying to meet him, just relieved from one absurd anxiety about his safety and indulging another on the subject of his wet feet. A smile of tender amusement visited his lips as he took hold of the door-handle. Exactly as he touched it, the key on the other side turned. The lock had been stiff, but it had shot out in the nick of time, and he found himself brought up short in his impulsive career and hurtling against a solid barrier. He knocked, but no one answered. He could have fancied he heard panting breaths on the other side of the ill-fitting door.

"Mayn't I come in, darling?" he asked, gently, but with a shade of reproach in his voice.

"No, you can't," returned Milly's voice; hers, but with an accent of coldness and decision in it which struck strangely on his ear. He paused, bewildered. Then he remembered how often he had read that women were capricious, unaccountable creatures. Milly had made him forget that. Her attitude towards him had been one of unvarying gentleness and devotion. Vaguely he felt that there was a kind of feminine charm in this sudden burst of coldness, almost indifference.

"Is anything the matter, dear?" he asked. "Aren't you well?"

"Quite well, thank you," came the curt voice through the door. Then after a minute's hesitation: "What do you want?"

Ian smiled to himself as he answered:

"My feet are wet. I want to change."

He was a delicate man, and if he had a foible which Milly could be said to execrate, it was that of "sitting in wet feet." He expected the door to fly open; but it did nothing of the kind. There was not a trace of anxiety in the grudging voice which replied, after a pause:

"I suppose you want dry shoes and stockings. I'll give them to you if you'll wait."

He stood bewildered, a little pained, not noticing the noisy opening and shutting of several ill-fitting drawers in the room. Yet Milly always put away his things for him and should have known where to find them. The door opened a chink and the shoes and stockings came flying through on to the passage floor. He had a natural impulse to use his masculine strength, to push the door open before she could lock it again, but fortunately he restrained it. He went down-stairs slowly, shoes and stockings in hand; threw them down behind the big green stove in the smoking-room and lighted a meditative pipe. It was evidently a fact that women were difficult to understand; even Milly was. He had been uniformly kind and tender to her, and so far she had seemed more than content with him as a husband. But beneath this apparent happiness of hers had some instinct, incomprehensible to him, been whispering to her that he did not love her as many men, perhaps most, loved their young wives? That he had felt for her no ardor, no worship? If so, then the crisis had come at the right moment; at the moment when, by one of those tricks of nature which make us half acquiesce in the belief that our personality is an illusion, that we are but cosmic automata, the power of love had been granted to him again. Yet for all that—very fortunately, seeing that the crisis was more acute than he was aware—he did not fancy that his way lay plain before him. He began to perceive that the cementing of a close union between a man and woman, two beings with so abundant a capacity for misunderstanding each other, is a complex and delicate affair. That to marry is to be a kind of Odysseus advancing into the palace of a Circe, nobler and more humane than the enchantress of old, yet capable also of working strange and terrible transformations. That many go in there carrying in their hands blossoms which they believe to be moly; but the true moly is not easy to distinguish. And he hoped that he and Milly, in their different ways, had found and were both wearing the milk-white flower. Yet he knew that this was a matter which must be left to the arbitrament of time.

IX

On their return to Oxford the young couple were fêted beyond the common. People who had known Milly Flaxman in earlier days were surprised to think how little they had noticed her beauty or guessed what a fund of humor, what an extraordinary charm, had lurked beneath the surface of her former quiet, grave manner. The Master of Durham alone refused to be surprised. He merely affirmed in his short squeak that he had always admired Mrs. Stewart very much. She was now frequently to be found in the place of honor at those dinners of his, where distinguished visitors from London brought the stir and color of the great world into the austere groves, the rarefied atmosphere of Academe.

Wherever she appeared, the vivid personality of Mrs. Stewart made a kind of effervescence which that indescribable entity, a vivid personality, is sure to keep fizzing about it. She was devoutly admired, fiercely criticised, and asked everywhere. It is true she had quite given up her music, but she drew caricatures which were irresistibly funny, and was a tremendous success in charades. Everything was still very new to her, everything interesting and amusing. She was enchanted with her house, although Milly and Lady Thomson had chosen it, preferring to a villa in the Parks an old gray house of the kind that are every day recklessly destroyed by the march of modern vulgarity. She approved of the few and good pieces of old furniture with which they had provided it; although Lady Thomson could not entirely approve of the frivolity and extravagance of the chintzes with which she helped the sunshine to brighten the low, panelled rooms. But Aunt Beatrice, girt with principles major and minor, armed with so Procrustean a measure for most of her acquaintance, accepted Mildred's deviations with an astonishing ease. The secret of personal magnetism is not yet discovered. It may be that the *aura* surrounding each of us is no mystic vision of the Neo-Buddhists, but a physical fact; that Mildred's personality acted by a power not moral but physical on the nerves of those who approached her, exciting those of some, of the majority, pleasurably, filling others with a nameless uneasiness, to account for which they must accuse her manners or her character.

To Ian Stewart the old panelled house with the walled garden behind, where snowdrops and crocuses pushed up under budding orchard

MARGARET L. WOODS

boughs, was a paradise beyond any he had imagined. He found Mildred the most adorable of wives, the most interesting of companions. Her defects as a housekeeper, which Aunt Beatrice noted in silence but with surprise, were nothing to him. He could not help pausing sometimes even in the midst of his work, to wonder at his own good fortune and to reflect that whatever the future might have in store, he would have no right to complain, since it had been given to him to know the taste of perfect happiness.

Since his marriage he had been obliged to take more routine work, and the Long Vacation had become more valuable to him than ever. As soon as he had finished an Examination he had undertaken, he meant to devote the time to the preparation of a new book which he had in his mind. Mildred, seemingly as eager as himself that the book should be done, had at first agreed. Then some of her numerous friends had described the pleasures of Dieppe, and she was seized with the idea that they too might go there. Ian, she said, could work as well at Dieppe as at Oxford or in the country. Ian knew better; besides, his funds were low and Dieppe would cost too much. For the first time he opposed Mildred's wishes, and to her surprise she found him perfectly firm. There was no quarrel, but although she was silent he felt that she did not yield her opinion and was displeased with him.

Late at night as he sat over Examination papers, his sensitive imagination framed the accusations of selfishness, pedantry, scrupulosity, which his wife might be bringing against him in the "sessions of silent thought;" although it was clearly to her advantage as much as to his own that he should keep out of money difficulties and do work which counted. She had no fixed habits, and he flung down pipe and pen, hoping to find her still awake. But she was already sound asleep. The room was dark, but he saw her by the illumination of distant lightning, playing on the edge of a dark and sultry world. His appointed task was not yet done and he returned to the study, a long, low, dark-panelled room, looking on the garden. The windows were wide open on the hushed, warm, almost sulphurous darkness, from which frail white-winged moths came floating in towards the shaded lamp on his writing-table. He sat down to his papers and by an effort of will concentrated his mind upon them. Habit had made such concentration easy to him as a rule, but to-night, after half an hour of steady work, he was mastered by an invading restlessness of mind and body. The cause was not far to seek; he could hear all the time he worked the dull, almost continuous, roar of distant thunder. All else was very still, it was long past midnight and the town was asleep.

He got up and paced the room once or twice, grasping his extinguished pipe absently in his hand. Suddenly a blast seemed to spring out of nowhere and rush madly round the enclosed garden, tossing the gnarled and leafy branches of the old orchard trees and dragging at the long trails of creepers on wall and trellis. It blew in at the windows, hot as from the heart of the thunder-cloud, and waved the curtains before it. It rushed into the very midst of the old house with its cavernous chimneys, deep cellars, and enormous unexplored walls, filling it with strange, whispering sounds, as of half articulate voices, here menacing, there struggling to reveal some sinister and vital secret. The blast died away, but it seemed to have left those voices still muttering and sighing through the walls that had sheltered so many generations, such various lives of men. Ian was used to the creaking and groaning of the wood-work; he knew how on the staircase the rising of the boards, which had been pressed down in the day, simulated ghostly footsteps in the night. He was in his mental self the most rational of mortals, but at times the Highland strain in his blood, call it sensitive or superstitious, spoke faintly to his nerves—never before so strongly, so over-masteringly as to-night. A blue blaze of crooked lightning zigzagged down the outer darkness and seemed to strike the earth but a little beyond the garden wall. Following on its heels a tremendous clap of thunder burst, as it were, on the very chimneys. The solid house shook to its foundations. But the tide of horrible, irrational fear which swept over Ian's whole being was not caused by this mere exaggerated commonplace of nature. He could give no guess what it was that caused it; he only knew that it was agony. He knew what it meant to feel the hair lift on his head; he knew what the Psalmist meant when he said, "My bones are turned to water." And as he stood unable to move, afraid to turn his head, abject and ashamed of his abjectness, he was listening, listening for he knew not what.

At length it came. He heard the stairs creak and a soft padding footstep coming slowly down them; with it the brush of a light garment and intermittently a faint human sound between a sigh and a sob. He did not reflect that he could not really have heard such slight sounds through a thick stone wall and a closed door. He heard them. The steps stopped at the door; a hand seemed feeling to open it, and again there was a painful sigh. The physical terror had not passed from him, but the sudden though that it was his wife and that she was frightened or ill, made him able to master it. He seized the lamp, because he knew the light in the hall was extinguished, rushed to the door, opened it and looked out. There was no one there. He made a hasty but sufficient search and returned to the study.

The extremity of his fear was now passed, but an unpleasantly eery feeling still lingered about him and he had a very definite desire to find himself in some warm, human neighborhood. He had left the door open and was arranging the papers on his writing-table, when once again he heard those soft padding feet on the stairs; but this time they were much heavier, more hurried, and stumbled a little. He stood bent over the table, a bundle of papers in his hand, no longer overcome by mortal terror, yet somehow reluctant once more to look out and to see once more—nothing. There was a sound outside the door, louder, hoarser than the faint sob or sigh which he had heard before, and he seized the lamp and turned towards it. Before he had made a step forward, the door was pushed violently back and his wife came in, leaning upon it as though she needed support. She was barefooted and dressed only in a long night-gown, white, yet hardly whiter than her face. Her eyes did not turn towards him, they stared in front of her, not with the fixed gaze of an ordinary sleep-walker, but with purpose and intensity. She seemed to see something, to pursue something, with starting eyes and out-stretched arms; something she hated even more than she feared it, for her lips were blanched and tightened over her teeth as though with fury, and her smooth white forehead gathered in a frown. Again she uttered that low, fierce sound, like that he had heard outside the door. Then, loosing the handle on which she had leaned, she half sprung, half staggered, with uplifted hand, towards an open window, beyond which the rush of the thunder shower was just visible, sloping pallidly across the darkness. She leaned out into it and uttered to the night a hoarse, confused voice, words inchoate, incomprehensible, yet with a terrible accent of rage, of malediction. This transformation of his wife, so refined, so self-contained, into a creature possessed by an almost animal fury, struck Ian with horror, although he accepted it as a phenomenon of somnambulism. He approached but did not touch her, for he had heard that it was dangerous to awaken a somnambulist. Her voice sank rapidly to a loud whisper and he heard her articulate—"My husband! Mine! Mine!"—but in no tone of tenderness, rather pronouncing the words as a passionate claim to his possession. Then suddenly she drooped, half kneeling on the deep window-seat, half fallen across the sill. He sprang to catch her, but not before her forehead had come down sharply on the stone edge of the outer window. He kneeled upon the window-seat and gathered her gently in his arms, where she lay quiet, but moaning and shuddering.

"My husband!" she wailed, no longer furious now but despairing. "Ian! My love! Ian! My life!—my life! My own husband!"

Even in this moment it thrilled him to hear such words from her lips. He had not thought she loved him so passionately. He lifted her on to a deep old sofa at the end of the room, wrapped her in a warm Oriental coverlet which hung there, and held her to his heart, murmuring love and comfort in her cold little ear. It seemed gradually to soothe her, although he did not think she really awoke. Then he put her down, lighted the lamp outside, and, not without difficulty, carried her up to bed. Her eyes were half closed when he laid her down and drew the bedclothes over her; and a minute or two later, when he looked in from his dressing-room, she was evidently asleep.

When he got into bed she did not stir, and while he lay awake for another hour, she remained motionless and breathing regularly. He assured himself that the whole curious occurrence could be explained by the electrical state of the atmosphere, which had affected his own nerves in a way he would never humiliate himself by confessing to any one. Those mysterious footsteps on the stairs which he had heard, footsteps like his wife's yet not hers; that hand upon the door, that voice of sighs, were the creation of his own excited brain. In time he would doubtless come to believe his own assurances on the point, but that night at the bottom of his heart he did not believe them.

X

Next morning, if Ian himself slept late, Milly slept later still. The strained and troubled look which he had seen upon her face even in sleep the night before, had passed away in the morning, but she lay almost alarmingly still and white. He was reassured by remembering that once when they were in Switzerland she had slept about sixteen hours and awakened in perfect health. He remained in the house watching over her, and about four o'clock she woke up. But she was very pale and very quiet; exhausted, he thought, by her strange mental and physical exertions of the night before.

She came down to tea with her pretty hair unbecomingly twisted up, and dressed in a brownish-yellow tea-gown, which he fancied he remembered hearing her denounce as only fit to be turned into a table-cloth. He did not precisely criticise these details, but they helped in the impression of lifelessness and gloom that hung about her. It was a faint, gleamy afternoon, and such sun as there was did not shine into the study. The dark panelling looked darker than usual, and as she sat silent and listless in a corner of the old sofa, her hair and face stood out against it almost startling in their blondness and whiteness. She was strangely unlike herself, but Stewart comforted himself by remembering that she had been odd in her manner and behavior, though in a different way, after her long sleep in Switzerland. After he had given her tea, he suggested that they should walk in the garden, as the rain was over.

"Not yet, Ian," she said. "I want to try and tell you something. I can do it better here."

Her mouth quivered. He sat down by her on the sofa.

"Must you tell me now?" he asked, smiling. "Do you really think it matters?"

"Yes—it does matter," she answered, tremulously, pressing her folded hands against her breast. "It's something I ought to have told you before you married me—but indeed, indeed I didn't know how dreadful it was—I didn't think it would happen again."

He was puzzled a moment, then spoke, still smiling:

"I suppose you mean the sleep-walking. Well, darling, it is a bit creepy, I admit, but I shall get used to it, if you won't do it too often."

"Did I really walk?" she asked—and a look of horror was growing on her face. "Ah! I wasn't sure. No—it's not that—it is—oh, don't think me mad, Ian!"

"Tell me, dearest. I promise I won't."

"I've not been here at all since you've been living in this house. I've not seen you, my own precious husband, since I went to sleep in Switzerland, at the Hôtel du Chalet—don't you remember—when we had been that long walk up to the glacier and I was so tired?"

Stewart was exceedingly startled. He paused, and then said, very gently but very firmly:

"That's nonsense, dearest. You have been here, you've been with me all the time."

"Ah! You think so, but it was not *I*—no, don't interrupt me—I mean to tell you, I must, but I can't if you interrupt me. It was awfully wrong of me not to tell you before; but I tried to, and then I saw you wouldn't believe me. Do you remember a dinner-party at the Fletchers', the autumn before we were engaged—when Cousin David had just bought that picture?"

"That portrait of Lady Hammerton, which is so like you? Yes, I remember it perfectly."

"You know I wanted my First so much and I had been working too hard, and then I was told that evening that you had said I couldn't get it—"

"Silly me!"

"And I felt certain you didn't love me—"

"Silly you!"

"Don't interrupt me, please. And I wasn't well, and I cried and cried and I couldn't leave off, and then I allowed Tims to hypnotize me. We both knew she had no business to do it, it was wrong of us, of course, but we couldn't possibly guess what would happen. I went to sleep, and so far as I knew I never woke again for more than six months, not till the Schools were over."

"But, my darling, I skated with you constantly in the Christmas Vacation, and took your work through the Term. I assure you that you were quite awake then."

"I remember nothing about it. All I know is that some one got my First for me."

"But, Mildred—"

"Why do you call me Mildred? That's what they called me when I woke up last time; but my own name's Milly."

Stewart rose and paced the room, then came back.

"It's simply a case of collapse of memory, dear. It's very trying, but don't let's be fanciful about it."

"I thought it was only that—I told you, didn't I, something of that sort? But I didn't know then, nobody told me, that I wasn't like myself at all those months I couldn't remember. Last night in my sleep I knew—I knew that some one else, something else—I can't describe it, it's impossible—was struggling hard with me in my own brain, my own body, trying to hold me down, to push me back again into the place, whatever it was, I came out of. But I got stronger and stronger till I was quite myself and the thing couldn't really stop me. I dare say it only lasted a few seconds, then I felt quite free—free from the struggle, the pressure; and I saw myself standing in the room, with some kind of white floating stuff over my head and about me, and I saw myself open the door and go out of the room. I wasn't a bit surprised, but I just lay there quiet and peaceful. Then suddenly it came to me that I couldn't have seen myself, that the person, the figure I had seen go out of the door was the other one, the creature I had been struggling with, who had stolen my shape; and it came to me that she was gone to steal you—to steal your heart from me and take you away; and you wouldn't know, you would think it was I, and you would follow her and love her and never know it was not your own wife you were loving. And I was mad with anger; I never knew before what it meant, Ian, to be as angry as that. I struggled hard to get up, and at last I managed it, and I came down-stairs after her, but I couldn't find her, and I was sure that she had gone and had taken you away with her. And you say I really did come down-stairs."

"Yes, darling, and if you had been awake instead of asleep, as you obviously were, you would have seen that this nightmare of yours was nothing but a nightmare. You would have seen that I was alone here, quietly arranging my papers before going to bed. You gave me a fright coming down as you did, for there was a tremendous thunderstorm going on, and I am ashamed to say how queer my own nerves were. The electrical state of the atmosphere and a very loud clap of thunder just overhead, account for the whole business, which probably lasted only a few seconds from beginning to end. Be reasonable, little woman, you are generally the most reasonable person I know—except when you talk about going to Dieppe."

Milly gave him a strange look.

"Why am I not reasonable when I talk about going to Dieppe?"

He drew her to him and kissed her hair.

"Never mind why. We aren't going to excite ourselves to-day or do anything but make love and forget nightmares and everything disagreeable."

She drew herself away a little and looked with frightened eyes in his.

"But I can't forget, Ian, that I don't remember anything that has happened since we were on our honeymoon in Switzerland. And now we are in Oxford, and I can see it's quite late in the summer. How can I forget that somehow I am being robbed of myself—robbed of my life with you?"

"Wait till to-morrow and you'll remember everything right enough."

But Milly was not to be convinced. She was willing to submit on the question of last night's experiences, but she assured him that Tims would bear her out in the assertion that she had never recovered her recollection of the months preceding her engagement. Ian ceased trying to convince her that she was mistaken on this point; but he argued that the memory was of all functions of the brain the most uncertain, that there was no limit to its vagaries, which were mere matters of nerves and circulation, and that Dr. Norton-Smith, the nerve and brain specialist to whom he would take her, would probably turn out to have a dozen patients subject to the same affliction as herself. One never hears of half the ills that flesh is heir to until the inheritance falls to one's own lot.

Milly was a common-sense young woman, and his explanation, especially as it was his, pacified her for the time. The clouds had been rolling away while they talked, the space of deep blue sky overhead growing larger, the sunshine fuller. There was a busy twittering and shaking of little wings in the tall pear-tree near the house, where the tomtits in their varied liveries loved to congregate. July was not far advanced and the sun had still some hours in which to shine. Ian and Milly went out and walked in the Parks. The tennis-club lawns were almost deserted, but they met a few acquaintances taking their constitutional, like themselves, and an exchange of ordinary remarks with people who took her normality for granted, helped Milly to believe in it herself. So long as the blank in her memory continued, she could not be free from care; but she went to sleep that night in Ian's arms, feeling herself protected by them not only from bodily harm, but from all those dreadful fears and evil fantasies that "do assault and hurt the soul."

XI

I an had been so busy persuading Milly to view her own case as a simple one, and so busy comforting her with an almost feminine intuition of what would really afford her comfort, that it was only in the watches of the night that certain disquieting recollections forced their way into his mind. It was of course now part of his creed that he had loved Milly Flaxman from the first—only he had never known her well till that Christmas Vacation when they had skated so much together. Later on, such disturbing events as engagement and marriage had seemed to him enough to explain any changes he had observed in her. Later still, he had been too much in love to think about her at all, in the true sense of the word. She had been to him "all a wonder and a wild desire."

Now, taking the dates of her collapses of memory, he made, despite himself, certain notes on those changes. It is to be feared he did not often want to see Miss Timson; but on the day after Milly's return to the world, he cycled out to visit her friend. Tims was spending the summer on the wild and beautiful ridge which has since become a suburb of Oxford. It was doubtful whether he would find her in, as she was herself a mighty cyclist, making most of her journeys on the wheel, happy in the belief that she was saving money at the expense of the railway companies.

The time of flowers, the freshness of trees, and the glory of gorse and broom was over. It was the season of full summer when the midlands, clothed with their rich but sheenless mantle of green, wear a self-satisfied air, as of dull people conscious of deserved prosperity. But just as the sea or a mountain or an adventurous soul will always lend an element of the surprising and romantic to the commonest corner of earth, so the sky will perpetually transfigure large spaces of level country, valley or plain, laid open to its capricious influences. Boars Hill looks over the wide valley of the narrow Og to the downs, and up to where that merges into the valley of the Upper Thames. By the sandy track which Ian followed, the tree still stood, though no longer alone, whence the poet of *Thyrsis* looking northward, saw the "fair city with her dreaming spires"; less fair indeed to-day than when he looked upon it, but still "lovely all times," in all its fleeting shades, whether blond and sharp-cut in the sunshine or dimly gray among its veiling trees. The blue waving line of the downs, crowned here and there by clumps of trees, ran far along the southwestern horizon, melting vaporously in the distance above "the Vale, the three lone weirs, the youthful Thames." Over the downs and over the wide valley of ripening cornfields, of indigo hedgerow-elms and greener willow and woodland, of red-roofed homesteads and towered churches, moved slowly the broad shadows of rolling clouds that journeyed through the intense blue above. Some shadows were like veils of pale gray gauze, through which the world showed a delicately softened face; others were dark, with a rich, indefinable hue of their own, and as they moved, the earth seemed to burst into a deeper glow of color behind them. Close by, the broken hill-side was set here and there with oak and thorn, was everywhere deep in bracken, on whose large fronds lay the bluish bloom of their maturity. It all gained a definiteness of form, an air of meaning by its detachment from the wide background floating behind.

Following steep and circuitous lanes, Ian arrived at the lodging-house and found Tims on the porch preparing to start on her bicycle. But flattered and surprised by his visit, she ordered tea in the bright little sitting-room she was inhabiting. He was shy of approaching the real object of his visit. They marked time awhile till the thunderstorm became their theme. Then he told something of Milly's sleep-walking, her collapse of memory; and watched Tims meantime, hoping to see in her face merely surprise and concern. But there was no surprise, hardly concern in the queer little face. There was excitement, and at last a flash of positive pleasure.

"Good old M.!" she observed. "I'm glad she has got back; though I'm a bit proud of the other one too. I expect you feel much the same, old boy, don't you?"

The speech was the reverse of soothing, even to its detail of "old boy." He looked at his teacup and drew his black brows together.

"I'm afraid I don't understand, Miss Timson. I suppose you think it a joke, but to me it seems rather a serious matter."

"Of course it is; uncommon serious," returned Tims, too much interested in her subject to consider the husband's feelings. "Bless you! *I* don't want to be responsible for it. At first I thought it was a simple case of a personality evolved by hypnotism; but if so it would have depended on the hypnotist, and you see it didn't after the first."

"I don't think we need bother about hypnotism"—there was a note of impatience in Ian's voice—"it's just a case of collapse of memory. But as you were with her the first time it happened, I want to know exactly how far the collapse went. There were signs of it every now and then in her work, but on the whole it improved."

"You never can tell what will happen in these cases," said Tims. "She remembered her book-learning pretty well, but she forgot her own name, and as to people and things that had happened, she was like a new-born babe. If I hadn't nursed her through she'd have been sent to a lunatic asylum. But it wasn't that, after all, that made it so exciting. It was the difference between Milly's two personalities. You don't mean to say, old chap, you've lived with her for seven months and can't see the difference?"

Tims looked at him. She held strong theoretical views as to the stupidity of the male, but circumstances had seldom before allowed her to put them to the test. Behold them more than justified; for Ian was far above the average in intelligence. He, for a fraction of a minute, paused, deliberately closing the shutter of his mind against an unpleasant search-light that shot back on the experiences of his courtship and marriage.

"Well, I suppose I'm not imaginative," he returned, with a dry laugh. "I only see certain facts about her memory and want more of them, to tell Norton-Smith when I take her up to see him."

"Norton-Smith!" exclaimed Tims. "What is the good? Englishmen are all right when it's a question of filling up the map of Africa, but they're no good on the dark continent of ourselves. They're cowards. That's what's the matter with them. Don't go to Norton-Smith."

Stewart made an effectual effort to overcome his irritation. He ought to have known better than to turn to an oddity like Tims for advice and sympathy.

"Whom ought I to go to, then?" he asked, good-humoredly, and looking particularly long as he rose from the depths of the low wicker chair. "A medicine-man with horns and a rattle?"

"Well," returned Tims with deliberation, pulling on a pair of thread gloves, "I dare say he could teach Norton-Smith a thing or two. Mind you, I'm not talking spiritualistic rot; I'm talking scientific facts, which every one knows except the English scientific men, who keep on clapping their glass to the blind eye like a lot of clock-work Nelsons. The effects of hypnotism are as much facts as the effects of a bottle of whiskey. But Milly's case is different. In my opinion she's developed an independent double personality. It's an inconvenient state of things, but I don't suppose it'll last forever. One or the other will get stronger and 'hold the fort.' But it's rather a bad business anyhow." Tims paused and sighed, drawing on the other glove. "I'm—I'm fond of them both myself, and I expect you'll feel the same, when you see the difference."

Ian laughed awkwardly, his brown eyes fixed scrutinizingly upon her.

"So long as the fort holds somebody, I sha'n't worry," he said, lightly.

They went out, and as he led his own bicycle towards the upper track, Tims spun down the steep drive, and, turning into the lane, kissed her hand to him in farewell from under the brim of her perennially crooked hat.

"That Timson girl's more than queer," he mused to himself, going on. "There's a streak of real insanity in her. I'm afraid it's not been good for a highly strung creature like Mildred to see so much of her; and why on earth did she?"

He tried to clear his mind of Tims's fantastic suggestions; of everything, indeed, except the freshness of the air rushing past him, the beauty of the wide view, steeped in the romance of distance. But memory, that strange, recalcitrant, mechanical slave of ours, kept diving, without connivance of his, into the recesses of the past twenty months of his life, and presenting to him unsolicited, circumstances, experiences, which he had thrust away unclassified—his own surprise, almost perplexity, when Mildred had brought him work for the first time after her illness that autumn Term before last; his disappointment and even boredom in his engagement and the first three weeks of his marriage; then the change in his own feelings after her long sleep at the Hôtel du Chalet; besides a score of disquieting trifles which meant nothing till they were strung on a thread. He felt himself beginning to be infected with Flora Timson's mania against his will, against his sober judgment; and he spun down Bagley Hill at a runaway speed, only saved by a miracle from collision with a cart which emerged from Hincksey Lane at the jolting pace with which the rustic pursues his undeviating course.

XII

M illy, too, had not been without a sharp reminder that the leaves in her life so blank to her, had been fully inscribed by another. She hardly yet felt mistress of the house, but it was pleasant to rest and read in the low, white-panelled drawing-room, which lowered awnings kept cool, although the afternoon sun struck a golden shaft across the flowering window-boxes of its large and deeply recessed bow-window. The whole room was lighter and more feminine than Milly would have made it, but at bottom the taste that reigned there was more severe than her own. The only pictures on the panels were a few eighteenth century colored prints, already charming, soon to be valuable, and one or two framed pieces of needlework which harmonized with them.

Presently the door-bell rang and a Mr. Fitzroy was announced by the parlor-maid, in a tone which implied that she was accustomed to his name. He looked about the age of an undergraduate and was extraordinarily well-groomed, in spite of, or perhaps because of, being in a riding-dress. His sleek dark hair was neatly parted in the middle and he was clean shaven, when to be so smacked of the stage; but his manners and expression smacked of nothing of the kind.

"I'm awfully glad to find you at home, Mrs. Stewart," he said. "I've been lunching at the Morrisons', and, you know, I'm afraid there's going to be a row."

The Morrisons? They lived outside Oxford, and Milly knew them by sight, that was all.

"What about?" she asked, kindly, thinking the young man had come for help, or at least sympathy, in some embarrassment of his own.

"Why, about your acting Galatea. Jim Morrison's been a regular fool about it. He'd no business to take it for granted that that was the part I wanted Mrs. Shaw for. Now it appears she's telling every one that she's been asked to play the lead at the Besselsfield theatricals; and, by Jove, he says she is to, too!"

Milly went rather pale and then quite pink.

"Then of course I couldn't think of taking the part," she said, gasping with relief at this providential escape.

Mr. Fitzroy in his turn flushed. He had an obstinate chin and the cares of stage-management had already traced a line right across his smooth forehead. It deepened to a furrow as he leaned forward out of his low wicker chair, clutching the pair of dogskin gloves which he held in his hand.

"Oh, come, I say now, Mrs. Stewart!" and his voice and eye were surprisingly stern for one so young. "That's not playing fair. You promised me you'd see me through this show, and you know as well as I do, Mrs. Shaw can no more act than those fire-irons."

"But I—" Milly was about to say "I've never acted in my life"—when she remembered that she knew less than any one in her acquaintance what she had or had not done in that recent life which was not hers. "I shouldn't act Galatea at all well," she substituted lamely; "and I shouldn't look the part nearly as well as Mrs. Shaw will."

"Excuse me, Mrs. Stewart, but I'm certain you're simply cut out for it all round, and you told me the other day you were particularly anxious to play it. You promised you'd stick to me through thick and thin and not care a twopenny—I mean a straw—what Jim Morrison and Mrs. Shaw—"

In the stress of conversation they had neither of them noticed the tinkle of the front-door bell. Now the door of the room, narrow and in the thickness of an enormous wall, was thrown open and Mrs. Shaw was announced.

Fitzroy, forgetful of manners in his excitement, stooped forward and gripping Milly's arm almost hissed:

"Remember! You've promised me."

The words filled Milly with misery. That any one should be able to accuse her of breaking a promise, however unreal her responsibility for it, was horrible to her.

Mrs. Shaw entered, no longer the seraph of twenty months ago. She had latterly put off the æsthetic raiment she had worn with such peculiar grace, and her dress and coiffure were quite in the fashion of the hour. The transformation somewhat shocked Milly, who could never help feeling a slight austere prejudice against fashionably dressed woman. Then, considering how little she knew Mrs. Shaw, it was embarrassing to be kissed by her.

"It's odd I should find you here, Mr. Fitzroy," said Mrs. Shaw, settling her rustling skirts on a chintzy chair. "I've just come to talk to Mrs. Stewart about the acting. I'm so sorry there's been a misunderstanding about it."

Her tone was civil but determined, and there was a fighting look in her eye.

"So am I, Mrs. Shaw, most uncommonly sorry," returned Fitzroy, patting his sleek hair and feeling that his will was adamant, however pretty Mrs. Shaw might be.

"Of course, I shouldn't have thought of taking the part away from Mrs. Stewart," she resumed, glancing at Milly, not without meaning, "but Mr. Morrison asked me to take it quite a fortnight ago. I've learned most of it and rehearsed two scenes already with him. He says they go capitally, and we both think it seems rather a pity to waste all that labor and change the part now."

Fitzroy cast a look at Mrs. Stewart which was meant to call up reinforcements from that quarter; but as she sat there quite silent, he cleared his throat and begun:

"It's an awful bore, of course, but I fancy it's about three weeks or a month since I first asked Mrs. Stewart to play the lead—isn't it, Mrs. Stewart?"

Milly muttered assent, horribly suspecting a lie. A flash of indignant scorn from Mrs. Shaw confirmed the suspicion.

"Mrs. Stewart said something quite different when I spoke to her about it at tennis on Friday. Didn't you, Mildred?" she asked.

Milly crimsoned.

"Did I?" she stammered. "I'm afraid I've got a dreadfully bad memory—for—for dates of that kind."

Mrs. Shaw smiled coldly. Mr. Fitzroy felt himself deceived in Mrs. Stewart as an ally. He had counted on her promised support, on her wit and spirit to carry him through, and her conduct was simply cowardly.

"The fact is, Mrs. Shaw," he said, "Jim Morrison's not bossing this show at all. That's where the mistake has come in. My aunt, Lady Wolvercote, is a bit of an autocrat, don't you know, and she doesn't like us fellows to arrange things on our own account. If she knew you I'm sure she'd see what a splendid Galatea you'd make, but as it is she's set her heart on getting Mrs. Stewart from the very first."

Had he stopped here his position would have been good, but an indignant instinct, urging him to push the reluctant Mrs. Stewart into the proper place of woman—that natural shield of man against all the social disagreeables he brings on himself—made Fitzroy rush into the fatal detail.

"My aunt told you so at the Masonic; didn't she, Mrs. Stewart?"

Milly, under the young man's imperious eye, assented feebly, but Mrs. Shaw laughed. She perfectly remembered Mildred having mentioned on that very occasion that she did not know Lady Wolvercote by sight.

"I'm afraid I've come just a few minutes too soon," she said, dryly. "You and Mr. Fitzroy don't seem to have talked things over quite enough."

The saying was dark and yet too clear. Milly, the meticulously truthful, saw herself convicted of some horrible falsehood. She blushed violently, gasped, and rolled her handkerchief into a tight ball. Mr. Fitzroy ignoring the insinuation, changed his line.

"The part we really wanted you to take, Mrs. Shaw, was that of a nymph in an Elizabethan masque which Lumley has written, with music by Stephen Bampton. It's to be played in the rose garden and there's a chorus of nymphs who sing and dance. We want them to look perfectly lovely, don't you know, and as there can't be any make-up to speak of, it's awfully difficult to find the right people."

Mrs. Shaw disdained the lure and mentally condemned his anxiously civil manner as "soapy."

"I shall ask Mr. Morrison to go to Lady Wolvercote at once," she said, "and see whether she really wishes me to give up the part. Time's getting on, and he says he won't be able to have many more rehearsals."

There was a sound as of a carriage stopping in the street below, the jingling of bits, and a high female voice giving an order. Fitzroy, inwardly exasperated by Mrs. Shaw's resistance and the abject conduct of his ally, sprang to his feet.

"I believe that's my aunt!" he exclaimed. "She wants me to call at Blenheim on the way home, and I suppose the Morrisons told her where I was."

He managed to slip his head out between the edge of an awning and the mignonette and geraniums of a window-box.

"It's my aunt, right enough. May I fetch her up, Mrs. Stewart?" He was down the stairs in a moment and voluble in low-voiced colloquy with the lady in the barouche.

Lady Wolvercote was organizing the great fancy fair for the benefit of the County Cottage Hospitals, and had left the dramatic part of the programme to her nephew to arrange. She was a tall, slight woman, of the usual age for aunts, and pleasant to every one; but she took it for granted that every one would do as she wished—naturally, since they always did in her neighborhood. As she stumbled up the stairs after Charlie Fitzroy—it was a dark staircase and narrow in proportion to its massive oak balusters—she felt faintly annoyed with him for dragging her into the quarrels of his middle-class friends, but confident that she could manage them without the least trouble.

Milly was relieved at the return of Mr. Fitzroy with his aunt. She had had an unhappy five minutes with Mrs. Shaw, who had been saying cryptic but unpleasant things and calling her "Mildred"; whereas she did not so much as know Mrs. Shaw's Christian name.

Seeing Mrs. Shaw, beautiful, animated, well-dressed, and Milly neatly clothed, since her clothes were not of her own choosing, but with her hair unbecomingly knotted, the brightness of her eyes, complexion, and expression in eclipse, Lady Wolvercote wondered at her nephew's choice. But that was his affair. She began to talk in a rather high-pitched voice and continuously, like one whose business it is to talk; so that it was difficult to interrupt without rudeness.

"So you're going to be kind enough to act Galatea for us at our fancy fair, Mrs. Stewart? We want it to be a great success, and Lord Wolvercote and I have heard so much about your acting. My nephew said the part of Galatea would suit you exactly; didn't you, Charlie?"

"Down to the ground," interpolated, or rather accompanied, Fitzroy. "We shall have the placards out on Wednesday, and people are looking forward already to seeing Mrs. Stewart. There'll be a splendid audience."

"Every one has promised to fill their houses for the fair," Lady Wolvercote was continuing, "and the Duke thinks he may be able to get down —," she mentioned a royalty. "You're going to help us too, aren't you, Mrs. Shaw? It's so very kind of you. We've got such a pretty part for you in a musical affair which Lenny Lumley wrote with somebody or other for the Duchess of Ulster's Elizabethan bazaar. There's a chorus of fairies—nymphs, Charlie? Yes, nymphs, and we want them all to be very pretty and able to sing, and there's a charming dance for them. I'm afraid that silly boy, Jim Morrison, made some mistake about it, and told you we wanted you to act Galatea. But of course we couldn't possibly do without you in the other thing, and Mrs. Stewart seems quite pointed out for that Galatea part. Jim's such a dear, isn't he? And such a splendid actor, every one says he really ought to go on the stage. But we none of us pay the least attention to anything the dear boy says, for he always does manage to get things wrong."

Mrs. Shaw had been making little movements preparatory to going. She had no gift for the stage except beauty, but that produces an illusion of success, and she took her acting with the seriousness of a Duse.

"I'm sorry I didn't know Mr. Morrison's habits better," she replied. "I've been studying the part of Galatea a good deal and rehearsing it with him as well. Of course, I don't for a moment wish to prevent Mrs. Stewart from taking it, but I've spent a good deal of time upon it and I'm afraid I can't undertake anything else. Of course, it's very inconvenient stopping in Oxford in August, and I shouldn't care to do it except for the sake of a part which I felt gave me a real opportunity—"

"But it's a very pretty part we've got for you," resumed Lady Wolvercote, perplexed. "And we were hoping to see you over at Besselsfield a good deal for rehearsals—"

It seemed to her a "part of nature's holy plan" that the prospect of Besselsfield should prove irresistibly attractive to the wives of professional men.

"Thanks, so much, but I'm sure you and Mr. Fitzroy must know plenty of girls who would do for that sort of part," returned Mrs. Shaw.

Milly here broke in eagerly:

"Please, Lady Wolvercote, do persuade Mrs. Shaw to take Galatea; I'm sure I sha'n't be able to do it a bit; and I would try and take the nymph. I should love the music, and I know I could do the singing, anyhow."

She rose because Mrs. Shaw had risen and was looking for her parasol and shaking out her plumes. But why did Mr. Fitzroy and Mrs. Shaw both stare at her in an unvarnished surprise, touched with ridicule on the lady's side?

"No, no, Mrs. Stewart, that won't do!" cried he, in obvious dismay. At the same moment Mrs. Shaw exclaimed, ironically:

"That's very brave of you Mildred! I thought you hated music and were never going to try to sing again."

She and Fitzroy had both been present on an occasion when Mildred, urged on by Milly's musical reputation, had committed herself to an experiment in song which had not been successful.

"Thank you very much," Mrs. Shaw went on, "for offering to change, but of course Lady Wolvercote must arrange things as she likes; and, to speak frankly, I'm not particularly sorry to give the acting up, as my husband was rather upset at my not being able to go to Switzerland with him on the 28th. No, please don't trouble; I can let myself out. Good-bye, Lady Wolvercote; I hope the fair and the theatricals will be a great success. Good-bye, Mr. Fitzroy, good-bye."

Lady Wolvercote's faint remonstrances were drowned in the adieus, and Mrs. Shaw sailed out with flying colors, while Milly sank back abjectly into the seat from which she had risen. Every minute she was realizing with a more awful clearness that she, whose one appearance on the stage had been short and disastrous, was cast to play the leading part in a public play before a large and brilliant audience. She hardly heard Fitzroy's bitter remarks on Mrs. Shaw—not forgetting Jim Morrison—or Lady Wolvercote exclaiming in a voice almost dreamy with amazement:

"Really it's too extraordinary!"

"I'm very sorry Mrs. Shaw won't take the part," said Milly, clasping and unclasping her slender fingers, "for I know I can't do it myself."

Fitzroy was protesting, but she forced herself to continue: "You don't know what I'm like when I'm nervous. When we had *tableaux vivants* at Ascham I was supposed to be Charlotte putting a wreath on Werther's urn, and I trembled so much that I knocked the urn down. It was only card-board, so it didn't break, but every one laughed and the tableau was spoiled."

Fitzroy and his aunt cried out that that was nothing, a first appearance; any one could see she had got over that now. Pale, with terrified eyes, she looked from one to the other of her tormentors, who continued to sing the praises of her past prowess on the boards and to foretell the unprecedented harvest of laurels she would reap at Besselsfield. The higher their enthusiasm rose, the more profound became her dejection. There seemed no loop-hole for escape, unless the earth would open and swallow her, which however much to be desired was hardly to be expected.

The ting of a bicycle-bell below did not seem to promise assistance, for cyclists affected the quiet street. But it happened that this bicycle bore Ian to the door. He did not notice the coronet on the carriage which stood before it, and assumed it to belong to one of the three or four ladies in Oxford who kept such equipages. Yet in the blank state of Milly's memory, he was sorry she had not denied herself to visitors, which Mildred had already learned to do with a freedom only possible to women who are assured social success. Commonly the sight of a carriage would have sent him tiptoeing past the drawing-room, but now, vaguely uneasy, he came straight in. He looked particularly tall in the frame of the doorway, so low that his black hair almost touched the lintel; particularly handsome in the shaded, white-panelled room, into which the dark glow of his sunburned skin and brown eyes, bright with exercise, seemed to bring the light and warmth of the summer earth and sky.

Milly sprang to meet him. Lady Wolvercote was surprised to learn that this was Mrs. Stewart's husband. She had no idea a Don could be so young and good-looking. Judging of Dons solely by the slight and slighting references of her undergraduate relatives, she had imagined them to be weird-looking men, within various measurable distances of the grave.

"Lady Wolvercote and Mr. Fitzroy want me to act Galatea at the Besselsfield theatricals," said Milly, clinging to his sleeve and looking up at him with appealing eyes. "Please tell them I can't possibly do it. I'm—I'm not well enough—am I?"

"We're within three weeks of the performance, sir," put in Fitzroy. "Mrs. Stewart promised she'd do it, and we shall be in a regular fix now if she gives it up. Mrs. Shaw's chucked us already."

"Yes, and every one says how splendidly Mrs. Stewart acts," pleaded Lady Wolvercote.

Stewart had half forgotten the matter; but now he remembered that Mildred had been keen to have the part only a week ago, and a little pettish because he had advised her to leave it alone, on account of Mrs. Shaw. Now she was hanging on him with desperate eyes and that worried brow which he had not seen once since he had married her.

"I'm extremely sorry, Lady Wolvercote," he said, "but my wife's had a nervous break-down lately and I can't allow her to act. She's not fit for it."

"Ah, I see—I quite understand!" returned Lady Wolvercote. "But we'd take great care of her, Mr. Stewart. She could come and stay at Besselsfield."

Fitzroy's gloom lifted. His aunt was a trump. Surely an invitation to Besselsfield must do the job. But Stewart, though apologetic, was inflexible. He had forbidden his wife to act and there was an end of it. The perception of the differences between the two personalities of Milly which had been thrust to-day on his unwilling mind, made him grasp the meaning of her frantic appeals for protection. He relieved her of all responsibility for her refusal to act.

Lady Wolvercote observed, as she and her nephew went sadly on their way, that Mr. Stewart seemed a very, very odd man in spite of his presentable manners and appearance; and Fitzroy replied gloomily that of course he was a beast. Dons always were beasts.

XIII

The diplomatic incident of the theatricals was not the only minor trouble which Milly found awaiting her. The cook's nerves were upset by a development of rigid economy on the part of her mistress, and she gave notice; the house parlor-maid followed suit. No one seemed to have kept Ian's desk tidy, his papers in order, or his clothes properly mended. It was a joy to her to put everything belonging to him right.

When all was arranged to her satisfaction: "Ian," she said, sitting on his knee with her head on his shoulder, "I can't bear to think how wretched you must have been all the time I was away."

Ian was silent a minute.

"But you haven't been away, and I don't like you to talk as though you had."

Wretched? It would have been absurd to think of himself as wretched now; yet compared with the wonderful happiness that had been his for more than half a year, what was this "house swept and garnished"? An empty thing. Words of Tims's which he had thought irritating and absurd at the time, haunted him now. "*You don't mean to say you haven't seen the difference?*" He might not have seen it, but he had felt it. He felt it now.

There was at any rate no longer any question of Dieppe. They took lodgings at Sheringham and he made good progress with his book. Yet not quite so good as he had hoped. Milly was indefatigable in looking up points and references, in preventing him from slipping into the small inaccuracies to which he was prone; but he missed the stimulus of Mildred's alert mind, so quick to hit a blot in logic or in taste, so vivid in appreciation.

Milly meantime guessed nothing of his dissatisfaction. She adored her husband more every day, and her happiness would have been perfect had it not been for the haunting horror of the possible "change" which might be lurking for her round the corner of any night—that "change," which other people might call what they liked, but which meant for her the robbery of her life, her young happy life with Ian. He had taken her twice to Norton-Smith before the great man went for his holiday. Norton-Smith had pronounced it a peculiar but not unprecedented case of collapse of memory, caused by overwork; and had spent most of the consultation time in condemning the higher education of women. Time, rest, and the fulfilment of woman's proper function of maternity would, he affirmed, bring all right, since there was no sign of disease in Mrs. Stewart, who appeared to him, on the contrary, a perfectly healthy young woman. When Ian, alone with him, began tentatively to bring to the doctor's notice the changes in character and intelligence that had accompanied the losses of memory, he found his remarks set aside like the chatter of a foolish child.

If maternity would indeed exorcise the Invader, Milly had lost no time in beginning the exorcism. And she did believe that somehow it would; not because the doctor said so, but because she could not believe God would let a child's mother be changed in that way, at any rate while she was bearing it. To do so would be to make it more motherless than any little living thing on earth. Milly had always been quietly but deeply religious, and she struggled hard against the feeling of peculiar injustice in this strange affliction that had been sent to her. She prayed earnestly to God every night to help and protect her and her child, and the period of six or seven months, at which the "change" had come before, passed without a sign of it. In April a little boy was born. They called him Antonio, after a learned Italian, a friend and teacher of Ian's.

The advent of the child did something to explain the comparative seclusion into which Mrs. Stewart had retired, and the curious dulling of that brilliant personality of hers. The Master of Durham was among the few of Mrs. Stewart's admirers who declined to recognize the change in her. He had been attracted by the girl Milly Flaxman, by her gentle, shy manners and pretty face, combined with her reputation for scholarship; the brilliant Invader had continued to attract him in another way. The difference between the two, if faced, would have been disagreeably mysterious. He preferred to say and think that there was none; Mrs. Stewart was probably not very well.

Milly's shyness made it peculiarly awkward for her to find herself in possession of a number of friends whom she would not have chosen herself, and of whose doings and belongings she was in complete ignorance. However, if she gave offence she was unconscious of it, and it came very naturally to her to shrink back into the shadow of her household gods. Ian and the baby were almost sufficient in themselves to fill her life. There was just room on the outskirts of it for a few relations and old friends, and Aunt Beatrice still held her honored place. But it was through Aunt Beatrice that she was first to learn the feel of a certain dull heartache which was destined to grow upon her like some fell disease, a thing of ceaseless pain.

She was especially anxious to get Aunt Beatrice, who had been in America all the Summer Vacation, to stay with them in the Autumn Term as Lady Thomson had been with them in May, and Milly did not like to think of the number of things, all wrong, which she was sure to have noticed in the house. Besides, what with theatricals and other engagements, it was evident that a good many people had been "in and out" in the Summer Term—a condition of life which Lady Thomson always denounced. Milly was anxious for her to see that that phase was past and that her favorite niece had settled down into the quiet, well-ordered existence of which she approved.

Aunt Beatrice came; but oh, disappointment! If it had been possible to say of Lady Thomson, whose moods were under almost perfect control, that she was out of temper, Milly would have said it. She volunteered no opinion, but when asked, she compared Milly's new cook unfavorably with her former one. When her praise was anxiously sought, she observed that it was undesirable to be careless in one's housekeeping, but less disagreeable than to be fussy and house-proud. She added that Milly—whom she called Mildred—must be on her guard against relaxing into domestic dulness, when she could be so extremely clever and charming if she liked. Milly was bewildered and distressed. She felt sure that she had passed through a phase of which Aunt Beatrice ought to have disapproved. She had evidently been frivolous and neglectful of her duties; yet it seemed as though her aunt had been better pleased with her when she was like that. What could have made Aunt Beatrice, of all women, unkind and unjust?

In this way more than a year went by. The baby grew and was short-coated; the October Term came round once more, and still Milly remained the same Milly. To have wished it otherwise would have seemed like wishing for her death.

But at times a great longing for another, quite another, came over Ian. It was like a longing for the beloved dead. Of course it was mad—mad! He struggled against the feeling, and generally succeeded in getting back to the point of view that the change had been more in himself, in his own emotional moods, than in Milly.

October, the golden month, passed by and November came in, soft and dim; a merry month for the hunting men beside the coverts, where the red-brown leaves still hung on the oak-trees and brushwood, and among the grassy lanes, the wide fresh fields and open hill-sides. No ill month either for those who love to light the lamp early and open their books beside a cheerful fire. But then the rain came, a persistent, soaking rain. Milly always went to her district on Tuesdays, no matter what the weather, and this time she caught a cold. Ian urged her to stop in bed next morning. He himself had to be in College early, and could not come home till the afternoon.

It was still raining and the early falling twilight was murky and brown. The dull yellow glare of the street-lamps was faintly reflected in the muddy wetness of pavements and streets. He was carrying a great armful of books and papers under his dripping mackintosh and umbrella. As he walked homeward as fast as his inconvenient load allowed, he became acutely conscious of a depression of spirits which had been growing upon him all day. It was the weather, he argued, affecting his nerves or digestion. The vision of a warm, cosey house, a devoted wife awaiting him, ought to have cheered him, but it did not. He hoped he would not feel irritable when Milly rushed into the hall as soon as his key was heard in the front door, to feel him all over and take every damp thread tragically. Poor dear Milly! What a discontented brute of a husband she had got! The fault was no doubt with himself, and he would not really be happy even if some miracle did set him down on a sunny Mediterranean shore, with enough money to live upon and nothing to think of but his book. Mildred used to say that she always went to a big dinner at Durham in the unquenchable hope of meeting and fascinating some millionaire who had sense enough to see how much better it would be to endow writers of good books than readers of silly ones.

With the recollection there rang in the ears of his mind the sound of a laugh which he had not heard for seventeen months. Something seemed to tighten about his heart. Yes, he could be quite happy without the millionaire, without the sunny skies, without even the pretty, comfortable home at whose door he stood, if somewhere, anywhere, he could hope to hear that laugh again, to hold again in his arms the strange bright bride who had melted from them like snow in spring-time—but that way madness lay. He thrust the involuntary longing from him almost with horror, and turned the latch-key in his door.

The hall lamp was burning low and the house seemed very chilly and quiet. He put his books down on the oak table, threw his streaming mackintosh upon the large chest, and went up to his dressing-room, to

　　　　　　　　　　　　　　MARGARET L. WOODS

change whatever was still damp about him before seeking Milly, who presumably was nursing her cold before the study fire. When he had thrown off his shoes, he noticed that the door leading to his wife's room was ajar and a faint red glow of firelight showed invitingly through the chink. A fire! It was irresistible. He went in quickly and stirred the coals to a roaring blaze. The dancing flames lit up the long, low room with its few pieces of furniture, its high white wainscoting, and paper patterned with birds and trellised leaves. They lit up the low white bed and the white figure of his sleeping wife. Till then he had thought the room was empty. She lay there so deathly still and straight that he was smitten with a sudden fear; but leaning over her he heard her quiet, regular breathing and saw that if somewhat pale, she was normal in color. He touched her hand. It was withdrawn by a mechanical movement, but not before he had felt that it was warm.

A wild excitement thrilled him; it would have been truer to say a wild joy, only that it held a pang of remorse for itself. So she had lain at the Hôtel du Chalet when he had left her for that long walk over the crisp mountain snow. And when he had returned, she—what She? No, his brain did not reel on the verge of madness; it merely accepted under the compulsion of knowledge a truth of those truths that are too profound to admit of mere external proof. For our reason plays at the edge of the universe as a little child plays at the edge of the sea, gathering from its fringes the flotsam and jetsam of its mighty life. But miles and miles beyond the ken of the eager eye, beyond the reach of the alert hand, lies the whole great secret life of the sea. And if it were all laid bare and spread at the child's feet, how could the little hand suffice to gather its vast treasures, the inexperienced eye to perceive and classify them?

Alone in the firelit, silent room, with this tranced form before him, Ian Stewart knew that the woman who would arise from that bed would be a different woman from the one who had lain down upon it. By what mysterious alchemy of nature transmuted he could not understand, any more than he could understand the greater part of the workings of that cosmic energy which he was compelled to recognize, although he might be cheated with words into believing that he understood them. Another woman would arise and she his Love. She had been gone so long; his heart had hungered for her so long, in silence even to himself. She had been dead and now she was about to be raised from the dead. He lighted the candles, locked the doors, and paced softly up and down, stopping to look at the figure on the bed from time to time. Far around him, close about him, life was moving at its usual jog-trot pace. People were going back to their College rooms or domestic hearths, grumbling about the weather or their digestions or their colds, thinking of their work for the evening or of their dinner engagements—and suddenly a door had shut between him and all that outside world. He was no longer moving in the driven herd. He was alone, above them in an upper chamber, awaiting the miracle of resurrection.

In the visions that passed before his mind's eye the face of Milly, pale, with pleading eyes, was not absent; but with a strange hardness which he had never felt before, he thrust the sighing phantom from him. She had had her turn of happiness, a long one; it was only fair that now they two, he and that Other, should have their chance, should put their lips to the full cup of life. The figure on the bed stirred, turned on one side, and slipped a hand under the pure curve of the young cheek. He was by the bed in a moment; but it still slept, though less profoundly, without that tranced look, as though the flame of life itself burned low within.

How would she first greet him? Last time she had leaned into the clear sunshine and laughed to him from the cloud of her amber hair; and a spirit in his blood had leaped to the music of her laugh, even while the rational self knew not it was the lady of his love. But however she came back it would be she, the Beloved. He felt exultantly how little, after all, the frame mattered. Last time he had found her, his love had been set in the sunshine and the splendor of the Alpine snows, with nothing to jar, nothing to distract it from itself. And that was good. To-day, it was opening, a sudden and wonderful bloom, in the midst of the murky discomfort of an English November, the droning hum of the machinery of his daily work. And this, too, was good.

Yes, it was better because of the contrast between the wonder and its environment, better because he himself was more conscious of his joy. He sat on the bed a while watching her impatiently. In his eyes she was already filled with a new loveliness, but he wanted her hair, her amber hair. It was brushed back and imprisoned tightly in a little plait tied with a white ribbon—Milly's way. With fingers clumsy, yet gentle, he took off the ribbon and cautiously undid the plait. Then he took a comb and spread out the silk-soft hair more as he liked to see it, pleased with his own skill in the unaccustomed task. She stirred again, but still she did not wake. He was pacing up and down the room when she raised

MARGARET L. WOODS

herself a little on her pillow and looked fixedly at the opposite wall. Ian held his breath. He stood perfectly still and watched her. Presently she sat up and looked about her, looked at him with a faint, vague smile, like that of a baby. He sat down at the foot of the bed and took her hand. She smiled at him again, this time with more definite meaning.

"Do you know who it is, sweetheart?" he said in a low voice. She nodded slightly and went on smiling, as though quietly happy.

"Ian," she breathed, at length.

"Yes, darling."

"I've been away a long, long time. How long?"

He told her.

She uttered a little "Ah!" and frowned; lay quiet awhile, then drew her hand from Ian's and sat up still more.

"I sha'n't lie here any longer," she said, in a stronger voice. "It's just waste of time." She pushed back the clothes and swung her feet out of bed. "Oh, how glad I am to be back again! Are you glad I'm back, Ian? Say you are, do say you are!"

And Ian on his knees before her, said that he was.

XIV

I an was leaning against the high mantel-piece of his study. Above it, let into the panelling, was an eighteenth-century painting of the Bridge and Castle of St. Angelo, browned by time. He was wondering how to tell Mildred about the child, and whether she would resent its presence. She, too, was meditating, chin on hand. At length she looked up with a sudden smile.

"What about the baby, Ian? Don't you take any notice of it yet?"

He was surprised.

"How do you know about him?"

She frowned thoughtfully.

"I seem to know things that have happened in a kind of way—rather as though I had seen them in a dream. But they haven't happened to me, you know."

"Was it the same last time?"

"No; but the first time I came, and especially just at first, I seemed to remember all kinds of things—" She paused as though trying in vain to revive her impressions—"Odd things, not a bit like anything in Oxford. I can't recall them now, but sometimes in London I fancy I've seen places before."

"Of course you have, dear."

"And the first time I saw that old picture there I knew it was Rome, and I had a notion that I'd been there and seen just that view."

"You've been seeing pictures and reading books and hearing talk all your life, and in the peculiar state of your memory, I suppose you can't distinguish between the impressions made on it by facts and by ideas."

Mildred was silent; but it was not the silence of conviction. Then she jumped up.

"I'm going to see Baby. You needn't come if you don't want."

He hesitated.

"I'm afraid it's too late. Milly doesn't like—" He broke off with a wild laugh. "What am I talking about!"

"I suppose you were going to say, Milly doesn't like people taking a candle into the room when Baby is shut up for the night. I don't care what Milly likes. He's my baby now, and he's sure to look a duck when he's asleep. Come along!"

She put her arm through his and together they climbed the steep staircase to the nursery.

Mildred had returned to the world in such excellent spirits at merely being there, that she took those awkward situations which Milly had inevitably bequeathed to her, as capital jokes. The partial and external acquaintance with Milly's doings and points of view which she had brought back with her, made everything easier than before; but her derisive dislike of her absent rival was intensified. It pained Ian if she dropped a hint of it. Tims was the only person to whom she could have the comfort of expressing herself; and even Tims made faces and groaned faintly, as though she did not enjoy Mildred's wit when Milly was the subject of it. She gave Milly's cook notice at once, but most things she found in a satisfactory state—particularly the family finances. More negatively satisfactory was the state of her wardrobe, since so little had been bought. Mildred still shuddered at the recollection of the trousseau frocks.

Once more Mrs. Stewart, whose social career had been like that of the proverbial rocket shot up into the zenith. But a life of mere amusement was not the fashion in the circle in which she lived, and her active brain and easily aroused sympathies made her quick to take up more serious interests.

It seemed wiser, too, to make no sudden break with Milly's habits. Still, Emma, the nurse, opined that Baby got on all the better since Mrs. Stewart had become "more used to him like"—wasn't always changing his food, taking his temperature, wanting him to have bandages and medicine, forbidding him to be talked to or sung to, and pulling his little, curling-up limbs straight when he was going to sleep. He was a healthy little fellow and already pretty, with his soft dark hair—softer than anything in the world except a baby's hair—his delicate eyebrows and bright dark eyes. Mildred loved playing with him. Sometimes when Ian heard the tiny shrieks of baby laughter, he used to think with a smile and yet with a pang of pity, how shocked poor Milly would have been at this titillation of the infant brain. But he did not want thoughts of Milly—so far as he could he shut the door of his mind against them. She would come back, no doubt, sooner or later; and her coming back would mean that Mildred would be robbed of her life, his own life robbed of its joy.

At the end of Term the Master of Durham sent a note to bid the Stewarts to dine with him and meet Sir Henry Milwood, the rich

Australian, and Maxwell Davison, the traveller and Orientalist. Ian remarked that Davison was a cousin, although they had not met since he was a boy. Maxwell Davison had gone to the East originally as agent for some big firm, and had spent there nearly twenty years. He was an accomplished Persian and Arabic scholar, and gossip related that he had run off with a fair Persian from a Constantinople harem and lived with her in Persia until her death. But that was years ago.

When the Stewarts entered the Master's bare bachelor drawing-room, they found besides the Milwoods, only familiar faces. Maxwell Davison was still awaited, and with interest. He came, and that interest did not appear to be mutual, judging from the Oriental impassivity of his long, brown face, with its narrow, inscrutable eyes. He was tall, slight, sinewy as a Bedouin, his age uncertain, since his dry leanness and the dash of silver at his temples might be the effect of burning desert suns.

Mildred was delighted at first at being sent into dinner with him, but she found him disappointingly taciturn. In truth, he had acquired Oriental habits and views with regard to women. If a foolish Occidental custom demanded that they should sit at meat with the lords of creation, he, Maxwell Davison, would not pretend to acquiesce in it. Mildred, to whom it was unthinkable that any man should not wish to talk to her, merely pitied his shyness and determined to break it down; but Davison's attitude was unbending.

After dinner the Master, his mortar-board cap on his head, opened the drawing-room door and invited them to come across to the College Library to see some bronzes and a few other things that Mr. Davison had temporarily deposited there. He had divined that Maxwell Davison would be willing to sell, and in his guileful soul the little Master may have had schemes of persuading his wealthy friend Milwood to purchase any bronzes that might be of value to the College or the University. Of the ladies, only Mildred and Miss Moore, the archæologist, braved the chill of the mediæval Library to inspect the collection. Davison professed to no artistic or antiquarian knowledge of the bronzes. They had come to him in the way of trade and had all been dug up in Asia Minor—no, not all, for one he had picked up in England. Nevertheless he had succeeded in getting a pretty clear notion of the relative value of his bronzes—the Oriental curios with them it was his business to understand. He could not help observing the sure instinct with which Mrs. Stewart selected what was best among all these different objects.

She had the *flair* of the born collector. The learned archæologists present leaned over the collection discussing and disputing, and took no notice of her remarks as she rapidly handled each article. But Davison did, and when at length she took up a small figure of Augustus—the bronze that had not come from Asia Minor—and looked at it with a peculiar doubtful intentness, he began to feel uncomfortable.

"Anything wrong with that?" he asked, in spite of himself.

She laughed nervously.

"Oh, Mr. Davison, please ask some one who knows! I don't. Only I—I seem to have seen something like it before, that's all."

Sanderson, roaming around the professed archæologists, took the bronze from her hands.

"I'll tell you where you've seen it, Mrs. Stewart. It's engraved in Egerton's *Private Collections of Great Britain*. I picked that up the other day—first edition, 1818. I dare say the book's here. We'll see."

Sanderson took a candle and went glimmering away down the long, dark room.

"What can this be?" asked Mildred, taking up what looked like a glass ball.

"Please stand over here and look into it for five minutes," returned Davison, evasively. "Perhaps you'll see what it is then."

He somehow wanted to get rid of Mildred's appraisal of his goods.

"Mr. Davison, your glass ball has gone quite cloudy!" she exclaimed, in a minute or two.

"That's all right. Go on looking and you'll see something more," he returned.

Presently she said:

"It's so curious. I see the whole room reflected in the glass now, but it's much lighter than it really is, and the windows seem larger. It all looks so different. There is some one down there in white."

Sanderson came up the room carrying a large quarto, open.

"Here's your bronze, right enough," he said, putting the book down on the table. "It's under the heading, *Hammerton Collection*."

He pointed to a small engraving inscribed, "Bronze statuette of Augustus. *Very rare.* "

"But some fellow's been scribbling something here," continued Sanderson, turning the book around to read a note written along the margin. He read out: "'A forgery. Sold by Lady Hammerton to Mr. Solomons, 1819. See case Solomons *versus* Hammerton, 1820.'"

The turning of the book showed Mildred a full-page engraving entitled, "The Gallery, Hammerton House." It represented a long room somewhat like the one in which they stood, but still more like the room she had seen in the crystal; and in the middle distance there was a slightly sketched figure of a woman in a light dress. Half incredulous, half frightened, she pored over the engraving which reproduced so strangely the image she had seen in Maxwell Davison's mysterious ball.

"How funny!" she almost whispered.

"You may call it funny, of course, that Lady Hammerton succeeded in cheating a Jew, which is what it looks like," rejoined Sanderson, bent on hunting down his quarry; "but it was pretty discreditable to her too."

"Not at all," Maxwell Davison's harsh voice broke in. "That was Solomons's look out. I sha'n't bring a lawsuit against the fellow who sold me that Augustus, if it is a forgery. A man's a fool to deal in things he doesn't understand."

"What is this glass ball, Mr. Davison?" asked Miss Moore, in her turn taking up the uncanny thing Mildred had laid down.

"It's a divining-crystal. In the East certain people, mostly boys, look in these crystals and see all sorts of things, present, past, and to come."

Miss Moore laughed.

"Or pretend they do!"

"Who knows? It isn't of any interest, really. The things that have happened have happened, and the things that are to happen will happen just as surely, whether we foresee them or not."

Miss Moore turned to the Master.

"Look, Master—this is a divining-crystal, and Mr. Davison's trying to persuade me that in the East people really see visions in it."

The Master smiled.

"Mr. Davison has a poor opinion of ladies' intelligence, I'm afraid. He thinks they are children, who will believe any fairy tale."

Davison had drawn near to Mildred as the Master spoke; his eyes met hers and the impassive face wore a faint, ironical smile.

"The Wisdom of the West speaks!" he exclaimed, in a low voice. "I'd almost forgotten the sound of it."

Then scrutinizing her pale face: "I'm afraid you've had a scare. What did you see?"

"I saw—well, I fancy I saw the Gallery at Hammerton House and my ancestress, Lady Hammerton. It was burned, you know, and she was burned with it, trying to save her collections. I expect she condescended to give me a glimpse of them because I've inherited her mania. I'd be a collector, too, if I had the money."

She laughed nervously.

"You should take Ian to the East," returned Davison. "You could make money there and learn things—the Wisdom of the East, for instance."

Mildred, recovering her equanimity, smiled at him.

"No, never! The Wisdom of the West engrosses us; but you'll come and tell us about the other, won't you?"

XV

Maxwell Davison settled in Oxford for six months, in order to see his great book on Persian Literature through the press. His advent had been looked forward to as promising a welcome variety, bringing a splash of vivid color into a somewhat quiet-hued, monotonous world. But there was doomed to be some disappointment. Mr. Davison went rather freely to College dinners but seldom into general society. It came to be understood that he disliked meeting women; Mrs. Stewart, however, he appeared to except from his condemnation or rule. Ian was his cousin, which made a pretext at first for going to the Stewarts' house; but he went because he found the couple interesting in their respective ways. Some Dons, unable to believe that a man without a University education could teach them anything, would lecture him out of their little pocketful of knowledge about Oriental life and literature. Ian, on the contrary, was an admirable producer of all that was interesting in others; and in Davison that all was much. At first he had tried to keep Mrs. Stewart in what he conceived to be her proper place; but as time went on he found himself dropping in at the old house with surprising frequency, and often when he knew Ian to be in College or too busy to attend to him.

He had brought horses with him and offered to give Mildred a mount whenever she liked. Milly had learned the rudiments of the art, but she was too timid to care for riding. Mildred, on the other hand, delighted in the swift motion through the air, the sensation of the strong bounding life almost incorporated with her own, and if she had moments of terror she had more of ecstatic daring. She and Davison ended by riding together once or twice a week.

Interesting as Mildred found Maxwell Davison's companionship, it did not altogether conduce to her happiness. She who had been so content to be merely alive, began now to chafe at the narrow limits of her existence. He opened the wide horizons of the world before her, and her soul seemed native to them. One April afternoon they rode to Wytham together. The woods of Wytham clothe a long ridge of hill around which the young Thames sweeps in a strong curve and through them a grass ride runs unbroken for a mile and a half. Now side by side, now passing and repassing each other, they had "kept the great pace" along the track, the horses slackening their speed somewhat as they went down the dip, only to spring forward with fresh impetus, lifting their hind-quarters gallantly to the rise; then given their heads for the last burst along the straight bit to the drop of the hill, away they went in passionate competition, foam-flecked and sending the clods flying from their hurrying hoofs.

A mile and a half of galloping only serves to whet the appetite of a well-girt horse, and the foaming rivals hardly allowed themselves to be pulled up at the edge of a steep grassy slope, where already here and there a yellow cowslip bud was beginning to break its pale silken sheath. At length their impatient dancing was over, and they stood quiet, resigned to the will of the incomprehensible beings who controlled them. But Mildred's blood was dancing still and she abandoned herself to the pleasure of it, undistracted by speech. Beyond the shining Thames, wide-curving through its broad green meadows, and the gray bridge and tower of Eynsham, that great landscape, undulating, clothed in the mystery of moving cloud-shadows, gave her an agreeable impression of being a view into a strange country, hundreds of miles away from Oxford and the beaten track. But Maxwell's eyes were fixed upon her.

The wood about them was just breaking into the various beauty of spring foliage, emerald and gold and red; a few trees still holding up naked gray branches among it; here and there a white cloud of cherry blossom, shining in a clearing or floating mistily amid bursting tree-tops below them. They turned to the right, down a narrow ride, mossy and winding, where perforce they trod on flowers as they went; for the path and the wood about it were carpeted with blue dog-violets and the pale soft blossoms of primroses, opening in clusters amid their thick fresh foliage and the brown of last year's fallen leaves. The sky above wore the intense blue in which dark clouds are seen floating, and as the gleams of travelling sunshine passed over the wooded hill, its colors also glowed with a peculiar intensity. The horses, no longer excited by a vista of turf, were walking side by side. But the beauty of earth and sky were nothing to Maxwell, whose whole being was intent on the beauty of the woman in the saddle beside him; the rose and the gold of cheek and hair, the lithe grace of the body, lightly moving to the motion of her horse.

She turned to him with a sudden bright smile.

"How perfectly delightful riding is! I owe all the pleasure of it to you."

"Do you?" he asked, smiling too, but slightly and gravely, narrowing on her his inscrutable eyes. "Well, then, will you do what I want?"

"I thought you were a fatalist and never wanted anything. But if you condescend to want me to do something, your slave obeys. You see I'm learning the proper way for a woman to talk."

"I want you to remove the preposterous black pot with which you've covered up your hair. I'll carry it for you."

"Oh, Max! What would people think if they met me riding without my hat? Fancy Miss Cayley! What she'd say! And the Warden of Canterbury! What he'd feel!"

She laughed delightedly.

"They never ride this way. It's the 'primrose path,' you see, and they're afraid of the 'everlasting bonfire.' I'm not; you're not. You're not afraid of anything."

"I am. I'm afraid of old maids and—most butlers."

Maxwell laughed, but his laugh was a harsh one.

"Humbug! If you really wanted to do anything you'd do it. I know you better than you know yourself. If you won't take your hat off it's because you don't really want to do what I want; and when you say pretty things to me about your gratitude for the pleasure I'm giving you, you're only telling the same old lies women tell all the world over."

"There! Catch my reins!" cried Mildred, leaning over and holding them out to him. "How do you suppose I can take my hat off if you don't?"

He obeyed and drew up to her, stooping near, a hand on the mane of her horse. The horses nosed together and fidgeted, while she balanced herself in the saddle with lifted arms, busy with hat-pins. The task accomplished, she handed the hat to him and they cantered on. Presently she turned towards him, brightening.

"You were quite right about the hat, Max. It's ever so much nicer without it; one feels freer, and what I love about riding is the free feeling. It's as though one had got out of a cage; as though one could jump over all the barriers of life; as though there were nobody and nothing to hinder one from galloping right out into the sky if one chose. But I can't explain what I mean."

"Of course you don't mean the sky," he answered. "What you really mean is the desert. There's space, there's color, glorious, infinite, with an air purer than earthly. Such a life, Mildred! The utter freedom of it! None of this weary, dreary slavery you call civilization. That would be the life for you."

It was true that Mildred's was an essentially nomadic and adventurous soul. Whether the desert was precisely the most suitable sphere for her wanderings was open to doubt, but for the moment as typifying freedom, travel, and motion—all that really was as the breath of life to her—it fascinated her imagination. Maxwell, closely watching that sunshine-gilded head, saw her eyes widen, her whole expression at once excited and meditative, as though she beheld a vision. But in a moment she had turned to him with a challenging smile.

"I thought slavery was the only proper thing for women."

"So it is—for ordinary women. It makes them happier and less mischievous. But I don't fall into the mistake—which causes such a deal of unnecessary misery and waste in the world—the mistake of supposing that you can ever make a rule which it's good for every one to obey. You've got to make your rule for the average person. Therefore it's bound not to fit the man or woman who is not average, and it's folly to wish them to distort themselves to fit it."

"And I'm not average? I needn't be a slave? Oh, thank you, Max! I am so glad."

"Confound it, Mildred, I'm not joking. You are a born queen and you oughtn't to be a slave; but you are one, all the same. You're a slave to the 'daily round, the common task,' which were never meant for such as you; you're a slave to the conventional idiocy of your neighbors. You daren't even take your hat off till I make you; and now you see how nice it is to ride with your hat off."

They had been slowly descending the steep, stony road which leads to Wytham Village, but as he spoke they were turning off into a large field to the right, across which a turfy track led gradually up to the woods from which they had come. The track lay smooth before them, and the horses began to sidle and dance directly their hoofs touched it. Mildred did not answer his remarks, except by a reference to the hat.

"Don't lose it, that's all!" she shouted, looking back and laughing, as she shot up the track ahead of him. He fancied she was trying to show him that she could run away from him if she chose; and with a quiet smile on his lips and a firm hand on his tugging horse, he kept behind her until she was a good way up the field. Then he gave his horse its head and it sprang forward. She heard the eager thud of the heavy hoofs drawing up behind, and in a few seconds he was level with her. For a minute they galloped neck and neck, though at a little distance from each other. Then she saw him ahead, riding with a seat looser than most Englishmen's, yet with an assurance, a grace of its own, the hind-quarters of his big horse lifting powerfully under him, as it sped with great bounds over the flying turf. Her own mare saw it, too, and vented her annoyance in a series of kicks, which, it must be confessed, seriously disturbed Mildred's equilibrium. Then settling to business, she sprang after her companion. Maxwell heard her following him up the long grass slope towards the gate which opens into the main ride by which they had started. He fancied he had the improvised race well in hand, but suddenly the hoofs behind him hurried their beat; Mildred flew past him at top speed and flung her mare back on its haunches at the gate.

"I've won! Hurrah! I've won!" she shouted, breathlessly, and waved her whip at him.

Maxwell was swearing beneath his breath, in a spasm of anger and anxiety.

"Don't play the fool!" he cried, savagely, as he drew rein close to her. "You might have thrown the mare down or mixed her in with the gate, pulling her up short like that. It's a wonder you didn't come off yourself, for though you're a devil to go, you know as well as I do you're a poor horse-woman."

He was violently angry, partly at Mildred's ignorant rashness, partly because, after all, she had beaten him. She, taking her hat from his hand and fastening it on again, uttered apologies, but from the lips only; for she had never seen a man furious before, and she was keenly interested in the spectacle. Maxwell's eyes were not inscrutable now; they glittered with manifest rage. His harsh voice was still harsher, his hard jaw clinched, the muscles of his lean face, which was as pale as its brownness allowed it to be, stood out like cords, and the hand that grasped her reins shook. Mildred felt somewhat as she imagined a lion-tamer might feel; just the least bit alarmed, but mistress of the brute, on the whole, and enjoying the contact with anything so natural and fierce and primitive. The feeling had not had time to pall on her, when going through the gate, they were joined by two other members of the little clan of Wytham riders, and all rode back to Oxford together, through flying scuds of rain.

XVI

There is a proverbial rule against playing with fire, but it is one which, as Davison would have said, was evidently made by average people, who would in fact rather play with something else. There are others to whom fire is the only really amusing plaything; and though the by-stander may hold his breath, nine times out of ten they will come out of the game as unscathed as the professional fire-eater. This was not precisely true of Mildred, who had still a wide taste in playthings; but in the absence of anything new and exciting in her environment, she found an immense fascination in playing with the fiery elements in Maxwell Davison's nature, in amusing her imagination with visions of a free wandering life, led under a burning Oriental sky, which he constantly suggested to her. Yet dangerously alluring as these visions might appear, appealing to all the hidden nomad heart of her, her good sense was never really silenced. It told her that freedom from the shackles of civilization might become wearisome in time, besides involving heavier, more intolerable forms of bondage; although she did not perceive that Maxwell Davison's dislike to her being a slave was only a dislike to her being somebody else's slave. He was a despot at heart and had accustomed himself to a frank despotism over women. Mildred's power over him, the uncertainty of his power over her, maddened him. But Mildred did not know what love meant. At one time she had fancied her affection for Ian might be love; now she wondered whether her strange interest in the society of a man for whom she had no affection, could be that. She did not feel towards Ian as an ordinary wife might have done, yet his feelings and interests weighed much with her. Milly, too, she must necessarily consider, but she did that in a different, an almost vengeful spirit.

One evening Ian, looking up from his work, asked her what she was smiling at so quietly to herself. And she could not tell him, because it was at a horrible practical joke suggested to her by an impish spirit within. What if she should prepare a little surprise for the returning Milly? Let her find herself planted in Araby the Blest with Maxwell Davison? Mildred chuckled, wondering to herself which would be in the biggest rage, Milly or Max; for however Tims might affirm the contrary, Mildred had a fixed impression that Milly could be in a rage.

The fire-game was hastening to its close; but before Mildred could prove herself a real mistress of the dangerous element, the sleep fell upon her.

Except a sensation of fatigue, for which it was easy to find a reason, there was no warning of the coming change. But Ian had dreams in the night and opened his eyes in the morning with a feeling of uneasiness and depression. Mildred could never sleep late without causing him anxiety, and on this morning his first glance at her filled him with a dread certainty. She was sleeping what was to her in a measure the sleep of death. He had a violent impulse to awaken her forcibly; but he feared it would be dangerous. With his arm around her and his head close to hers on the pillow, he whispered her name over and over again. The calmness of her face gradually gave way to an expression of struggle approaching convulsion, and he dared not continue. He could only await the inevitable in a misery which from its very nature could find no expression and no comforter.

Milly, unlike Mildred, did not return to the world in a rapture of satisfaction with it. The realization of the terrible robbery of life of which she had again been the victim, was in itself enough to account for a certain sadness even in her love for Ian and for her child. The hygiene of the nursery had been neglected according to her ideas, yet Baby was bonny enough to delight any mother's heart, however heavy it might be. Ian, she said, wanted feeding up and taking care of; and he submitted to the process with a gentle, melancholy smile. Just one request he made; that she would not spoil her pretty hair by screwing it up in her usual unbecoming manner. She understood, studying a certain photograph in a drawer—what drawer was safe from Milly's tidyings?—and dressed her hair as like it as she knew how, with a secret bitterness of heart.

Mildred had found a diary, methodically kept by Milly, of great use to her, and although incapable herself of keeping one regularly, she had continued it in a desultory manner, noting down whatever she thought might be useful for Milly's guidance. For whatever the feelings of the two personalities towards each other, there was a terrible closeness of union between them. Their indivisibility in the eyes of the world made their external interests inevitably one. New friends and acquaintances Mildred had noted down, with useful remarks upon them. She was not confidential on the subject of Maxwell Davison, but she gave the bare necessary information.

It was now late in the Summer Term and her bedroom chimney-

MARGARET L. WOODS

piece was richly decorated with invitation cards. Among others there was an invitation to a garden-party at Lady Margaret Hall. Milly put on a fresh flowered muslin dress, apparently unworn, that she found hanging in one of the deep wall-cupboards of the old house, and a coarse burnt-straw hat, trimmed with roses and black ribbon, which became her marvellously well. All the scruples of an apostle of hygienic dress, all the uneasiness of an economist at the prospect of unpaid bills, disappeared before the pleasure of a young woman face to face with an extremely pretty reflection in a pier-glass. That glass, an oval in a light mahogany frame, of the Regency period, if not earlier, was one of Mildred's finds in the slums of St. Ebbes.

She walked across the Parks, where the Cricket Match of the season was drawing a crowd, meaning to come out by a gate below Lady Margaret Hall, the gardens and buildings of which did not then extend to the Cherwell. In their place were a few tennis-grounds and a path leading to a boat-house, shared by a score or more of persons. While she was still coming across the grass of the Parks, a man in flannels, very white in the sun, came towards her from the gate for which she was making. He must have recognized her from a long way off. He was a striking-looking man of middle age, walking with a free yet indolent stride that carried him along much faster than it appeared to do.

Milly had no idea who the stranger was, but he greeted her with: "Here you are at last, Mildred! Do you know how much behind time you are?"—he took out his watch—"Exactly thirty-five minutes. I should have given you up if I hadn't known that breaking your promise is not among your numerous vices, and unpunctuality is."

Who on earth was he? And why did he call her by her Christian name? Milly went a beautiful pink with embarrassment.

"I'm so sorry. I thought the party would have just begun," she replied.

"You don't mean to say you want to keep me kicking my heels while you go to a confounded party? I thought you knew I was off to Paris to-night, after that Firdusi manuscript, and I think of taking the Continental Express to Constantinople next week. I don't know when I shall be back. Surely, Mildred, it's not a great deal to ask you to spare half an hour from a wretched party to come on the river with me before I go?" It struck Maxwell as he ended that he was falling into the whining of the Occidental lover. He was determined that he would clear the situation this afternoon; the more determined because he was conscious of a feeling odiously resembling fear which had before now held him back from plain dealing with Mildred. Afraid of a woman? It was too ridiculous.

Milly, meanwhile, felt herself on firmer ground. This must be Ian's cousin, Maxwell Davison, the Orientalist. But there was nothing nomadic in her heart to thrill to the idea of being on the Cherwell this afternoon, in London this evening, in Paris next morning, in Constantinople next week.

"Of course I'll come on the river with you," she said. "I'm sorry I'm late. I'm afraid I—I'd forgotten."

Forgotten! How simply she said it! Yet it was surely the veriest impudence of coquetry. He looked at her slowly from the hat downward, as he lounged leisurely at her side.

"War-paint, I see!" he remarked. "Armed from head to heel with all the true and tried female weapons. They're just the same all the world over—'plus ça change, plus c'est la même chose,'—though no doubt you fancy they're different. Who's the frock put on for, Mildred? For the party, or—for me?"

Milly was conscious of such an extreme absence of intention so far as Maxwell was concerned, that it would have been rude to express it. She went very pink again, and lifting forget-me-not blue eyes to his inscrutable ones, articulated slowly:

"I'm sure I don't know."

Her eyes were like a child's and a shy smile curved her pink lips adorably as she spoke. Such mere simplicity would not in itself have cast a spell over Maxwell, but it came to him as a new, surprising phase of the eternal feminine in her; and it had the additional charm that it caused that subjugated feeling resembling fear, with which Mildred could inspire him, to disappear entirely. He was once more in the proper dominant attitude of Man. He felt the courage now to make her do what he believed she wished to do in her heart; the courage, too, to punish her for the humiliation she had inflicted upon him. Six months ago he would have had nothing but a hearty contempt for the man who could beat thirty yards of gravel-path for half an hour, watch in hand, in a misery of impatience, waiting on the good pleasure of a capricious woman.

Meantime he laughed good-humoredly at Milly's answer and began to talk of neutral matters. If her tongue did not move as nimbly as usual, he flattered himself it was because she knew that the hour of her surrender was at hand.

Milly knew the boat-house well, the pleasant dimness of it on hot summer days; how the varnished boats lay side by side all down its length, and how the light canoes rested against the walls as it were on shelves. How, when the big doors were opened on to the raft and the slowly moving river without, bright circles of sunlight, reflected from the running water, would fly in and dance on wall and roof. She stood there in the dimness, while Maxwell lifted down a large canoe and, opening one of the barred doors, took it out to the water. Mildred would have felt a half-conscious æsthetic pleasure in watching his movements, superficially indolent but instinct with strength. Milly had not the same æsthetic sensibilities, and she was still disagreeably embarrassed at finding herself on such a familiar footing with a man whom she had never seen before. Then, although she followed Aunt Beatrice's golden rule of never allowing a question of feminine dress to interfere with masculine plans, she could not but feel anxious as to the fate of her fresh muslin and ribbons packed into a canoe. Maxwell, however, had learned canoeing years ago on the Canadian lakes, and did not splash. His lean, muscular brown arms and supple wrists took the canoe rapidly through the water, with little apparent effort.

It was the prime of June and the winding willow-shaded Cherwell was in its beauty. White water-lilies were only just beginning to open silver buds, floating serenely on their broad green and red pads; but prodigal masses of wild roses, delicately rich in scent and various in color, overhung the river in brave arching bowers or starred bushes and hedgerows so closely that the green briers were hardly visible. Beds of the large blue water forget-me-not floated beside the banks, and above them creamy meadow-sweet lifted its tall plumes among the reeds and grasses. Small water-rats swam busily from bank to bank or played on the roots of the willows, and bright wings of birds and insects fluttered and skimmed over the shining stream.

The Cherwell, though not then the crowded waterway it has since become, was usually popular with boaters on such an afternoon. But there must have been strong counter-attractions elsewhere, for Milly and Davison passed only one, a party of children working very independent oars, on their way to the little gray house above the ferry, where an old Frenchman dispensed tea in arbors.

There was a kind of hypnotic charm in the gliding motion of the canoe and the water running by. Milly was further dazed by Maxwell's talk. It was full of mysterious references and couched in the masterful tone of a person who had rights over her—a tone which before he had been more willing than able to adopt; but now the bit was between his teeth. Perhaps absorbed in his own intent, he hardly noticed how little she answered; but he did notice every point of her beauty as she leaned back on the cushions in the light shade of her parasol, from the soft brightness of her hair to the glimpse of delicate white skin which showed through the open-work stocking on her slender foot.

When they were in the straight watery avenue between green willow walls, which leads up to the ferry, he slackened the pace.

"And what are you going to do next week?" he asked, as one of a series of ironical questions.

"A great deal; much more than I care to do. I'm going up to town to see the new Savoy opera, and I'm going to a dance, and to several garden-parties, and to dine with the Master of Durham."

"Quite enough for some people; but not for you, Mildred. Think of it—year after year, always the same old run. October Term, Lent Term, Summer Term! A little change in Vacations, say a month abroad, when you can afford it. You aren't meant for it, you know you're not, any more than a swallow's meant for the little hopping, pecketing life of a London sparrow."

"Indeed, I don't see the likeness either way. I'm quite happy as I am."

He smiled mockingly.

"Quite happy! As it's very proper you should be, of course. Come, Mildred, no humbug! Think how you'd feel if you knew that instead of going to all those idiotic parties next week you were going to Constantinople."

"Isn't it dreadfully hot at this time of year?"

"I like it hot. But at any rate one can always find some cool place in the hottest weather. How would you like to go in a caravan from Cairo to Damascus next autumn?"

"I dare say it would be delightful, if the country one passed through were not too wild and dangerous. But Ian would never be able to leave his work for an expedition like that."

Maxwell smiled grimly.

"I'd no idea you'd want him. I shouldn't. Do be serious. If you fancy I'm the sort of man you can go on playing with forever, you're most confoundedly mistaken."

Milly was both offended and alarmed. Was this strange man mad? And she alone with him on the river!

"I don't know what you mean," she said, coldly.

"Don't you?" he returned, and he still wore his ironic smile—"Well, I know what you mean all the time. You say I only know Oriental women, but, by Allah, there's not a pin to choose between the lot of you, except that there's less humbug about them, and over here you're a set of trained, accomplished hypocrites!"

Indignation overcame fear in Milly's bosom.

"We are nothing of the kind," she said. "How can you talk such nonsense?"

"Nonsense? I suppose being a woman you can't really be logical, although you generally pretend to be so. Why have you pranked yourself out, spent an hour I dare say in making yourself pretty to-day? For what possible reason except to attract the eyes of a crowd of men, young fools or doddering old ones—"

Milly uttered an expression of vehement denial, but he continued:

"Or else to whet my appetite for forbidden fruit. But there's no 'or' about it, is there? Most likely you had both of those desirable objects in view."

Milly was not a coward when her indignation was aroused. She took hold of the sides of the canoe and began raising herself.

"I don't know whether you mean to be insulting," she said; "but I don't wish to hear any more of this sort of thing. I'd rather you put me out, please."

"Sit down," he said, with authority—the canoe was rocking violently—"unless you're anxious to be drowned. I warn you I'm a very poor swimmer, and if we upset there's not a ghost of a chance of my being able to save you."

Milly was a poor swimmer, too, and felt by no means competent to save herself; neither was she anxious to be drowned. So she sat down again.

"Put me out at the ferry, please," she repeated, haughtily.

They were reaching the end of the willow avenue, just where the wire rope crosses the river. On the right was a small wooden landing-stage, and high above it the green, steep river-bank, with the gray house and the arbors on the top. The old Frenchman stood before the house in his shirt-sleeves, watching sadly for his accustomed prey, which for some inexplicable reason did not come. He took off his cap expectantly to Maxwell Davison, whom he knew; but the canoe glided swiftly under the rope and on.

"No, I sha'n't put you out, Mildred," Maxwell answered with decision, after a pause. "I'm sorry if I've offended you. I've forgotten my manners, no doubt, and must seem a bit of a brute to you. I didn't bring you here just to quarrel, or to play a practical joke upon you, and send you on a field-walk in that smart frock and shoes—" he smiled at her, and this time she was obliged to feel a certain fascination in his smile—"nor yet to go on with the game you've been playing with me all these months. You forget; I've been used to Nature for so many years that I find it hard to realize how natural the most artificial conditions of life appear to you. I'll try to remember; but you must remember, too, that the most civilized beings on earth have got to come right up against the hard facts of Nature sometimes. They've got to be stripped of their top layer and see it stripped off other people, and to recognize the fact that every one has got a core of Primitive Man or of Primitive Woman in them; a perfectly unalterable, indestructible core. And the people who refuse to recognize that aren't elevated and refined, but simply stupid and obstinate and no good."

Milly, if she would have no compromise with principles, was always quick to accept an apology. She did not follow the line of Maxwell's argument, but she remembered it was noted in a certain deplorably irregular Diary, that he had lived for many years in the East and was quite Orientalized in many of his ways and ideas. With gentle dignity she signified that in her opinion civilized European manners and views were to be commended in opposition to barbarous and Oriental ones. Maxwell, his face bent towards the turning paddle, hardly heard what she was saying. He was paddling fast and considering many things.

They came to where the river ran under a narrow grass field, rising in a steep bank and shut off from the world by a tall hedge and a row of elms, that threw long shadows down the grass and were reflected in the water. A path led through it, but it was little frequented. On the other side was a wide, green meadow, where the long grass was ripening under rose-blossoming hedges, and far beyond was the blueness of distant hills and woods. Maxwell ran the bow of the canoe into a thick bed of forget-me-nots, growing not far from the bank. He laid the dripping paddle aside, and, resting his elbows on his knees, held his head in his hands for a minute or more. When he turned his face towards her it was charged with passion, but most of all with a grave masterfulness. He had been sitting on a low seat, but now he knelt so as to come nearer to her, and, stretching out his long arms, laid a hand, brown, long-fingered, smooth, on her two slight, gray-gloved ones.

"Mildred," he said, and his voice seemed to have lost its harshness,

"I've brought you here to make you decide what you are going to do with me and with yourself. I want you—you know I want you, but I don't come begging for you as an alms. I say, just compare the life, the free, glorious life I can give you, and the wretched, petty round of existence here. Come with me, won't you? Don't be afraid I shall treat you like a slave; I follow Nature, and Nature made you a queen. Come with me to-night, come to Paris, to Constantinople, to all the East! Never mind about love yet, we won't talk about that, for I don't really flatter myself you love me; I'm only sure you don't love Ian—"

Milly had listened to him so far, drawing herself back to the farthest end of the canoe, half petrified with amazement, half dominated by his powerful personality. At these words her pallor gave way to a scarlet flush.

"How dare you!" she cried, in a voice tremulous with indignation. "How dare you talk to me like this? How dare you name my husband? You brought me out here on purpose to say such things to me? Oh, it's abominable, it's disgraceful!"

There was no room for doubt as to the sincerity of her indignation. Maxwell drew back and his face changed. There were patches of dull red on his cheeks, almost as though he had been struck, and his narrow eyes glittered. Looking at him, Milly felt physical fear; she thought once more of insanity. There was a silence; then she spoke again.

"Put me on to the bank here, please. I'll walk back."

"I shall let you go when I choose," returned he, in a grating voice. "I have something to say to you first."

He paused and his frown darkened upon her. "You asked me how I 'dared.' Dare! Do you take me for a dog, to be chained up and tantalized with nice bits, and hardly allowed to whine for them? I say, how dare you entice me with your beauty—it's decked out now for me—entice me with all your beguiling ways, your pretence of longing to go away and to live the free life in the East as I live it? Now, when you've made me want you—what else have you been aiming at? You pretend to be surprised, you pretend even to yourself, to be dreadfully shocked. What damned humbug! With us only the dancing-girls venture to play such tricks as you do, and they daren't go too far, because the men are men and wear knives. But here you proper women, with your weakness unnaturally protected, you go about pretending you don't know there's such a thing in the world as desire—oh, of course not!—and all the while you're deliberately exciting it and playing upon it."

Mildred had been right in saying that the gentle Milly could be in a rage; though it was a thing that had happened to her only once or twice before since her childhood. It happened now. Anger, burning anger, extinguished the fear that had held her silent while he was speaking.

"It's false!" she cried, with burning face and blazing eyes. "It's disgraceful of you to say such things—it's degrading for me to have to hear them. I will get away from you, if I have to jump into the river."

She started forward, but Maxwell, with his tall, lithe body and long arms, had a great reach. He leaned forward and his iron hands were upon her shoulders, forcing her back.

"Don't be a fool," he said, still fierce in eye and voice.

Her lips trembled with fury so that she could hardly speak.

"Do you consider yourself a gentleman?"

He laughed scornfully.

"I don't consider the question at all. I am a man; you are a woman, and you have presumed to make a plaything of me. You thought you could do it with impunity because we are civilized, because you are a lady; for bar-maids and servant-girls do get their throats cut sometimes still. Don't be frightened, I'm not going to kill you, but I mean to make you understand for once that these privileges of weakness are humbug, that they're not in nature. I mean to teach you that a man is a better animal—"

He suddenly withdrew his hands from her with a sharp exclamation. Milly's teeth were pearly white and rather small, but they were pointed, and they had met in the flesh of the right hand which rested so firmly on her shoulder. He fell back and put his hand to his mouth. A boat-hook lay within her reach, and her end of the canoe had drifted near enough to the river-bank for her to be able to catch hold with the hook and to pull it farther in. Braced to the uttermost by rage and fear, she bounded to her feet without upsetting the canoe. It lurched violently, but righted itself, swinging out once more into the stream. Maxwell looked up and saw her standing on the river-bank above him. She did not stay to parley, but with lifted skirt hurried up the steep meadow, through the sun-flecked shadows of the elm-trees, towards the path. When she was half-way up a harsh, sardonic laugh sounded behind her, and instinctively she looked back. Maxwell held up his wounded hand:

"Primitive woman at last, Mildred!" he shouted. "Don't apologize, I sha'n't."

XVII

Ian only came home just in time to scramble into his evening dress-suit for a dinner at the Fletchers'. He needed not to fear delay either from that shirt-button at the back, refractory or on the last thread, or from any other and more insidious trap for the hurrying male. Milly looked after him in a way which, if the makers of traditions concerning wives were not up to their necks in falsehood, must have inspired devotion in the heart of any husband alive. She had already observed that he had been allowed to lose most of the pocket-handkerchiefs she had marked for him in linen thread. That trifles such as this should cause bitterness will seem as absurd to sensible persons as it would to be told that our lives are made up of mere to-morrows—if Shakespeare had not happened to put that in his own memorable way. For it takes a vast deal of imagination to embrace the ordinary facts of life and human nature. But even the most sensible will understand that it was annoying for Milly regularly to find her own and the family purse reduced to a state that demanded rigid economy. The Invader, stirring in that limbo where she lay, might have answered that rigid economy was Milly's forte and real delight, and that it was well she should have nothing to spend in ridiculously disguising the fair body they were condemned to share. Mildred certainly left behind her social advantages which both Ian and Milly enjoyed without exactly realizing their source, while her bric-à-brac purchases, from an eighteenth-century print to a Chinese ivory, were always sure to be rising investments. But all such minor miseries as her invasion might multiply for Milly, were forgotten in the horror of the abyss that had now opened under her feet. For long after that second return of hers, on the night of the thunderstorm, a shadow, a dreadful haunting thought, had hovered in the back of her mind. Gradually it had faded with the fading of a memory; but to-night the colors of that memory revived, the thought startled into a more vivid existence.

In the press and hurry of life, not less in Oxford than in other modern towns, the Stewarts and Fletchers did not meet so often and intimately as to make inevitable the discovery of Mildred Stewart's dual personality by her cousins. They said she had developed moods; but with the conservatism of relations, saw nothing in her that they had not seen in her nursery days.

Ian and Milly walked home from dinner, according to Oxford custom, but a Durham man walked with them, talking over a College question with Ian, and they did not find themselves alone until they were within the wainscoted walls of the old house. Milly had looked so pale all the evening that Ian expected her to go to bed at once; but she followed him into the study, where the lamp was shedding its circle of light on the heaped books and papers of his writing-table. Making some perfunctory remarks which she barely answered, he sat down to work at an address which he was to deliver at the meeting of a learned society in London.

Milly threw off her white shawl and seated herself on the old, high-backed sofa. Her dress was of some gauzy material of indeterminate tone, interwoven with gold tinsel, and a scarf of gauze embroidered with gold disguised what had seemed to her an over-liberal display of dazzling shoulders. Ian, absorbed in his work, hardly noticed his wife sitting in the penumbra, chin on hand, staring before her into nothingness, like some Cassandra of the hearth, who listens to the inevitable approaching footsteps of a tragic destiny. At last she said:

"I've got something awful to tell you."

Ian startled, dropped his pen and swung himself around in his pivot chair.

"What about? Tony?"—for it was to this diminutive that Mildred had reduced the flowing syllables of Antonio.

"No, your cousin, Maxwell Davison."

Now, Ian liked his cousin well enough, but by no means as well as he liked Tony.

"About Max!" he exclaimed, relieved. "What's happened to him?"

"Nothing—but oh, Ian! I—hate even to speak of such a thing—"

"Never mind. Just tell me what it is."

"I was on the river with him this afternoon, and he—he made love to me."

The lines of Ian's face suddenly hardened.

"Did he?" he returned, significantly, playing with a paper-knife. Then, after a pause: "I'm awfully sorry, Milly. I'd no idea he was such a cad."

"He—he wanted me to run away with him."

Ian's face became of an almost inhuman severity.

"I shall let Maxwell Davison know my opinion of him," he said.

"But it's worse—it's even more horrible than that. He was expecting me. I—*I* of course knew nothing about it; I only knew about the garden-party at Lady Margaret. But he said I'd promised to come; he said all kinds of shocking, horrid things about my having dressed myself up for him—"

"Please don't tell me what he said, Milly," Ian interrupted, still coldly, but with a slight expression of disgust. "I'd rather you didn't. I suppose I ought to have taken better care of you, my poor little girl, but really here in Oxford one never thinks of anything so outrageous happening."

"I must tell you one thing," she resumed, almost obstinately. "He said he knew I didn't love you—that *I* didn't love *you*, my own darling husband. Some one, some one—must be responsible for his thinking that. How do I know what happens when—when I'm away. My poor Ian! Left with a creature who doesn't love you!"

Ian rose. His face was cold and hard still, but there was a faint flush on his cheek, the mark of a frown between his black brows. He walked to a window and looked out into the moonlit garden, where the gnarled apple-trees threw weird black shadows on grass and wall, like shapes of grotesque animals, or half-hidden spectres, lurking, listening, waiting.

"We're getting on to a dangerous subject," he answered, at length. "Don't give me pain by imagining evil about—about yourself. You could never, under any aspect, be anything but innocent and loyal and all that a man could wish his wife to be."

He smoothed his brow with an effort, went up to her, and taking her soft face between his hands kissed her forehead.

"There!" he exclaimed, with a forced smile. "Don't let's talk about it any more, darling. Go to bed and forget all about it. It won't seem so bad to-morrow morning."

But Milly did not respond. When he released her head she threw it back against her own clasped hands, closing her eyes. She was ghastly pale.

"No," she moaned, "I can't bear it by myself. It's too, too awful. It's not Me; it's something that takes my place. I saw it once. It's an evil spirit. O God, what have I done that such a thing should happen to me! I've always tried to be good."

There was a clash of pity and anger in Ian's breast. Pity for Milly's case, anger on account of her whom his inmost being recognized as another, whatever his rational self might say to the matter. He sat down beside his wife and uttered soothing nothings. But she turned upon him eyes of wild despair, the more tragic because it broke through a nature fitted only for the quietest commonplaces of life. She flung herself upon him, clutching him tight, hiding her face upon him.

"What have I done?" she moaned again. "You know I always believed in God, in God's love. I wouldn't have disbelieved even if He'd taken you away from me. But now I can't believe in anything. There must be wicked spirits, but there can't be a good God if He allows them to take possession of a poor girl like me, who's never done any one any harm. O Ian, I've tried to pray, and I can't. I don't believe in anything now."

Ian was deeply perplexed. He himself believed neither in a God nor in evil spirits, and he knew not how to approach Milly's mind. At length he said, quietly:

"I should have expected you, dear, to have reasoned about this a little more. What's the use of being educated if we give way to superstition, like savages, directly something happens that we don't quite understand? Some day an eclipse of conscious personality, like yours, will come to be understood as well as an eclipse of the moon. Don't let's make it worse by conjuring up superstitious terrors."

"At first I thought it was like that—an eclipse of memory. But now I feel more and more it's a different person that's here, it's not I. To-night Cousin David said that sometimes when he met me he expected to find when he got home that his Lady Hammerton had walked away out of the frame. And, Ian, I looked up at that portrait, and suddenly I was reminded of—that fearful night when I came back and saw—something. I am descended from that woman, and you know how wicked she was."

Again the strange irritation stirred in the midst of Ian's pity.

"Wicked, darling! That's an absurd word to use."

"She left her husband. And it's awful that I, who can't understand how any woman could be so wicked as to do that, should be so terribly like her. I feel as though it had something to do with this appalling thing happening to me. Perhaps her sins are being visited on me." She held the lapels of his coat and looked tenderly, yearningly, in his face. "And I could bear it better if—But oh, my Ian! I can't bear to think of you left with something wicked, with some one who doesn't love you, who deceives you, and—"

"Milly," he broke in, "I won't have you say things like that. They are absolutely untrue, and I won't have them said."

There was a note of sternness in his voice that Milly had never heard before, and she saw a hard look come into his averted face which was new to her. When she spoke it was in a gasp.

"You love her? You love that wicked, bad woman so much you won't let me tell you what she is?"

He drew himself away from her with a gesture, and in a minute answered with cold deliberation:

"I cannot cease to love my own wife because—because she's not always exactly the same."

They sat silent beside each other. At length Milly rose from the sofa. The tinselled scarf, that other woman's delicate finery, had slipped from the white beauty of her shoulders. She drew it around her again slowly, and slowly with bowed head left the room.

XVIII

B etween noon and one o'clock on a bright June morning there is
no place in the world quite so full of sunshine and summer as the
quadrangle of an Oxford College. Not Age but Youth of centuries
smiles from gray walls and aery pinnacles upon the joyous children
of To-day. Youth, in a bright-haired, black-winged-butterfly swarm,
streams out of every dark doorway, from the austere shade of study, to
disport itself, two by two, or in larger eddying groups, upon the worn
gravel, even venturously flits across the sacred green of the turf. There
is an effervescence of life in the clear air, and the sun-steeped walls of
stone are resonant with the cheerful noise of young voices. Here and
there men already in flannels pass towards the gate; Dons draped in
the black folds of the stately gown, stand chatting with their books
under their arms; and since the season of festivity has begun, scouts
hurry cautiously to and fro from buttery and kitchen, bearing brimming
silver cups crowned with blue borage and floating straws, or trays of
decorated viands. The scouts are grave and careworn, but from every
one else a kind of physical joy and contentment seems to breathe as
perfume breathes from blossoms and even leaves, in the good season
of the year.

Ian Stewart did not quite resist this atmosphere of physical
contentment. He stood in the sunshine exchanging a few words with
passing pupils; yet at the back of his mind there was a deep distress. He
had been brought up in the moral refinement, the honorable strictness
of principle with regard to moral law, common to his academic class,
and, besides, he had an innate delicacy and sensibility of feeling. If
his intelligence perceived that there are qualities, individualities which
claim exemption from ordinary rules, he had no desire to claim any such
exemption for himself. Yet he found himself occupying the position of a
man torn on the rack between a jealous wife for whom he has affection
and esteem, and a mistress who compels his love. Only here was not
alone a struggle but a mystery, and the knot admitted of no severance.

He looked around upon his pupils, upon the distant figures of his
fellow Dons, robed in the same garb, seemingly living the same life as
himself. Where was fact, where was reality? In yonder phantasmagoric
procession of Oxford life, forever repeating itself, or in this strange tragi-
comedy of souls, one in two and two in one, passing behind the thick

MARGARET L. WOODS

walls of that old house in the street nearby? There he stood among the rest, part and parcel apparently of an existence as ordinary, as peaceful, as monotonous as the Victorian era could produce. Yet if he were to tell any one within sight the plain truth concerning his life, it would be regarded as a fairy tale, the fantastic invention of an overwrought brain.

There is something in college life which fosters a reticence that is almost secretiveness; and this becomes a code, a religion; yet Stewart found himself seized with an intense longing to confide in someone. And at that moment, from under the wide archway leading into the quadrangle, appeared the Master of Durham. The Master was in cap and gown, and carried some large papers under his arm; he walked slowly, as he had taken to walking of late, his odd, trotting gait transformed almost to a hobble. Meditative, he looked straight before him with unseeing eyes. No artist was ever able to seize the inner and the outer verity of that round, pink baby face, filled with the power of a weighty personality and a penetrating mind. Stewart marked him in that minute, sagacity and benevolence, as it were, silently radiating from him; and the younger man in his need turned to the wise Master, the paternal friend whose counsels had done so much to set his young feet in the way of success.

When Stewart found himself in the Master's study, the study so familiar to his youth, with its windows looking out on the garden quadrangle, and saw the great little man himself seated before him at the writing-table, he marvelled at the temerity that had brought him there to speak on such a theme. But the cup was poured and had to be drunk. The Master left him to begin. He sat with a plump hand on each plump knee, and regarded his old pupil with silent benevolence.

"I've come to see you, Master," said Stewart, "because I feel very bewildered, very helpless, in a matter which touches my wife even more than myself. You were so kind about my marriage, and you have always been good to her as well as to me."

"Miss Flaxman was a nice young lady," squeaked the Master. "I knew you married wisely."

"Something happened shortly before we were engaged which she— we didn't quite grasp—its importance, I mean," Stewart began. He then spoke of those periodical lapses of memory in his wife which he had come to see involved real and extraordinary variations in her character—a change, in fact, of personality. He mentioned their futile visits to Norton-Smith, the brain and nerve specialist. The Master heard him without either moving or interrupting. When he had done there was a silence. At length the Master said:

"I suspect we don't understand women."

"Perhaps not. But, Master, haven't you yourself noticed a great difference in my wife at various times?"

"Not more than I feel in myself—not of another character, that is. We live among men; we live among men who, generally speaking, know nothing about women. That's why women appear to us strange and unnatural. Your wife's quite normal, really."

"But the memory alone, surely—"

"That's made you nervous; but I've known cases not far different. You remember meeting Sir Henry Milwood here? When I knew him he was a young clergyman. He had an illness; forgot all about his clerical life, and went sheep-farming in Australia, where he made his fortune."

"But his personality?" asked Stewart, with anxiety. "Was that changed?"

"Certainly. A colonial sheep-farmer is a different person from a young Don just in orders."

"I don't mean that, Master. I mean did he rise from his bed with ideas, with feelings quite opposite to those which had possessed him when he lay down upon it? Did he ever have a return of the clerical phase, during which he forgot how he became a sheep-farmer and wished to take up his old work again?"

"No—no."

There was a pause. The Master played with his gold spectacles and sucked his under lip. Then:

"Take a good holiday, Stewart," he said.

Stewart's clear-cut face hardened and flushed momentarily. "These are not fancies of my own, Master. Cases occur in which two, sometimes more than two, entirely different personalities alternate in the same individual. The spontaneous cases are rare, of course, but hypnotism seems to develop them pretty freely. The facts are there, but English scientists prefer to say nothing about them."

The Master rose and trotted restlessly about.

"They're quite right," he returned, at length. "Such ideas can lead to nothing but mischief."

"Surely that is the orthodox theologian's usual objection to scientific fact."

The Master lifted his head and looked at his rebel disciple. For although he was an officiating clergyman, he and the orthodox theologians were at daggers drawn.

"Views, statements of this kind are not knowledge," he said, after a while, and continued moving uneasily about without looking at Stewart.

Stewart did not reply; it seemed useless to go on talking. He recognized that the Master's attitude was what his own had been before the iron of fact had entered into his flesh and spirit. Yet somehow he had hoped that his Master's large and keen perception of human things, his judicial mind, would have lifted him above the prejudices of Reason. He sat there cheerless, his college cap between his knees; and was seeking the moment to say good-bye when the Master suddenly sat down beside him. To any one looking in at the window, the two seated side by side on the hard sofa would have seemed an oddly assorted pair. Stewart's length of frame, the raven black of his hair and beard, the marble pallor of his delicate features, made the little Master look smaller, pinker, plumper than usual; but his face, radiating wisdom and affection, was more than beautiful in the eyes of his old disciple.

"I took a great interest in your marriage, Stewart," he said. "I always think of you and your wife as two very dear young friends. You must let me speak to you now as a father might—and probably wouldn't."

Stewart assented with affectionate reverence.

"You are young, but your wife is much younger. A man marries a girl many years younger than himself and has not the same feeling of responsibility towards her as he would have towards a young man of the same age. He seldom considers her youth. Yet his responsibility is much greater towards her than towards a pupil of the same age; she needs more help, she will accept more in forming her mind and character. Now you have married a young lady who is very intelligent, very pleasing; but she has a delicate nervous system, and it has been overstrained. She lets this peculiar weakness of her memory get on her nerves. You have nerves yourself, you have imagination, and you let your mind give way to hers. That's not wise; it's not right. Let her feel that these moods do not affect you; be sure that they do not. What matters mainly is that your mutual love should remain unchanged. When your wife finds that her happiness, her real happiness, is quite untouched by these changes of mood, she will leave off attributing an exaggerated importance to them. So will you, Stewart. You will see them in their right proportion; you will see the great evil and danger of giving way to imagination, of accepting perverse psychological hypotheses as guides in life. Reason and Religion are the only true guides."

The Master did not utter these sayings continuously. There were pauses which Stewart might have filled, but he did not offer to do so. The spell of his old teacher's mind and aspect was upon him. His spirit was, as it were, bowed before his Master in a kind of humility.

He walked home with a lightened heart, feeling somewhat as a devout sinner might feel to whom his confessor had given absolution. For about twenty-four hours this mood lasted. Then he confronted the fact that the beloved Master's advice had been largely, though not altogether, futile, because it had not dealt with actuality. And Ian Stewart saw himself to be moving in the plain, ordinary world of men as solitary as a ghost which vainly endeavors to make its presence and its needs recognized.

XIX

Tims had ceased to be an inhabitant of Oxford. She was studying physiology in London and luxuriating in the extraordinary cheapness of life in Cranham Chambers. Not that she had any special need of cheapness; but the spinster aunt who brought her up had, together with a comfortable competence, left her the habit of parsimony. If, however, she did not know how to enjoy her own income, she allowed many women poorer than herself to benefit by it.

She was no correspondent; and an examination, followed by the serious illness of her next-door neighbor—Mr. Fitzalan, a solitary man with a small post in the British Museum—had prevented her from visiting Oxford during Mildred's last invasion. She had imagined Milly Stewart to have been leading for two undisturbed years the busily tranquil life proper to her; adoring Ian and the baby, managing her house, and going sometimes to church and sometimes to committees, without wholly neglecting the cultivation of the mind. A letter from Milly, in which she scented trouble, made her call herself sternly to account for her long neglect of her friend.

It was now the Long Vacation, but Miss Burt was still at Ascham and Lady Thomson was spending a week with her. She had stayed with the Stewarts in the spring, and resolutely keeping a blind eye turned towards whatever she ought to have disapproved in Mildred, had lauded her return to bodily vigor, and also to good sense, in ceasing to fuss about the health of Ian and the baby. Aunt Beatrice would have blushed to own a husband and child whose health required care. This time when she dined with the Stewarts she had found Milly reprehensibly pale and dispirited. One day shortly afterwards she came in to tea. The nurse happened to be out, and Tony, now a beautiful child of fifteen months, was sitting on the drawing-room floor.

The two women were discussing plans for raising money to build a gymnasium at Ascham, but Tony was not interested in the subject. He kept working his way along the floor to his mother, partly on an elbow and a knee, but mostly on his stomach. Arrived at his goal he would pull her skirt, indicate as well as he could a little box lying by his neglected picture-book, and grunt with much expression. A monkey lived inside the box, and Tony, whose memory was retentive, persevered in expecting to hear that monkey summoned by wild tattoos and subterranean growls until it jumped up with a bang—a splendidly terrible thing of white bristles, and scarlet snout—to dance the fandango to a lively if unmusical tune. Then Tony, be sure, would laugh until he rolled from side to side. Mummy never responded to his wishes now, but Daddy had pleaded for the Jack-in-the-box to be spared, and sometimes when quite alone with Tony, would play the monkey-game in his inferior paternal style, pleased with such modified appreciation as the young critic might bestow upon him.

"I'm sorry Baby's so troublesome," apologized the distressed Milly, for the third time lifting Tony up and replacing him in a sitting posture, with his picture-book. "I'm trying to teach him to sit quiet, but I'm afraid he's been played with a great deal more than he should have been."

"To tell the truth, I thought so the last time I was here," replied Aunt Beatrice. "But he's still young enough to be properly trained. It's such waste of a reasonable person's time to spend it making idiotic noises at a small baby. And it's a thousand times better for the child's brain and nerves for it to be left entirely to itself."

Tony said nothing, but his face began to work in a threatening manner.

"I perfectly agree with you, Aunt Beatrice," responded Milly, eagerly.

Lady Thomson continued:

"Children should be spoken to as little as possible until they are from two to two and a half years old; then they should be taught to speak correctly."

Milly chimed in: "Yes, that's always been my own view. I do feel it so important that their very first impressions should be the right ones, that the first pictures they see should be good, that they should never be sung to out of tune and in general—"

Apparently this programme for babies did not commend itself to Tony; certainly the first item, enjoining silent development, did not. His face had by this time worked the right number of minutes to produce a roar, and it came. Milly picked him up, but the wounds of his spirit were not to be immediately healed, and the roar continued. Finally he had to be handed over to the parlor-maid, and so came to great happiness in the kitchen, where there were no rules against infantile conversation. Milly was flushed and disturbed.

"Baby has not been properly brought up," she said. "He's been allowed his own way too much."

"Since you say so, Milly, I must confess I noticed in the spring that you seemed to be bringing the child up in an easy-going, old-fashioned way I should hardly have expected of you. I hope you will begin now to study the theory of education. A mother should take her vocation seriously. I own I don't altogether understand the taste for frivolities which you have developed since you married. It's harmless, no doubt, but it doesn't seem quite natural in a young woman who has taken a First in Greats."

Milly's hands grasped the arms of her chair convulsively. She looked at her aunt with desolation in her dark-ringed eyes. The last thing she had ever intended was to mention the mysterious and disastrous fate that had befallen her; yet she did it.

"The person you saw here last spring wasn't I. Oh, Aunt Beatrice! Can't you see the difference?"

Lady Thomson looked at her in surprise:

"What do you mean? I was speaking of my visit to you in March."

"And don't you see the difference? Oh, how hateful you must have found me!"

"Really, Mildred, I saw nothing hateful about you. On the contrary, if you want the plain truth, I greatly prefer you in a cheerful, common-sense mood, as you were then, even if your high spirits do lead you into a little too much frivolity. I think it a more wholesome, and therefore ultimately a more useful, frame of mind than this causeless depression, which leads you to take such a morbid, exaggerated view of things."

Every word pierced Milly's heart with a double pang.

"You liked her better than me?" she asked, piteously. "Yet I've always tried to be just what you wanted me to be, Aunt Beatrice, to do everything you thought right, and she—Oh, it's too awful!"

"What do you mean, Mildred?"

"I mean that the person you prefer to me as I am now, the person who was here in March, wasn't I at all."

The fine healthy carnation of Lady Thomson's cheek paled. In her calm, rapid way she at once found the explanation of Milly's unhealthy, depressed appearance and manner. Poor Mildred Stewart was insane. Beyond the paling of her cheek, however, Lady Thomson allowed no sign of shock to be visible in her.

"That's an exaggerated way of talking," she replied. "I suppose you mean your mood was different."

Milly was looking straight in front of her with haggard eyes.

"No; it simply wasn't I at all. You believe in the Bible, don't you?"

"Not in verbal inspiration, of course, but in a general way, yes," returned Lady Thomson, puzzled but guarded.

"Do you believe in the demoniacs? In possession by evil spirits?"

Milly was not looking at vacancy now. Her desperate hands clutched the arms of her chair, as she leaned forward and fixed her aunt with hollow eyes, awaiting her reply.

"Certainly not! Most certainly not! They were obviously cases of epilepsy and insanity, misinterpreted by an ignorant age."

"No—it's all true, quite literally true. Three times, and for six months or more each time, I have been possessed by a spirit that cannot be good. I know it's not. It takes my body, it takes the love of people I care for, away from me—" Milly's voice broke and she pressed her handkerchief over her face. "You all think her—But she's bad, and some day she'll do something wicked—something that will break my heart, and you'll all insist it was I who did it, and you'll believe I'm a wicked woman."

Lady Thomson looked very grave.

"Mildred, dear," she said, "try and collect yourself. It is really wicked of you to give way to such terrible fancies. Would God permit such a thing to happen to one of His children? We feel sure He would not."

Milly shook her head, but the struggle with her hysterical sobs kept her silent. Lady Thomson walked to the window, feeling more "upset" than she had ever felt in her life. The window was open, but an awning shut out the view of the street. From the window-boxes, filled with pink geraniums and white stocks, a sweet, warm scent floated into the room, and the rattle of the milkman's cart, the chink of his cans, fell upon Lady Thomson's unheeding ears. So did voices in colloquy, but she did not particularly note a female one of a thin, chirpy quality, addressing the parlor-maid with a familiarity probably little appreciated by that elegantly decorous damsel.

Milly had scarcely mastered her tears and Lady Thomson had just begun to address her in quiet, firm tones, when Tims burst unannounced into the room. Her hat was incredibly on one side, and her sallow face almost crimson with heat, but bright with pleasure at finding herself once more in Oxford.

"Hullo, old girl!" she cried, blind to the serious scene into which she was precipitated. "How are you? Now don't kiss me"—throwing herself into an attitude of violent defence against an embrace not yet offered—

"I'm too hot. Carried my bag myself all the way from the station and saved the omnibus."

Lady Thomson fixed Tims with a look of more than usually cold disapproval. Milly proffered a constrained greeting.

"Anything gone wrong?" asked Tims, after a minute, peering at Milly's tear-stained eyes with her own short-sighted ones.

Milly answered with a forced self-restraint which appeared like cold deliberation.

"Aunt Beatrice thinks I'm mad because I say I'm not the same person she found in my place last March. I want you to tell her that it's not just my fancy, but that you know that sometimes a quite different person takes my place, and I'm not responsible for anything she says or does."

"Yes, that's a solemn Gospel fact, right enough," affirmed Tims.

Lady Thomson could hardly control her indignation, but she did, although she spoke sternly to Tims.

"Do I understand you to say, Miss Timson, that it's a 'solemn Gospel fact'—Gospel! Good Heavens—that Milly is possessed by a devil?"

Tims plumped down on the sofa and stared at Lady Thomson.

"Possessed by a devil? Good Lord, no! What do you mean?"

"Mildred believes herself to be possessed by an evil spirit."

Tims turned to Milly in consternation.

"Milly, old girl! Come! Poor old Milly! I never thought you were so superstitious as all that. Besides, I know more about it than you do, and I tell you straight, you mayn't be quite such a good sort when you're in your other phase, but as to there being a devil in it—well, devil's all nonsense, but if that were so, I should like to have a devil myself, and the more the merrier."

Milly turned on her a face pale with horror and indignation. Her eyes flashed and she raised a remonstrating hand.

"Hush!" she cried. "Hush! You don't know what dreadful things you're saying. I don't know exactly what this spirit is that robs me of my life; I'm only sure it's not Me and it's not good."

"Whatever may be the matter with you, Mildred," said Lady Thomson, "it can't possibly be that. I suppose you have suffered from loss of memory again and it's upset your nerves. Why will people have nerves? I should advise you to go to Norton-Smith at once."

Milly's tears were flowing again but she managed to reply:

"I've been to Dr. Norton-Smith, Aunt Beatrice. He doesn't seem to understand."

"He doesn't want to," interjected Tims, scornfully. "You don't suppose a respectable English nerve-doctor wants to know anything about psychology? They'd be interested in the case in France, or in the United States, but they wouldn't be able to keep down Milly Number Two."

"Then what use would they be to me?" asked Milly, despairingly. "I can only trust in God; and He seems to have forsaken me."

"No, no, my dear child!" cried Lady Thomson. "Don't talk in this painful way. I can't imagine what you mean, Miss Timson. It all sounds dreadfully mad."

"I can explain the whole case to you perfectly," stated Tims, with eager confidence.

"I'd better go away," gasped Milly between her convulsive sobs. "I can't bear any more. But Aunt Beatrice must know now. Tell her what you like, only—only it isn't true."

Milly fled to her bedroom; the long, low room, so perfect in its simplicity, its windows looking away into the sunshine over the pleasant boughs of orchards and garden-plots and the gray shingled roofs of old houses—the room from which on that November evening Milly's spirit had been absent while Ian, the lover whom she had never known, had watched his Beloved, the Desire of his soul and sense, returning to him from the unimagined limbo to which she had again withdrawn.

XX

When Ian came back from the Bodleian Library, where he was working, he heard voices talking in raised tones before he entered the drawing-room. He found no Milly there, but Lady Thomson and Miss Timson seated at the extreme ends of the same sofa and engaged in a heated discussion.

"It can't be true," Lady Thomson was stating firmly. "If it were, what becomes of Personal Immortality?"

Miss Timson had just time to convey the fact that Personal Immortality was not the affair of a woman of science, before she rose to greet Ian, which she did effusively.

"Hullo!" he remarked, cheerfully, when her effusion was over. "No Milly and no tea!"

"We don't want either just yet," returned Lady Thomson. "I'm terribly anxious about Mildred, Ian, and Miss Timson has not said anything to make me less so. I want a sound, sensible opinion on the state of her—her nerves."

Ian's brow clouded.

"Tell me frankly, do you notice so great a difference in her from time to time, as to account for the positively insane delusion she has got into her head?"

"What do you mean, Aunt Beatrice?" asked Ian, shortly, sternly eying Tims, whom he imagined to have let out the secret.

"Mildred has made an extraordinary statement to me about not being the same person now as she was in March. Of course I see she—well, she is not so full of life as she was then. Yes, I do admit she is in a very different mood. But do you know the poor unfortunate child has got it into her head that she is possessed by an evil spirit? I can't think how you could have allowed her to come to that state of—of mental aberration, without doing anything."

Ian was silent. He looked gaunt and sombrely dark in the low, awning-shaded room, with its heavy beams and floor of wavelike unevenness.

"You'll have to put her under care next, if you don't take some steps. Send her for a sea-voyage."

"I'd take her myself if I thought it would do her any good," said Tims. "But I'll lay my bottom dollar it wouldn't."

"I'm afraid I think Miss Timson's view of the matter as insane as Milly's," returned Lady Thomson, tartly.

Ian lifted his bowed head and addressed Tims:

"I should like to know exactly what your view of the matter is, Miss Timson. We need not discuss poor Milly's; it's too absurd and also too painful."

"It's no doubt a case of disintegration of personality," replied Tims, after a pause. "Somewhere inside our brains must be a nerve-centre which co-ordinates most of our mental, our sensory and motor processes, in such a manner as to produce consciousness, volition, what we call personality. But after all there are always plenty of activities within us going on independent of it. Your heart beats, your stomach digests—even your memory works apart from your consciousness sometimes. Now suppose some shock or strain enfeebles your centre of consciousness, so that it ceases to be able to co-ordinate all the mental processes it has been accustomed to superintend. What you call your personality is the outcome of your memory and all your other faculties and tendencies working together, checking and balancing each other. Suppose your centre of consciousness so enfeebled; suppose at the same time an enfeeblement of memory, causing you to completely forget external facts: certain of your faculties and tendencies are left working and they are co-ordinated without an important part of the memory, without many other faculties and tendencies which checked and balanced them. Naturally you appear to yourself and to every one else a totally different person; but it's not a new personality really, it's only a bit of the old one which goes on its own hook, while the rest is quiescent."

"This is the most abominably materialistic theory of the human mind I ever heard," exclaimed Lady Thomson, indignantly. "The most degrading to our spiritual natures."

Ian leaned against the high, carved mantel-piece and pushed back the black hair from his forehead.

"I'm not concerned with that," he replied, deliberately, discussing this case so vitally near to him with an almost terrible calmness. "But I can't feel that this disintegration theory altogether covers the ground. There is no development of characteristics previously to be found in Milly; on the contrary, the qualities of mind and character which she exhibits when—when the change comes over her, are precisely the opposite of those she exhibits in what I presume we ought to call her normal state."

"There must be some reason for it, old chap, you know," returned Tims; "and it seems to me that's the line you've got to move along, unless you're an idiot and go in for devils or spiritualistic nonsense."

"I believe I've followed what you've been saying, Miss Timson," said Lady Thomson, in her fullest tones; "and I can assure you I feel under no necessity to become either a materialist or an idiot in consequence."

Ian spoke again.

"I don't profess to be scientific, but I do seem to see another possible line, running parallel with yours, but not quite the same. It's evident we can inherit faculties, characteristics, from our ancestors which never become active in us; but we know they must have been present in us in a quiescent state, because we can transmit them to children in whom they become active. Mildred's father and mother, for example, are not scholars, although her grandfather and great-grandfather were; yet in one of her parents at least there must be a germ of the scholar's faculty which has never been developed, because Mildred has inherited it. Now why can't we develop all the faculties, the germs of which lie within our borders? Perhaps because we have each only a certain amount of what I'll call vital current. If the Nile could overflow the whole desert it would all be fertilized, and perhaps if we had sufficient vital force we could develop all the faculties whose germs we inherit. Suppose by some accident, owing to a shock or strain, as you say, the flow of this vital current of ours is stopped in the direction in which it usually flows most strongly; its course is diverted and it fertilizes tracts of our brain and nervous system which before have been lying quiescent, sterile. If we lose the memory of our former lives, and if at the same time hereditary faculties and tendencies, of the existence of which we were unaware, suddenly become active in us, we are practically new personalities. Then say the vital current resumes its old course; we regain our memories, our old faculties, while the newly developed ones sink again into quiescence. We are once more our old selves. No doubt this is all very unscientific, but so far Science seems to have nothing to say on the question."

"It certainly has not," commented Lady Thomson, decisively. "I ought to know what Science is, considering how often I've met Mr. Darwin and Professor Huxley. Hypnotism and this kind of unpleasant talk is not Science. It's only a new variety of the hocus-pocus that's been imposing on human weakness ever since the world began. I'd sooner believe with poor Milly that she's possessed by a devil. It's less silly to accept inherited superstitions than to invent brand-new ones."

"But we've got to account somehow for the extraordinary changes which take place in Milly," sighed Ian, wearily.

The light lines across his forehead were showing as furrows, and Tims's whole face was corrugated.

"No hocus-pocus about them, anyway," she said.

"There's a great deal of fancy about them," retorted Lady Thomson. "A nervous, imaginative man like you, Ian, ought to be on your guard against allowing such notions to get hold of you. It's so easy to fancy things are as you're afraid they may be, and then you influence Milly and she goes from bad to worse. I think I may claim to understand her if any one does, and all I see is that she gives way to moods. At first I thought it was a steady development of character; but I admit that when she is unwell and out of spirits, she becomes just her old timid, over-conscientious self again. She's always been very easily influenced, very dependent, and now—I hardly like to say such a thing of my own niece—but I fear there's a touch of hysteria about her. I've always heard that hysterical people, even when they've been perfectly frank and truthful before, become deceitful and act parts till it's impossible to tell fact from falsehood with regard to them. I would suggest your letting Mildred come to me for a month or two, Ian. I feel sure I should send her back to you quite cured of all this nonsense."

At this point Milly came in. Ian stretched out his hand towards her with protective tenderness; but even at the moment when his whole soul was moved by an impulse of compassion so strong that it seemed almost love, a spirit within him arose and mocked at all hypotheses, telling him that this poor stricken wife of his, seemingly one with the lady of his heart, was not she, but another.

"Aunt Beatrice was just saying you ought to get away from domestic cares for a month or two, Milly," he said, as cheerfully as he could.

Lady Thomson explained.

"What you want is a complete change; though I don't know what people mean when they talk about 'domestic cares.' I should like to have you up at Clewes for the rest of the Long. Ian can look after the baby."

Milly smiled at her sweetly, but rather as though she were talking nonsense.

"It's very kind of you, Aunt Beatrice, but Ian and I have never been parted for a day since we were married; I mean not when—and I don't feel as though I could spare a minute of his company. And poor Baby, too! Oh no! But of course it's very good of you to think of it."

"Then you must all come to Clewes," decided Aunt Beatrice, after some remonstrance. "That'll settle it."

"But my work!" exclaimed Ian in dismay. "How am I to get on at Clewes, away from the libraries?"

"There are some things in life more important than books, Ian," returned Lady Thomson.

"But it won't do a penn'orth of good," broke in Tims, argumentatively. "I don't pretend to have more than a working hypothesis, but whoever else may prove to be right, Lady Thomson's on the wrong line."

Lady Thomson surveyed her in silence; Ian took no notice of her remark. He was looking before him with a sadness incomprehensible to the uncreative man—to the man who has never dreamed dreams and seen visions; with the sadness of one who just as the cloudy emanations of his mind are beginning to take form and substance sees them scattered, perhaps never again to reunite, by some cold breath from the relentless outside world of circumstance. He made his renunciation in silence; then, with a quiet smile, he turned to Lady Thomson and answered her.

"You're very kind, Aunt Beatrice, and quite right. There are things in life much more important than books."

XXI

So the summer went by; a hot summer, passed brightly enough to all appearance in the spacious rooms and gardens of Clewes and in expeditions among the neighboring fells. But to Ian it seemed rather an anxious pause in life. His work was at a stand-still, yet whatever the optimistic Aunt Beatrice might affirm, he could not feel that the shadow was lifting from his wife's mind. To others she appeared cheerful in the quiet, serious way that had always been hers, but he saw that her whole attitude towards life, especially in her wistful, yearning tenderness towards himself and Tony, was that of a woman who feels the stamp of death to be set upon her. At night, lying upon his breast, she would sometimes cling to him in an agony of desperate love, adjuring him to tell her the truth as to that Other: whether he did not see that she was different from his own Milly, whether it were possible that he could love that mysterious being as he loved her, his true, loving wife. Ian, who had been wont to hold stern doctrines as to the paramount obligation of truthfulness, perjured himself again and again, and hoped the Recording Angel dropped the customary tear. But, however deep the perjury, before long he was sure to find himself obliged to renew it.

To a man of his sensitive and punctilious nature the situation was almost intolerable. The pity of this tender, innocent life, his care, which seemed like some little inland bird, torn by the tempest from its native fields and tossed out to be the plaything of an immense and terrible ocean whose deeps no man has sounded! The pity of that other life, so winged for shining flight, so armed for triumphant battle, yet held down helpless in those cold ocean depths, and for pity's sake not to be helped by so much as a thought! Yet from the thorns of his hidden life he plucked one flower of comfort which to him, the philosopher, the man of Abstract Thought, was as refreshing as a pious reflection would be to a man of Religion. He had once been somewhat shaken by the dicta of the modern philosophers who relegate human love to the plane of an illness or an appetite. But where was the physical difference between the woman he so passionately loved and the one for whom he had never felt more than affection and pity? If from the strange adventure of his marriage he had lost some certainties concerning the human soul, he had gained the certainty that Love at least appertains to it.

One hot afternoon Milly was writing her Australian letter under a spreading ilex-tree on the lawn. Lady Thomson and Ian were sitting there also; he reading the latest French novel, she making notes for a speech she had to deliver shortly at the opening of a Girls' High School.

It is sometimes difficult to find the right news for people who have been for some years out of England, and Milly, in the languor of her melancholy, had relaxed the excellent habit formed under Aunt Beatrice of always keeping her mind to the subject in hand. She sat at the table with one hand propping her chin, gazing dreamily at the bright flower-beds on the lawn and the big, square, homely house, brightened by its striped awnings. At length Aunt Beatrice looked up from her notes.

"Mooning, Milly!" she exclaimed, in her full, agreeable voice. "Now I suppose you'll be telling your father you havn't time to write him a long letter."

"Milly's not mooning; she's making notes, like you," Ian replied, for his wife.

Milly looked around at him in surprise, and then at her right hand. It held a stylograph and had been resting on some scattered sheets of foolscap that Ian had left there in the morning. She had certainly been scrawling on it a little, but she was not aware of having written anything. Yet the scrawl, partly on one sheet and partly on another, was writing, very bad and broken, but still with a resemblance to her own handwriting. She pored over it; then looked Ian in the eyes, her own eyes large with a bewilderment touched with fear.

"I—I don't know what it means," she said, in a low, anxious tone.

"What's that?" queried Aunt Beatrice. "Can't read what you've written? You remind me of our old writing-master at school, who used to say tragically that he couldn't understand how it was that when that happened to a man he didn't just take a gun and shoot himself. I recommend you the pond, Mildred. It's more feminine."

"Please don't talk to Milly like that," retorted Ian, not quite lightly. "She always follows your advice, you know. It—it's only scrabbles."

He had left his chair and was leaning over the table, completely puzzled, first by Milly's terrified expression, then by what she had written, illegibly enough, across the two sheets of foolscap. He made out: "You are only miserab. . ."—the words were interspersed with really illegible scrawls—". . . Go. . . go. . . Let me. . . I want to live, I want to. . . Mild. . ."

Milly now wrote in her usual clear hand: "Who wrote that?"

He scribbled with his pencil: "You."

She replied in writing: "No. I know nothing about it."

Lady Thomson had taken up the newspaper, a thing she never did except at odd minutes, although she contrived to read everything in it that was really worth reading. Folding it up and looking at her watch, she exclaimed:

"A quarter of an hour before the carriage is round! Now don't go dawdling there, young people, and keep it standing in the sun."

Milly stood up and gathered her writing-materials together. Aunt Beatrice's tall figure, its stalwart handsomeness disguised in uncouth garments, passed with its usual vigorous gait across the burning sunlight on the lawn and broad gravel walk, to disappear under the awning of a French window. Milly, very pale, had closed her eyes and her hands were clasped. She trembled, but her voice and expression were calm and even resolute.

"The evil spirit is trying to get possession of me in another way now," she said. "But with God's help I shall be able to resist it."

Ian too was pale and disturbed. It was to him as though he had suddenly heard a beloved voice calling faintly for help.

"It's only automatic writing, dear," he replied. "You may not have been aware you were writing, but it probably reflects something in your thoughts."

"It does not," returned she, firmly. "However miserable I may sometimes be, I could never wish to give up a moment of my life with you, my own husband, or to leave you and our child to the influence of this—this being."

She stretched out her arms to him.

"Please hold me, Ian, and will as I do, that I may resist this horrible invasion. I have a feeling that you can help me."

He hesitated. "I, darling? But I don't believe—"

She approached him, and took hold of him urgently, looking him in the eyes.

"Won't you do it, husband dear? Please, for my sake, even if you don't believe, promise you'll will to keep me here. Will it, with all your might!"

What madness it was, this fantastic scene upon the well-kept lawn, under the square windows of the sober, opulent North Country house! And the maddest part of it all was the horrible reluctance he felt to comply with his wife's wish. He seemed to himself to pause noticeably before answering her with a meaningless half-laugh:

"Of course I'll promise anything you like, dear."

He put his arms around her and rested his face upon her golden head.

"Will!" she whispered, and the voice was one of command rather than of appeal. "Will! You have promised."

He willed as she commanded him.

The triple madness of it! He did not believe—and yet it seemed to him that the being he loved best in all the world was struggling up from below, calling to him for help from her tomb; and he was helping her enemy to hold down the sepulchral stone above her. He put his hand to his brow, and the sweat stood upon it.

Aunt Beatrice's masculine foot crunched the gravel. She stood there dressed and ready for the drive, beckoning them with her parasol. They came across the lawn holding each other by the hand, and Milly's face was calm, even happy. Aunt Beatrice smiled at them broadly with her large, handsome mouth and bright brown eyes.

"What, not had enough of spooning yet, you foolish young people! The carriage will be round in one minute, and Milly won't be ready."

XXII

There is a joy in the return of every season, though the return of spring is felt and celebrated beyond the rest. The gay flame dancing on the hearth where lately all was blackness, the sense of immunity from the "wrongs and arrows" of the skies and their confederate earth, the concentration of the sense upon the intimate charms which four walls can contain, bring to civilized man consolation for the loss of summer's lavish warmth and beauty. Children are always sensible of these opening festivals of the seasons, but many mature people enjoy without realizing them.

To Mildred the world was again new, and she looked upon its most familiar objects with the delighted eyes of a traveller returning to a favorite foreign country. So she did not complain because when she had left the earth it had been hurrying towards the height of June, and she had returned to find the golden boughs of October already stripped by devastating winds. The flames leaped merrily under the great carved mantel-piece in her white-panelled drawing-room, showing the date 1661, and the initials of the man who had put it there, and on its narrow shelf a row of Chelsea figures which she had picked up in various corners of Oxford. The chintz curtains were drawn around the bay-window and a bright brass *scaldino* stood in it, filled with the yellows and red-browns, the silvery pinks and mauves of chrysanthemums. The ancient charm, the delicate harmony of the room, in which every piece of furniture, every picture, every ornament, had been chosen with an exactness of taste seldom found in the young, made it more pleasurable to a cultivated eye than the gilded show drawing-rooms into which wealth too commonly crowds a medley of incongruous treasures and costly nullities.

It was a free evening for Ian, and as it was but the second since the Desire of his Eyes had returned to him, his gaze followed her movements in a contented silence, as she wandered about the room in her slight grace, the whiteness of her skin showing through the transparency of a black dress, which, although it was old, Milly would have thought unsuitable for a domestic evening. When everything was just where it should be, she returned to the fire and sank into a chair thoughtfully.

"How I should like some rides," she said; "but I suppose I can't have them, not unless Maxwell Davison's still in Oxford."

Ian's face clouded.

"He's not," he returned, shortly; and knocked the ashes out of his pipe, hesitating as to how he should put what he had to say about Maxwell Davison.

Mildred put her hand over her eyes and leaned back in her chair. Suddenly the silence was broken by a burst of rippling laughter. Ian started; his own thoughts had not been so diverting.

"What's the joke, Mildred?"

"Oh, Ian, don't you know? Max made love to Milly and she—she bit him! Wasn't it frightfully funny?" She laughed again, with a more inward enjoyment.

"I didn't know you bit him, although he richly deserved it; but of course I knew he made love to you. How do you know?"

"It came to me just now in a sort of flash. I seemed to see him—to see her, floundering out of the canoe; and both of them in such a towering rage. It really was too funny."

Ian's face hardened.

"I am afraid I can't see the joke of a man making love to my wife."

"You old stupid! He'd never have dared to behave like that to me; but Milly's such an ass."

"Milly was frightened, shocked, as any decent woman would be to whom such a thing happened. She certainly didn't encourage Maxwell; but she found an appointment already made for her to go on the river with him. No doubt she took an exaggerated view of her—of your—good God, Mildred, what am I to say?—well, of your relations with him."

Mildred had closed her eyes. A strange knowledge of things that had passed during her suppression was coming to her in glimpses.

"I know," she returned, in a kind of wonder at her own knowledge. "Absurd! But Max did behave abominably. I couldn't have believed it of him, even with that silly little baa-lamb. Of course she couldn't manage him. She won't be able to manage Tony long."

"Please don't speak of—of your other self in that way, Mildred. You're very innocent of the world in both your selves, and you must have been indiscreet or it would never have occurred to Maxwell to make love to you."

Ian was actually frowning, his lips were tight and hard, the clear pallor of his cheek faintly streaked with red. Mildred, leaning forward, looked at him, interested, her round chin on her hands.

"Are you angry, Ian? I really believe you are. Is it with me?"

"No, not with you. But of course I'm angry when I think of a fellow like that, my own cousin, a man who has been a guest in my house over and over again, being cad enough to make love to my wife."

Mildred was smiling quietly to herself.

"How primitive you are, Ian!" she said. "I suppose men are primitive when they're angry. I don't mind, but it does seem funny *you* should be."

He looked at her, surprised.

"Primitive? What do you mean?"

"What difference does it make, Max being your cousin, you silly old boy? You'd hardly ever seen him till last winter. Clans aren't any use to us now, are they? And when a man's got a house of his own, as Max had, or even a hotel, why should he be so grateful as all that for a few decent meals? He's not in the desert, depending on you for food and protection. Anyhow, it seems curious to expect him to weigh little things like that in the balance against what is always said to be such a very strong feeling as a man's love for a woman."

Men often deplore that they have failed in their attempts fundamentally to civilize Woman. They would use stronger language if Woman often made attempts fundamentally to civilize them.

"Please don't look at me like that," Mildred said, tremulously, after a pause. And the tears rushed to her eyes.

Ian's face softened, as leaning against the tall white mantel-piece he looked down and met the tear-bright gaze of his beloved.

"Poor sweetheart!" he exclaimed. "You're just a child for all your cleverness, and you don't half understand what you're talking about. But listen to me—" He kneeled before her, bringing their heads almost on a level. "I won't have any more affairs like this of Maxwell's. I dare say it was as much my fault as yours, but it mustn't happen again."

She dabbed away two tears that hung on her eyelashes, and looked at him with such a bright alluring yet elusive smile as might have flitted across the face of Ariel.

"How can I help it if Milly flirts? I don't believe I can help it if I do myself. But I can tell you this, Ian—yes, really—" Her soft white arms went about his neck. "I've never seen a man yet who was a patch upon you for cleverness and handsomeness and goodness and altogetherness. No! You really are the very nicest man I ever saw!"

XXIII

I n spite of the deepening dislike between the two egos which struggled for the possession of Mildred Stewart's bodily personality, they had a common interest in disguising the fact of their dual existence. Yet the transformation never occurred without producing its little harvest of inconveniences, and the difficulty of disguising the difference between the two was the greater because of the number of old acquaintances and friends of Milly Flaxman living in Oxford.

This was one reason why, when Ian was offered the headship of the Merchants' Guild College in London, Mildred encouraged him to take it. The income, too, seemed large in comparison to their Oxford one; and the great capital, with its ever-roaring surge of life, drew her with a natural magnetism. The old Foundation was being reconstructed, and was ambitious of adorning itself with a name so distinguished as Ian Stewart's, while at the same time obtaining the services of a man with so many of his best years still before him. Stewart, although he could do fairly well in practical administration, if he gave his mind to it, had won distinction as a student and man of letters, and feared that, difficult as it was to combine the real work of his life with bread-and-butter-making in Oxford, it would be still more difficult to combine it with steering the ship of the Merchants' Guild College. But he had the sensitive man's defect of too often deferring to the judgment of others, less informed or less judicious than himself. He found it impossible to believe that the opinion of the Master of Durham was not better than his own; and his old friend and tutor was strongly in favor of his accepting the headship. His most really happy and successful years had been those later ones in which he had shone as the Head of the most brilliant College in Oxford, a man of affairs and, in his individual way, a social centre. Accordingly he found it impossible to believe that it might be otherwise with Ian Stewart. The majority of Ian's most trusted advisers were of the same opinion as the Master, since the number of persons who can understand the conditions necessary to the productiveness of exceptional and creative minds is always few. Besides, most people at bottom are in Martha's attitude of scepticism towards the immaterial service of the world.

Lady Thomson voiced the general opinion in declaring that a man could always find time to do good work if he really wanted to do it.

She rejoiced when Ian put aside the serious doubts which beset him and accepted the London offer. Mildred also rejoiced, although she regretted much that she must leave behind her, and in particular the old panelled house.

This was, however, the one part of Oxford that Milly did not grieve to have lost, when she awoke once more from long months of sleep, to find herself in a new home. For she had grown to be silently afraid of the old house, with the great chimney-stacks like hollowed towers within it, made, it seemed, for the wind to moan in; its deep embrasures and panelling, that harbored inexplicable sounds; its ancient boards that creaked all night as if with the tread of mysterious feet. Awake in the dark hours, she fancied there were really footsteps, really knockings, movements, faint sighs passing outside her door, and that some old wicked life which should long since have passed away through the portals of the grave, clung to those ancient walls with a horrible tenacity, still refusing the great renunciation of death.

It was true that in the larger, more hurried world of London it was easier to dissimulate her transformations than it had been in Oxford. The comparative retirement in which Milly lived was easily explained by her delicate health. It seemed as though in her sojourns—which more and more encroached upon those of the original personality—the strong, intrusive ego consumed in an unfair degree the vitality of their common body, leaving Milly with a certain nervous exhaustion, a languor against which she struggled with a pathetic courage. She learned also to cover with a seldom broken silence the deep wound which was ever draining her young heart of its happiness; and for that very reason it grew deeper and more envenomed.

That Ian should love her evil and mysterious rival as though they two were really one was horrible to her. Even her child was not unreservedly her own, to bring up according to her own ideas, to love without fear of that rival. Tony was like his father in the sweetness of his disposition, as well as in his dark beauty, and he accented with surprising resignation the innumerable rules and regulations which Milly set about his path and about his bed. But although he was healthy, his nerves were highly strung, and it seemed as though her feverish anxiety for his physical, moral, and intellectual welfare reacted upon him and made him, after a few weeks of her influence, less vigorous in appearance, less gay and boylike than he was during her absence. Ian dared not hint a preference for the animal spirits that Mildred encouraged, with their attendant noise and nonsense, considered by Milly so undesirable. But one day Tims observed, cryptically, that "A watched boy never boils"; and Emma, the nurse, told Mrs. Stewart bluntly that she thought Master Tony wasn't near so well and bright when he was always being looked after, as he was when he was let go his own way a bit, like other children. Then a miserable fear beset Milly lest the boy, too, should notice the change in his mother; lest he should look forward to the disappearance of the woman who loved him so passionately, watched over him with such complete devotion, and in his silent heart regret, invoke, that other. It was at once soothing and bitter to her to be assured by Ian and by Tims that they had never been able to discover the least sign that Tony was aware when the change occurred between the two personalities of his mother.

Two years passed in London, two years out of which the original owner enjoyed a total share of only nine months; and this, indeed, she could not truly have been said to have enjoyed, since happiness was far from her. Death would have been a sad but simple catastrophe, to be met with resignation to the will of God. What resignation could be felt before this gradual strangulation of her being at the hands of a nameless yet surely Evil Thing? Her love for Ian was so great that his sufferings were more to her than her own, and in the space of those two years she saw that on him, too, sorrow had set its mark. The glow of his good looks and the brilliancy of his mind were alike dulled. It was not only that his shoulders were bent, his hair thinned and touched with gray, but his whole appearance, once so individual, was growing merely typical; that of the middle-aged Academic, absorbed in the cares of his profession. His real work was not merely at a stand-still, but a few more such years and his capacity for it would be destroyed. She felt this vaguely, with the intuition of love. If the partnership had been only between him and her, he surely would have yielded to her prayer to give up the headship of the Merchants' Guild College after a set term; but he put the question by. Evidently that Other, who cared for nothing but her own selfish interests and amusements, who spent upon them the money that he ought to be saving, would never allow him to give up his appointment unless something better offered. It was not only her own life, it was the higher and happier part of his that she was struggling to save in those desperate hours when she sought around her for some weapon wherewith to fight that mortal foe. She turned to priests, Anglican, Roman Catholic; but they failed her. Both believed her to be suffering under an insane delusion, but the Roman Catholic priest would have attempted to exorcise the evil spirit if she would have joined his Communion. She was too honest to pretend to a belief that was not hers.

When she returned from her last vain pilgrimage to the Church of the Sacred Heart and stood before the glass, removing a thick black veil from the pale despair of her face, she was suddenly aware of a strange, unfamiliar smile lifting the drooped lines of her lips—an elfish smile which transformed her face to something different from her own. And immediately those smiling lips uttered words that fell as unexpectedly on her ears as though they had proceeded from the mouth of another person.

"Never mind," they said, briskly. "It wouldn't have been of the least use."

For a minute a wild terror made her brain swim and she fled to the door, instinctively seeking protection; but she stayed herself, remembering that Ian, who was sleeping badly at night, was now asleep in his study. Weak and timid though she was, she would lay no fresh burden on him, but fight her battle, if battle there was to be, alone.

She walked back deliberately to the glass and looked steadily at her own reflection. Her brows were frowning, her eyes stern as she had never before seen them, but they were assuredly hers, answering to the mood of her own mind. Her lips were cold, and trembled so that although she had meant solemnly to defy the Power of Evil within her she was unable to articulate. As she looked in the glass and saw herself—her real self—so evidently there, the strange smile, the speech divorced from all volition of hers which had crossed her lips, began to lose reality. Still her lips trembled, and at length a convulsion shook them as irresistible as that of a sob. Words broke stammeringly out which were not hers:

"Struggle for life—the stronger wins. I'm stronger. It's no use struggling—no use—no use—no use!"

Milly pressed her lips hard against her teeth with her hands, stopping this utterance by main force. Her heart hammered so loud it seemed as though some one must hear it and come to ask what was the matter. But no one came. She was left alone with the Thing within her.

It may have been a long while, it may have been only a few seconds that she remained standing at her dressing-table, her hands pressed hard against her convulsed mouth. She had closed her eyes, afraid to look longer in the glass, lest something uncanny should peer out of it. She did not pray—she had prayed so often before—but she fought with her whole strength against the encroaching power of the Other. At length she gradually released her lips. They were bruised, but they had ceased to move. It was she herself who spoke, low but clearly and with deliberation:

"I shall struggle. I shall never give in. You think you're the stronger. I won't let you be. I'm fighting for my husband's happiness—do you hear?—as well as my own. You're strong, but we shall be stronger, he and I, in the end."

There was no answer, the sense of struggle was gone from her; and suddenly she felt how mad it was to be talking to herself like that in an empty room. She took off the little black toque which sat on her bright head with an alien smartness to which she was now accustomed, and forced herself to look in the glass while she pinned up a stray lock of hair. Beyond an increased pallor and darker marks under her eyes, she saw nothing unusual in her appearance.

It was five o'clock, and Ian would probably be awake and wanting his tea. She went softly into the study and leaned over him. Sleep had almost smoothed away the lines of effort and worry which had marred the beauty of his face; in the eyes of her love he was always the same handsome Ian Stewart as in the old Oxford days, when he had seemed as a young god, so high above her reach.

She went to an oak table behind the sofa, on which the maid had set the tea-things without awakening him, and sat there quietly watching the kettle. The early London twilight began to veil the room. Ian stirred on the sofa and sat up, with his back to her, unconscious of her presence. She rose, vaguely supposing herself about to address some gentle word to him. Then suddenly she had thrown one soft hand under his chin and one across his eyes, and with a *brusquerie* quite unnatural to her pulled him backwards, while a ripple of laughter so strange as to be shocking in her own ears burst from her lips, which cried aloud with a defiant gayety:

"Who, Ian? Guess!"

Ian, with a sudden force as strange to her as her own laughter, her own gay cry, pulled her hands away, held them an instant fast; then, kneeling on the sofa, he caught her in his long arms across the back of it, and after the pressure of a kiss upon her lips such as she had never felt before, breathed with a voice of unutterable gladness: "Mildred! Darling! Dearest love!"

A hoarse cry, almost a shriek, broke from the lips of Milly. The woman he held struggled from his arms and stared at him wildly in the veiling twilight. A strange horror fell upon him, and for several seconds he remained motionless, leaning over the back of the sofa. Then, groping towards the wall, he switched on the electric light. He saw it plainly, the white mask of a woman smitten with a mortal blow.

"Milly," he uttered, stammeringly. "What's the matter? You are ill."

She turned on him her heart-broken look, then pressing her hand to her throat, spoke as though with difficulty.

"I love you very much—you don't know how much I love you. I've tried so hard to be a good wife to you."

Ian perceived catastrophe, yet dimly; sought with desperate haste to remember why for a moment he had believed that that Other was come back; what irreparable thing he had said or done.

Meantime he must say something. "Milly, dear! What's gone wrong? What have I done, child?"

"You've let her take you—" She spoke more freely now, but with a startling fierceness—"You've let her take you from me."

"Ah, the old trouble! My poor Milly! I know it's terrible for you. I can only say that no one else really exists; that you are always you really."

"That's not true. You don't believe it yourself. That wicked creature has made you love her—her own wicked way. You want to have her instead of me; you want to destroy your own wife and to get her back again."

The cruel, ultimate truth that Milly's words laid bare—the truth which he constantly refused to look upon, in mercy to himself and her—paralyzed the husband's tongue. He tried to approach her with vague words and gestures of affection and remonstrance, but she motioned him from her.

"No. Don't say you love me; I can't believe it, and I hate to hear you say what's not true."

For a moment the fierce heart of Primitive Woman had blazed up within her—that fire which all the waters of baptism fail to quench. But the flame died down as suddenly as it had arisen, and appealing with outspread hands, as to some invisible judge, she wailed, miserably:

"Oh, what am I to do—what am I to do? I love you so much, and it's all no use."

Ian was as white as herself.

"Milly, my poor girl, don't break our hearts."

He stretched his arms towards her, but she turned away from him towards the door, made a few steps, then stopped and clutched her throat. He thought her struggling with sobs; but when once more, as though in fear, she turned her face towards him, he saw it strangely convulsed. He moved towards her in an alarmed silence, but before he could reach her and catch her in his arms, her head drooped, she swayed once upon her feet, and fell heavily to the ground.

XXIV

N ow be reasonable Tims. You can be if you choose."
Mildred was perched on a high stool in Tims's Chambers, breathing spring from a bunch of fresh Neapolitan violets, grown by an elderly admirer of hers, and wearing her black, winter toque and dress with that invincible air of smartness which she contrived to impart to the oldest clothes, provided they were of her own choosing. Tims, who from her face and attitude might have been taken for a victim of some extreme and secret torture, crouched, balancing herself on the top rail of her fender. She replied only by a horrible groan.

"Who do you suppose is the happier when Milly comes back?" continued Mildred.

"Well—the brat."

"Tony? He doesn't even know when she's there; but by the time she's done with him he's unnaturally good. He can't like that, can he?"

"Then there's Ian, good old boy!"

"That's humbug. You know it is."

"But it's Milly herself I really care about," cried Tims. "You've been a pig to her, Mil. She says you're a devil, and if I weren't a scientific woman I swear I should begin to believe there was something in it."

"No, Tims, dear," returned Mildred with earnestness. "I'm neither a pig nor a devil." She paused. "Sometimes I think I've lived before, some quite different life from this. But I suppose you'll say that's all nonsense."

"Of course it is—rot," commented Tims, sternly. "You're a physiological freak, that's what you are. You're nothing but Milly all the time, and you ought to be decent to her."

"I don't want to hurt her anyhow," apologized Mildred; "but you see when I'm only half there—well, I am only half there. I'm awfully rudimentary and I can't grasp anything except that I'm being choked, squeezed out of existence, and that I must make a fight for my life. Any woman becomes rudimentary who is fighting for her life against another woman; only I've more excuse for it, because as a scientist you must see that I can only be in very partial possession of my brain."

Tims had pulled her wig down over her eyes and glared at space. "That's all very well for you," she said; "but why should I help you to kill poor old M.?"

"Do try and understand! Every time she comes back she's more and more miserable; and that's not cheerful for Ian either, is it? Now, through that underhand trick of rudimentary Me—you see I don't try to hide my horrid ways—she knows Ian adores me and, comparatively speaking, doesn't care two straws about her. That will make her more miserable than she has ever been before. She'll only want to live so that I mayn't."

"I don't see how Ian's going to get on without her. *You* don't do much for him, my girl, except spend his money."

"Of course, that's quite true. I'm not in the least suited to Ian or his life or his income; but that's not my fault. How perverse men are! Always in love with the wrong women, aren't they?"

Tims's countenance relaxed and she replied with a slight air of importance:

"My opinion of men has been screwed up a peg lately. Every now and then you do find one who's got too much sense for any rot of that kind."

Mildred continued.

"Ian's perfectly wretched at what happened; can't understand it, of course. He doesn't say much, but I can see he dreads explanations with Milly. He's good at reserve, but no good at lies, poor old dear, and just think of all the straight questions she'll ask him! It'll be torture to both of them. Poor Milly! I've no patience with her. Why should she want to live? Life's no pleasure to her. She's known a long time that Tony's really jollier and better with me, and now she knows Ian doesn't want her. How can you pretend to think Milly happy, Tims? Hasn't she said things to you?"

"Yes," groaned Tims. "Poor old M.! She's pretty well down on her luck, you bet."

"And I enjoy every minute of my life, although I could find plenty to grumble at if I liked. Listen to me, Tims. How would it be to strike a bargain? Let me go on without any upsets from Milly until I'm forty. I'm sure I sha'n't care what happens to me at forty. Then Milly may have everything her own way. What would it matter to her? She likes to take time by the forelock and behaves already as though she were forty. I feel sure you could help me to keep her quiet if only you chose."

"If I chose to meddle at all, I should be much more likely to help her to come back," returned Tims, getting snappish.

"Alas! I fear you would, Tims, dear, in spite of knowing it would only make her miserable. That shows, doesn't it, how unreasonable even a distinguished scientific woman can be?"

This aspersion on Tims's reasoning powers had to be resented and the resentment to be soothed. And the soothing was so effectually done that Tims owned to herself afterwards there was some excuse for Ian's infatuation.

But Tims had no desire to meddle, and the months passed by without any symptoms of the change appearing. It seemed as if Mildred's hold upon life had never been so firm, the power of her personality never so fully developed. She belonged to a large family which in all its branches had a trick of throwing up successful men and brilliant women. But in reaction against Scottish clannishness, it held little together, and in the two houses whence Mildred was launched on her London career, she had no nursery reputation of Milly's with which to contend.

One of these houses was that of her cousin, Sir Cyril Meres, a fashionable painter with a considerable gift for art, and more for success—success social and financial. His beautiful house, stored with wonderful collections, had a reputation, and was frequented by every one of distinction in the artistic or intellectual world—by those of the world of wealth and rank who were interested in such matters, and the yet larger number who affected to be interested in them. For those Anglo-Saxon deities, Mammon and Snobbery, who have since conquered the whole civilized globe, had temporarily fallen back for a fresh spring, and in the eighties and early nineties Culture was reckoned very nearly as *chic* as motoring in the first years of the new century.

Several painters of various degrees of talent attempted to fix on canvas the extraordinary charm of Mrs. Stewart's appearance. Not one of them succeeded; but the peculiar shade of her hair, the low forehead and delicate line of the dark eyebrows, the outline of the mask, sometimes admired, sometimes criticised, made her portrait always recognized, whether simpering as a chocolate-box classicality, smiling sadly from the flowery circle of the Purgatorio, or breaking out of some rough mass of paint with the provocative leer of a *cocotte* of the Quartier Latin.

The magnetism of her personality defied analysis, as her essential beauty defied the painter's art. It was a magnetism which surrounded her with an atmosphere of adorations, admirations, enmities—all equally violent and irrational. Her wit had little to do with the making of her enemies, because it was never used in offence against friends or even harmless acquaintances; only against her foes she employed it with the efficiency and mercilessness of a red Indian wielding the tomahawk.

The other family where she found her niche awaiting her was of a different order. It was that of the retired Indian judge, Sir John Ireton, whose wife had chaperoned her through a Commemoration the summer she had taken her First in Greats. Ireton was not only in Parliament, but his house was a meeting-place where politicians cemented personal ties and plotted party moves. Milly in her brief appearances, had been of use to Lady Ireton, but Mildred proved socially invaluable. There were serious persons who suspected Mrs. Stewart of approaching politics in a flippant spirit; but on certain days she had revealed a grave and ardent belief in the dogmas of the party and a piety of attitude towards the person of its great apostle, which had convinced them that she was not really cynical or frivolous.

Lady Augusta Goring was the most important conquest of the kind Milly had made. She was the only child of the Marquis of Ipswich, and one of those rather stupid people whose energy of mind and character is often mistaken by themselves and others for cleverness. Lady Augusta was handsome in a dull, massive way, and so conscientious that she had seldom time to smile. Her friends said she would smile oftener if her husband caused her less anxiety; but considering who George Goring was and how he had been brought up, he might have been much worse. Where women were concerned, scandal had never accused him of anything more flagrant than dubious flirtations. It was his political intrigues, constantly threatening unholy *liaisons* in the most unthinkable directions; his sudden fits of obstinate idleness, often occurring at the very moment when some clever and promising political scheme of his own was ripe for execution, which so unendurably harassed the staid Marquis and the earnest Lady Augusta. They were highly irritating, too, to Sir John Ireton, who had believed himself at one time able to tame and tutor the tricksy young politician.

The late Lord Ipswich had been a "sport" in the Barthop family; a black sheep, but clever, and a well known collector. Accidental circumstances had greatly enriched him, and as he detested his brother and successor, he had left his pictures to the nation and all of his fortune which he could dispose of—which happened to be the bulk— to his natural son, George Goring. But his will had not been found for some weeks after his death, and while the present Marquis had believed himself the inheritor of the whole property, he had treated the nameless and penniless child of his brother with perfect delicacy and generosity. When George Goring found himself made rich at the expense of his uncle, he proposed to his cousin Lady Augusta and was accepted.

Mildred was partly amused and partly bored to discover herself on so friendly a footing with Lady Augusta. Putting herself into that passive frame of mind in which revelations of Milly's past actions were most often vouchsafed to her, she saw herself type-writing in a small, high-ceilinged room looking out on a foggy London park, and Lady Augusta seated at a neighboring table, surrounded by papers. Type-writing was not then so common as it is now, and Milly had learned the art in order to give assistance to Ian. Mildred was annoyed to find herself in danger of having to waste her time in a mechanical occupation which she detested, or else of offending a woman whom her uncle valued as a friend and political ally.

It was a slight compensation to receive an invitation to accompany the Iretons to a great ball at Ipswich House. There was no question of Ian accompanying her. He was usually too tired to care for going out in the evening and went only to official dinners and to the houses of old friends, or of people with whom he had educational connections. It did not occur to him that it might be wise to put a strain upon himself sometimes, to lay by his spectacles, straighten his back, have his beard trimmed and appear at Mildred's side in the drawing-rooms where she shone, looking what he was—a husband of whom she had reason to be proud. More and more engrossed by his own work and responsibilities, he let her drift into a life quite apart from his, content to see her world from his own fireside, in the sparkling mirror of her talk.

Ipswich House was a great house, if of little architectural merit, and the ball had all the traditional spectacular splendor common to such festivities. The pillared hall and double staircase, the suites of spacious rooms, were filled with a glittering kaleidoscopic crowd of fair and magnificently bejewelled women and presumably brave, certainly well-groomed and handsome men. The excellence of the music, the masses of flowers, the number of great names and well-advertised society beauties present, would subsequently provide material for long and eulogistic paragraphs in the half-penny press and the Ladies' Weeklies.

Mildred enjoyed it as a spectacle rather than as a ball, for she knew few people there, and the young political men whom she had met at her uncle's parties were too much engaged with ladies of more importance, to whom they were related or to whom they owed social attention, to write their names more than once on her programme. One of these, however, asked her if she had noticed how harassed both Lord Ipswich and Lady Augusta looked. Goring's speech, he said, at the Fothering by-election was reported and commented upon in all the papers, and had given tremendous offence to the leaders of his party; while the fact that he had not turned up in time for the ball must be an additional cross to his wife, who made such a firm stand against the social separation of married couples.

When Mildred returned to her uncle she found him the centre of a group of eminent politicians, all denouncing in more or less subdued tones the outrageous utterances and conduct of Goring, and most declaring that only consideration for Lord Ipswich and Lady Augusta prevented them from publicly excommunicating the hardened offender. Others, however, while admitting the outrage, urged that he was too brilliant a young man to be lightly thrown away, and advised patience, combined with the disciplinary rod. Sir John was of the excommunicatory party. Later in the evening he disappeared into some remote smoking or card-room, not so much forgetting his niece as taking it for granted that she was, as usual, surrounded by friends and admirers of both sexes. But a detached personality, however brilliant, is apt to be submerged in such a crowd of social eminences, bound together by ties of blood, of interests, and of habit, as filled the salons of Ipswich House. Mildred walked around the show contentedly enough for a time, receiving a smile here and a pleasant word there from such of her acquaintances as she chanced upon, but practically alone. And being alone, she found herself yielding to a vulgar envy of richer women's clothes and jewels. Her dress, with which she had been pleased, looked ordinary beside the creations of great Parisian *ateliers*, and the few old paste ornaments which were the only jewels she possessed, charming as they were, seemed dim and scant among the crowns and constellations of diamonds that surrounded her. Her pride rebelled against this envy, but could not conquer it.

More gnawing pangs, however, assailed her presently, the pangs of hunger; and no one offered to take her in to supper. The idea of taking herself in was revolting; she preferred starvation. But where could Uncle John have hidden himself? She sought the elderly truant with all the suppressed annoyance of a chaperon seeking an inconsiderate flirt of a girl. And it happened that a spirit in her feet led her to the door of a small room in which Milly and Lady Augusta had been wont to transact their business. A curious feeling of familiarity, of physical habit, caused her to open the big mahogany door. There was no air of public festivity about the room, which was furnished with a substantial, almost shabby masculine comfort. But oh, tantalizing spectacle! Under the illumination of a tall, crimson-shaded, standard lamp, stood a little, white-covered table, reminding her irresistibly of a little table in a fairy story, which the due incantation causes to rise out of the ground. A small silver-gilt tureen of soup smoked upon it and a little pile of delicate rolls lay beside the plate set for one. But alas! she might not, like the favored girl in the fairy story, proceed without ceremony to satisfy her hunger at the mysterious little table.

A door immediately opposite that of the small sitting-room opened noiselessly, and a young man entered with a light, quick step. He saw Mildred, but for a second or so she did not see him. He was at her side when she looked around and their eyes met. They had never seen each other before, but at that meeting of the eyes a curious feeling, such as two Europeans might experience, meeting in the heart of some dark continent, affected them both.

There was something picturesque about the young man's appearance, in spite of the impeccable cut and finish of his dress-suit and the waxed ends of his small blond mustache. His hair was of a ruddy nut-brown color, and had a wave in it; his bright hazel eyes seemed exactly to match it. His face had a fine warm pallor, and his under lip, which with his chin was somewhat thrust forward, was redder than the lip of a child. It was perhaps this noticeable coloring and something in his port which made him, in spite of the correct modernity of his dress, suggest some seventeenth-century portrait.

"Forgive my passing you," he said, at length; "but I'm starving."

"So am I," she returned, hardly aware of what she was saying. Some strange, almost hypnotic attraction seemed to rivet her whole attention on the mere phenomenon of this man.

"By Jove! Aren't they feeding the multitude down there?" he asked, nodding in the direction of the supper-room.

"Of course," she answered, with the simple gravity of a child, her blue eyes still fixed upon him. "But I can't ask for supper for myself, can I?"

Her need was distinctly material; yet the young man confronting her white grace, the strange look in her blue eyes, had a dreamlike feeling, almost as though he had met a dryad or an Undine between two of the prosaic, substantial doors of Ipswich House. And as in a dream the most extraordinary things seem familiar and expected, so the apparition of the Undine and her confidence in him seemed familiar, in fact just what he had been expecting during those hours of fog off the Goodwins, when the sirens, wild voices gathering up from all the seas of the world, had been screaming to each other across the hidden waters. That same inner concentration upon the mere phenomenon of a presence, an existence, which had given the childlike note to Mildred's speech, froze a compliment upon his lips; and they stood silent, eying each other gravely. A junior footman appeared, carrying a bottle of champagne in a bucket, and the young man addressed him in a vague, distracted tone, very unlike his usual manner.

"Look here, Arthur, here's a lady who can't get any supper."

The footman went quite pink at this personal reproach. He happened to have heard some one surmise, on seeing Mildred roaming about alone, that she was a newspaper woman.

"Please sir," he replied, "I don't know how it's happened, for her Ladyship told Mr. Mackintosh to be sure and see as the newspaper ladies and gentlemen were well looked after, and he thought as they'd all had supper."

It seemed incredible that Mildred should not have heard this reply, uttered so close to her; but though it fell upon her ears it did not penetrate to her mind.

"Bring up supper for two, Arthur," said Goring, in his usual decisive tone. "That'll do, won't it?" he added, and turned to Mildred, ushering her into the room. "You'll have supper with me, I hope? My name's Goring; I'm Lord Ipswich's son-in-law and I live in his house; so you see it's all right."

The corollary was not evident; but the mention of the name brought Mildred back to the ordinary world. So this was George Goring, the plague of his political party, the fly in the ointment of a respectable Marquis and his distinguished daughter. She had not fancied him like this. For one thing, she did not know him to be younger than his wife, and between the careworn solidity of Lady Augusta and this vivid restless personality, the five actual years of difference seemed stretched to ten.

"I'm convinced it's all right, Mr. Goring," she replied, throwing herself into a chair and smiling at him sparklingly. "It must be all right. I want my supper so much I should have to accept your invitation even if you were a burglar."

Goring, whose habit it was to keep moving, laughed as he walked about, one hand in his trousers pocket.

"Why shouldn't I be a burglar? A burglar, with an assistant disguised as a footman, sacking the bedrooms of Lord Ipswich's house while the ball proceeds? There's copy for you! Shall I do it? 'Mr. George Goring's Celebrated Black Pearls Stolen,' would make a capital head-line. Perhaps you've heard I'd do anything to keep my name in the newspapers."

"It certainly gets there pretty often," returned Mildred, politely; "and whenever it's mentioned it has an enlivening effect."

The footman had reappeared and they were unfolding their dinner-napkins, sitting opposite each other at the little table.

"As how, enlivening?"

"Like a bit of bread dropped into a glass of flat champagne."

"You think my party's like champagne? Why, it couldn't exist for a moment if it sparkled."

"I was talking of newspapers, not of your party; though there's no doubt you do enliven that."

"Do I? Like what? No odiously inoffensive comparisons, if you please."

"Well, I have heard people say like—like a blister on the back of the neck."

Goring laughed. "Thanks. That's better."

"The patient's using language, but he won't really tear it off, because he knows that would hurt him more, and the blister will do him good in the end, if he bears with it."

"But there's the blister's side to it, too. It's infernally tiring for a blister to be sticking on to such a fellow everlastingly. It'll fly off of itself before long, if he doesn't look out. Hullo! What am I saying? I suppose you'll have all this out in some confounded paper—'The Rebel Member Returns. A Chat with Mr. Goring'—Don't do that; but I'll give you some other copy if you like."

"You're very kind in giving me all this copy. What shall I do with it? Shall I keep it as a memento?"

"No, no. You can sell it; honor bright you can."

"Can I? Shall I get much for it? Enough money to buy me a tiara, do you think?"

"Do you really want to wear the usual fender? Now, why? I suppose because you aren't sufficiently aware how—" he paused on the edge of a compliment which seemed suddenly too full-flavored and ordinary to be addressed to this strangely lovely being, with her smile at once so sparkling and so mysterious. He substituted: "How much more distinguished it is to look like an Undine than like a peeress."

Mildred seemed slightly taken aback.

"Why do you say 'Undine?'" she asked, almost sharply. "Do I—do I look as if I came out of a Trafalgar Square fountain with fell designs on Lord Ipswich?"

"Of course not. But—I can't exactly define even to myself what I mean, only you do suggest an Undine to me. To some one else you might be simply Miss—Forgive me, I don't know your name."

He had not even troubled to glance at her left hand, and when the "Mrs." was uttered it affected him oddly. It was one of the peculiar differences between her two personalities that, casually encountered, Mildred was as seldom taken for a married woman as Milly for an unmarried one.

"Do I look as if I'd got no soul?" she persisted, leaning a little towards him, an intensity that might almost have been called anxiety in her gaze.

He could even have fancied she had grown paler. He, too, became serious. His eyes brightened, meeting hers, and a slight color came into his cheeks.

"Quite the contrary," he answered. "I should say you had a great deal—in fact, I shall begin to believe in detachable souls again. Fancy most people as just souls, without trimmings. It makes one laugh. But your body looks like an emanation from the spirit; as though it might flow away in a white waterfall or go up in a white fire; and as though, if it did, your soul could certainly precipitate another body, which must certainly be like this one, because it would be as this is, the material expression of a spirit."

She listened as he spoke, seriously, her eyes on his. But when he had done, she dropped her chin on her hand and laughed delightedly.

"You think I should be able to grow a fresh body, like a lobster growing a fresh claw? What fun!"

There was a sound without, not of the footman struggling with dishes and plates and the door-handle, but of middle-aged voices.

Instinctively Goring and Mildred straightened themselves and looked polite. Lord Ipswich and Sir John Ireton, deep in political converse, came slowly in and then stopped short in surprise. Mildred lost not a moment in carrying the war into their country. She turned about and addressed her uncle in a playful tone, which yet smacked of reproof.

"Here you are at last, Uncle John! I thought you'd forgotten all about me. I've been walking miles in mad pursuit of you, till I was so tired and hungry I think I should have dropped if Mr. Goring hadn't taken pity upon me and made me eat his supper."

Sir John defended himself, and Lord Ipswich was shocked to think that a lady had been in such distress in his house; although the apparition of Goring prevented him from feeling it as acutely as he would otherwise have done. His pleasant pink face took on an expression of severity as he responded to his son-in-law's somewhat too cheerful greeting.

"Sorry to be so late, but we were held up by a fog at the mouth of the Thames."

"It must have been very important business to take you all the way to Brussels so suddenly."

"It certainly wouldn't wait. I heard there was a whole set of Beauvais tapestries to be had for a mere song. I couldn't buy them without seeing them you know, and the big London and Paris dealers were bound to chip in if I didn't settle the matter pretty quick. I'm precious glad I did, for they're the finest pieces I ever saw and would have fetched five times what I gave for them at Christie's."

"Ah—really!" was all Lord Ipswich's response, coldly uttered and accompanied by a smile more sarcastic than often visited his neat and kindly lips. Sir John Ireton and Mildred, aware of the delicate situation, partly domestic and partly political, upon which they were intruding, took themselves away and were presently rolling through the empty streets in the gray light of early morning.

XXV

Not long afterwards Mildred received a letter the very address of which had an original appearance, looking as if it were written with a stick in a fist rather than with a pen between fingers. It caught her attention at once from half a dozen others.

Dear Mrs. Stewart,

Yesterday I was at Cochrane's studio and he told me Meres was the greatest authority in England on tapestry, and also a cousin of yours. Please remember (or forgive) the supper on Tuesday, and of your kindness, ask him to let me see his lot and give me his opinion on mine. Cochrane had a folly he called a portrait of you in his studio. I turned its face to the wall; and in the end he admitted I was right.

Yours sincerely,
George Goring

Accordingly, on a very hot day early in July, Goring met Mildred again, at Sir Cyril Meres's house on Campden Hill. The long room at one end of which stood the small dining-table looked on the greenness of a lawny, lilac-sheltered garden, so that such light as filtered through the green jalousies was green also. There was a great block of ice somewhere in the room, and so cool it was, so greenly dim there, that it seemed almost like a cavern of the sea. Mildred wore a white dress, and, as was the fashion of the moment, a large black hat shadowed with ostrich-feathers. Once more on seeing her he had a startled impression of looking upon an ethereal creature, a being somehow totally distinct from other beings; and for lack of some more appropriate name, he called her again in his mind "Undine." As the talk, which Cyril Meres had a genius for making general, became more animated, he half lost that impression in one of a very clever, charming woman, with a bright wit sailing lightly over depths of knowledge to which he was unaccustomed in her sex.

The party was not intended to number more than eight persons, of whom Lady Thomson was one, and they sat down seven. When Sir Cyril observed: "We won't wait any longer for Davison," Mildred was too much interested in Goring's presence to inquire who this Davison might be.

She sparkled on half through luncheon to the delight of every one but Miss Ormond the actress, who would have preferred to play the lead herself. Then came a pause. A door was opened at the far end of the dim room, and the missing guest appeared. Sir Cyril rose hastily to greet him. He advanced without any apologetic hurry in his gait; the same impassive Maxwell Davison as before, but leaner, browner, more silver-headed from three more years of wandering under Oriental suns. Mildred could hardly have supposed it possible that the advent of any human being could have given her so disagreeable a sensation.

Sir Cyril was unaware that she knew Maxwell Davison; surprised to hear that he was a cousin of Stewart's, between whom and himself there existed a mutual antipathy, expressing itself in terms of avoidance. His own acquaintance with Davison was recent and in the way of business. He had had the fancy to build for the accommodation of his Hellenic treasures a room in imitation of the court of a Græco-Roman house which he had helped to excavate in Asia Minor. He had commissioned Davison to buy him hangings for it to harmonize with an old Persian carpet in cream color and blue of which he was already possessed. Davison had brought these with him and a little collection of other things which he thought Meres might care to look at. He did not know the Stewarts had moved to London, and it was an unpleasant surprise to find himself seated at the same table with Mildred; he had not forgotten, still less forgiven, the lure of her coquetry, the insult of her rebuff.

Lady Thomson was next him and questioned him exhaustively about his book on Persian Literature and the travels of his lifetime. Miss Ormond took advantage of Mrs. Stewart's sudden silence to talk to the table rather cleverly around the central theme of herself. Goring conversed apart with Mrs. Stewart.

Coffee was served in the shrine which Sir Cyril had reared for his Greek collection, of which the gem was a famous head of Aphrodite—an early Aphrodite, divine, removed from all possible pains and agitations of human passion. The room was an absurdity on Campden Hill, said some, but undeniably beautiful in itself. The columns, of singular lightness and grace, were of a fine marble which hovered between creamy white and faint yellow, and the walls and floor were of the same tone, except for a frieze on a Greek model, very faintly colored, and the old Persian carpet. In fine summer weather the large skylight covering the central space was withdrawn, and such sky as London can show looked down upon it. The new hangings which Maxwell Davison had brought with him were already displayed on a tall screen, and his miscellaneous collection of antiquities, partly sent from Durham College, partly lately acquired, were arranged on a marble bench.

"I shouldn't have brought these things, Sir Cyril," he said; "if I'd known Mrs. Stewart was here. She's got a way of hinting that my most cherished antiquities are forgeries; and the worst of it is, she makes every one believe her, including myself."

Mildred protested.

"I don't pretend to know anything about antiquities, Mr. Davison. I'm sure I never suspected you of a forgery, and if I had, I hope I shouldn't have been rude enough to tell you so."

Maxwell Davison laughed his harsh laugh.

"Do you want me to believe you can't be rude, Mrs. Stewart?"

"I'm almost afraid she can't be," interposed Lady Thomson's full voice. "People who make a superstition of politeness infallibly lose the higher courtesy of truth."

Here Sir Cyril Meres called Davison away to worship at the shrine of the Aphrodite, while Goring invited Mrs. Stewart into a neighboring corridor where some tapestries were hanging.

The divining crystal was among the objects returned from Oxford, and had been included in the collection which Davison had brought with him, on the chance that the painter might fancy such curiosities. When Goring and Mildred returned from their leisurely inspection of the tapestries, Miss Ormond had it in her hand, and Lady Thomson was commenting on some remark of hers.

"I've no doubt, as you say, it has played a wicked part before now in Oriental intrigues. But of course the poor crystal is perfectly innocent of the things read into it by rascals, practising on the ignorant and superstitious."

"Sometimes, perhaps, Lady Thomson," returned Miss Ormond; "but sometimes people do see extraordinary visions in a crystal."

Lady Thomson sniffed.

"Excitable, imaginative people do, I dare say."

"On the contrary, prosaic people are far more likely to see things than highly strung imaginative creatures like myself. I've tried several times and have never seen anything. I believe having a great deal of brain-power and emotion and all that tells against it. I shouldn't be at all surprised now if Mrs. Stewart, who is—well, I should fancy, just a little cold, very bright and all that on the surface, you know—I shouldn't wonder if she could crystal-gaze very successfully. I should like to know whether she's ever tried."

"I'm sure she's not," replied Lady Thomson, firmly. "My niece, Mrs. Stewart, is a great deal too sensible and well-educated."

"Mrs. Stewart can't honestly say the same for herself," interposed Davison; "she gazed in this very crystal some years ago and certainly saw something in it."

Miss Ormond exclaimed in triumph. Mildred froze. She did not desire the rôle of Society Seer.

"What did I see, Mr. Davison?" she asked.

He shrugged his shoulders.

"Nothing of importance. You saw a woman in a light dress. Perhaps it was Lady Hammerton the collector, originally guilty, you remember, in the matter of the forged Augustus."

"Mildred had only to peep in any glass to see Lady Hammerton, or some one sufficiently like her," observed Meres.

"That idea was started when David Fletcher picked up the fancy picture which he chose to call a portrait of Lady Hammerton," cried Lady Thomson, who was just taking her leave. "Such nonsense! I protest against my own niece and a scholar of Ascham being likened to that scandalous woman."

Cyril Meres smiled and stroked his soft, silvery beard.

"Quite right of you to protest, Beatrice. Still, I'm glad Lady Hammerton didn't stick heroically to her Professor—as Mildred here does. We should never have been proud of her as an ancestress if she had."

"Heroically?" repeated Maxwell Davison under his breath, and laughed. But the meaning of his laugh was lost on every one except Mildred. She flushed hotly at the thought of having to bear the responsibility of that ridiculous scene on the Cherwell; it was humiliating, indeed. She took up the crystal to conceal her chagrin.

"Do please see something, Mrs. Stewart!" exclaimed Miss Ormond.

"What sort of thing?"

"Anything! Whatever you see, it will be quite thrilling.

"Please see me, Mrs. Stewart," petitioned Goring, wandering towards the crystal-gazer. "I should so like to thrill Miss Ormond."

"It's no good your trying that way," smiled the lady, playing fine eyes. "It's only shadows that are thrilling in the crystal; shadows of something happening a long way off; or sometimes a coming event casts a shadow before—and that's the most thrilling of all."

"A coming event! That's exactly what I am, a tremendous coming Political Event. You ask them in the House," cried Goring, thrusting out his chin and aiming a provocative side-smile at a middle-aged Under-Secretary of State who discreetly admired Miss Ormond.

"Modest creature!" exclaimed the Under-Secretary playfully with his lips; and in his heart vindictively, "Conceited devil!"

"Please see me, Mrs. Stewart!" pleaded Goring, half kneeling on a chair and leaning over the crystal.

"I do," she returned. "I'd rather not. You look so distorted and odd; and so do I, don't I? Dreadful! But the crystal's getting cloudy."

"Then you're going really to see something!" exclaimed Miss Ormond. "How delightful! Come away directly, Mr. Goring, or you'll spoil everything."

Sir Cyril and Davison looked up from some treasure of Greek art. The conversation was perfunctory, every one's curiosity waiting on Mildred and the crystal.

"Don't you see anything yet, Mrs. Stewart?" asked Miss Ormond at length, impatiently.

"No," replied Mildred, hesitatingly. "At least, not exactly. I see something like rushing water and foam."

"The reflection of clouds overhead," pronounced the Under-Secretary, dogmatically, glancing upward.

"I'm sure it's nothing of the kind," asserted Miss Ormond. "Please go on looking, Mrs. Stewart, and perhaps you'll see a water-spirit."

"Why do you want her to see a water-spirit?" asked Davison, ironically. "In all countries of the world they are reckoned spiteful, treacherous creatures. I was once bitten by one severely, and I have never wanted to see one since."

"Oh, Mr. Davison! Are you serious? What do you mean?" questioned Miss Ormond.

Mrs. Stewart hastily put down the crystal. "I don't want to see one," she said; "I'm afraid it might bring me bad luck, and, besides, I can't wait for it, I've got several calls to make before I go home, and I think there's a storm coming." She shivered. "I'm quite cold."

Miss Ormond said that must be the effect of the crystal, as the afternoon was still oppressively hot.

Goring caught up with Mrs. Stewart in the gravel drive outside the house and walked through Kensington Gardens with her. It seemed to them both quite natural that they should be walking together, and their talk was in the vein of old friends who have met after a long separation rather than in that of new acquaintances. When he left her and turned to walk across Hyde Park towards Westminster, he examined his impressions and perceived that he was in a state of mind foreign to his nature, and therefore the butt of his ridicule; a state in which, if he and Mrs. Stewart had been unmarried persons, he would have said to himself, "That is the woman I shall marry." It would not have been a passion or an emotion that would have made him say that; it would have been a conviction. As it was, the thing was absurd. Cochrane had told him, half in jest, that Mrs. Stewart was a breaker of hearts, but had not hinted that her own was on the market. Her appearance made it surely an interesting question whether she had a heart at all.

And for himself? He hated to think of his marriage, because he recognized in it the fatal "little spot" in the yet ungarnered fruit of his life. He was only thirty, but he had been married seven years and had two children, both of them the image of all the Barthops that had ever been, except his own father. In moments of depression he saw himself through all the coming years being gradually broken, crushed under a weight of Barthops—father-in-law, wife and children—moulded into a thin semblance of a Marquis of Ipswich, a bastard Marquis. No one but himself knew the weakness of his character—explosive, audacious in alarums or excursions, but without the something, call it strength or hardness or stupidity, which enables the man or woman possessing it to resist constant domestic pressure—the unconscious pressure of radically opposed character. The crowd applauds the marriage of such opposites because their side almost always wins; partly by its own weight and partly by their weight behind. But the truth is that two beings opposed in emotional temperament and mental processes are only a few degrees more able to help and understand each other in the close union of marriage than the two personalities of Milly Stewart in the closer union of her body.

From one point of view it was Goring's fatal weakness to have a real affection for his father-in-law, who was a pattern of goodness and good-breeding. Consequently, that very morning he had promised Lord Ipswich to walk in the straightest way of the party, for one year at least; and if he must slap faces, to select them on the other side of the House. Nevertheless, if he really wished to give sincere gratification to Lord Ipswich and to dear Augusta, he must needs give up his capricious and offensive tactics altogether. These things might give him a temporary notoriety in the House and country, but they were not in the traditions of the Ipswich family, which had held a high place in politics for two hundred years. The Marquis said that he had always tried to make George feel that he was received as a true son of the family and heir of its best traditions, if not of its name. There had been a great deal of good faith on both sides. Yet now a solitary young man, looking well in the frock-coat and tall hat of convention, might have been observed stopping and striking the gravel viciously as he reflected on the political future which his father-in-law was mapping out for him.

XXVI

S ir James Carus, the well-known scientist, had for some time been employing Miss Timson in the capacity of assistant, and spoke highly of her talents. She began to have a reputation in scientific circles, and owing to her duties with Carus she could not come to the Stewarts' as often as she had formerly done. But she preserved her habit of dismissing the parlor-maid at the door and creeping up to the drawing-room like a thief in the night.

On the day following Sir Cyril Meres's luncheon-party she arrived in her usual fashion. The windows were shaded against the afternoon sun, but the sky was now overcast, and such a twilight reigned within that at first she could distinguish little, and the drawing-room seemed to her to be empty. But in a minute she discerned a white figure supine in a large arm-chair—Mildred, and asleep.

She had a writing-board on her knee, and a hand resting on it still held a stylograph. She must have dozed over her writing; yet she did not stir when her name was uttered. Tims noticed a peculiar stillness in her, a something almost inanimate in her attitude and countenance, which suggested that this was no ordinary siesta. The idea that Milly might even now be resurgent fluttered Tims's pulses with a mixed emotion.

"Good old Milly! Poor old girl!" she breathed to the white figure in the arm-chair. "Don't be in a hurry! You won't find it all beer and skittles when you're here."

It seemed to her that a slight convulsion passed over the sleeper's face.

Tims seated herself on a low chair, in the attitude of certain gargoyles that crouch under the eaves of old churches, elbows on knees, chin on hands, and fixed her eyes in silence on her silent companion. In spite of her work along the acknowledged lines of science, she had pursued her hypnotic studies furtively, half in scorn and half in fear of her scientific brethren. What would she not have given to be enabled to watch, to comprehend the changes passing within that human form so close to her that she could see its every external detail, could touch it by the out-stretching of a hand! But its inner shrine, its secret place, remained barred against those feeble implements of sense with which nature has provided the explorative human intelligence. Its content was more mysterious, more inaccessible than that of the remotest star which yields the secret of its substance to the spectroscope of the astronomer.

Tims's thoughts had forsaken the personal side of the question, when she was recalled to it by seeing the right hand in which the stylograph had been lying begin to twitch, the fingers to contract. There was no answering movement in the face—even when the sleeper at length firmly grasped the pen and suddenly sat up. Tims rose quickly, and then perceived, lying on the writing-board, a directed envelope and a half-finished note to herself. She slipped the note-paper nearer to the twitching hand, and after a few meaningless flourishes, it wrote slowly and tentatively:

"Tims—Milly—cannot get back. Help me... Save Ian. Wicked creature—no conscience—"

Here the power of the hand began to fail, and the writing was terminated by mere scrawls. The sleeper's eyes were now open, but not wide. They had a strange, glassy look in them, nor did she show any consciousness of Tims's presence. She dropped the pen, folded the paper in the same slow and tentative manner in which she had written upon it, and placed it in the directed envelope lying there. Then her face contracted, her fingers slackened, and she fell back again to the depths of the chair.

"Milly!" cried Tims, almost involuntarily bending over her. "Milly!"

Again there was a slight contraction of the face and of the whole body.

At the moment that Tims uttered Milly's name, Ian was entering the room. His long legs brought him up to the chair in an instant, and he asked, without the usual salutation:

"What's the matter? Has—has the change happened?"

His voice unconsciously spoke dismay. Tims looked at him.

"No, not exactly," she articulated, slowly; and, after a pause: "Poor old Milly's trying to come back, that's all."

She paused again; then:

"You look a bit worried, old man."

He tossed back his head with a gesture he had kept from the days when the crest of raven-black hair had been wont to grow too long and encroach on his forehead. It was grizzled now, and much less intrusive.

"I'm about tired out," he said, shortly.

"Look here," she continued, "if you really want Milly back, just say so. She's kind of knocking at the door, and I believe I could let her in if I tried."

He dropped wearily into a chair.

"For Heaven's sake, Miss Timson, don't put the responsibility on me!"

"I can't help it," returned Tims. "She's managed to get this through to me—" She handed Milly's scrawled message to Ian.

He read it, then read it again and handed it back.

"Strange, certainly."

"Does it mean anything in particular?"

He shrugged his shoulders almost impatiently and sighed.

"Oh no! It's the poor child's usual cry when she's here. She's got it into her head that the self she doesn't know is frightfully wicked, and makes me miserable. I've tried over and over again to convince her, but it's all nonsense."

He thought to himself: "She is coming back still full of this mortal, heart-rending jealousy, and we shall have more painful scenes."

"Well, it's your business to say what I'm to do," insisted Tims. "I don't think she'd have troubled to write if she'd found she could get back altogether without my help; but the other one's grown a bit too strong for her. Do you want Milly back?"

The remorseless Tims forced on Ian a plain question which in his own mind he habitually sought to evade. He leaned back and shaded his eyes with his hand. After a silence he spoke, low, as if with effort:

"I can't honestly say I want the change to happen just now, Miss Timson. It means a great deal of agitation, a thorough upheaval of everything. We have an extremely troublesome business on at the Merchants' Guild—I've just come away from a four hours' meeting; and upon my word I don't think I can stand a—domestic revolution at the same time. It would utterly unfit me for my work."

He did not add that he had been looking forward to receiving helpful counsel from Mildred, with her clear common-sense, seasoned with wit.

Tims wagged her head and stared in his face.

"Poor old M.!" she exclaimed, slowly.

Miss Timson still possessed the rare power of irritating Ian Stewart. He grew restive.

"I suppose I am a selfish brute. Men always are, aren't they? But, after all, my wife enjoys life in her present state at least as much as she does in the other."

"Not for the same reason, dear boy," returned Tims. "Old M., bless her, just lives for you. You don't imagine, do you, that Mildred cares about you like that?"

Ian flushed slightly, and his face hardened.

"One can't very well discuss one's wife's feeling for one's self," he said. "I believe I have every reason to be happy, however things are. And I very much doubt, Miss Timson, whether you can really effect the change in her in any way. At any rate, I'd rather you didn't try, please. I'll have her moved to her room, where she'll most likely sleep till to-morrow."

Tims bent over the sleeper. Then:

"I don't believe she will, somehow. You'd better leave her with me for the present, and I'll let you know if anything happens."

He obeyed, and in a minute she heard the front door close after him. Tims sat down in the chair which he had vacated.

"Poor old M.!" she exclaimed again, presently, and added: "What idiots men are! All except old Carus and Mr. Fitzallan. He's sensible enough."

Her thoughts wandered away, until they were recalled by the door opening a mere chink to let a child slip into the room—a slim, tall child, in a blue smock—Tony. His thick, dark hair was cropped boywise now, and the likeness of the beautiful, sensitive child face to Ian's was more marked. It was evident that in him there was to be no blending of strains, but an exact reproduction of the paternal type.

Tims was in his eyes purely a comic character, but the ready grin with which he usually greeted her was replaced to-day by a little, inattentive smile. He went past her and stood by the sofa, looking fixedly at his mother with a grave mouth and a slight frown on his forehead. At length he turned away, and was about to leave the room as quietly as he had come, when Tims brought him to a stand-still at her knee. He held up an admonishing finger.

"Sh! Don't you wake my Mummy, or Daddy'll be angry with you."

"We sha'n't wake her; she's too fast asleep. Tell me why you looked so solemnly at her just now, Tony?"

Tony, his hands held fast, wriggled, rubbed his shoulder against his ear, and for all answer laughed in a childish, silly way. Such is the depth and secretiveness of children, whom we call transparent.

"Did you think Mummy was dead?"

"What's 'dead'?" asked Tony, with interest, putting off his mask of inanity.

"People are dead when they've gone to sleep and will never wake again," returned Tims.

Tony thought a minute; then his dark eyes grew very large. He whispered slowly, as though with difficulty formulating his ideas:

"Doesn't they *never* wake? Doesn't they wake up after ever so long, when peoples can't remember everything—and it makes them want to cry, only grown-up people aren't 'lowed?"

Tims was puzzled. But even in her bewilderment it occurred to her that if poor Milly should return, she would be distressed to find in what a slovenly manner Tony was allowed to express himself.

"I don't know what you mean, Tony. Say it again and put it more clearly."

Tims had around her neck a necklace composed of casts of coins in the British Museum. She did not usually wear ornaments, because she possessed none, except a hair-bracelet, two brooches, and a large gold cross which had belonged to her late aunt. Tony's soft, slender fingers went to the necklace, and ignoring her question, he asked: "Why have you got these funny things round your neck, Auntie Tims?"

"They're not funny. They're beautiful—copies of money which the old Greeks used to use. A gentleman gave it to me." Tims spoke with a grand carelessness. "I dare say if you're a good boy he'll tell you stories about them himself some day. But I want you to explain what it was you meant to say about dead people. Dead people don't come back, you know."

Tony touched her hand, which lay open on her knee, and played with the fingers a minute. Then raising his eyes he said, plaintively:

"I do so want my tea."

Once more he had wiped the conversational slate, and the baffled Tims dismissed him. He opened the door a little and slipped out; put his dark head in again with an engaging smile, said politely, "I sha'n't be away *very* long," and closed the door softly behind him. For that soft closing of the door was one of the things poor Milly had taught him which the little 'peoples' did contrive to remember.

The sleeper now began to stir slightly in her sleep, and before Tony's somewhat prolonged tea was over, she sat up and looked about her.

"Is that Tims?" she asked, in a colorless voice.

"Yes—is it you, Milly?"

"No. What makes you think so?"

"Milly's been trying to come back. I suppose she couldn't manage it."

"Ah!"—there was a deep satisfaction in Mildred's tone now; "I thought she couldn't!"

XXVII

G eorge Goring and Mildred Stewart did not move in the same social set, but their sets had points of contact, and it was at these that Goring was now most likely to be found; especially at the pleasant bachelor house on Campden Hill. Mrs. Stewart walked in the Park every morning at an unfashionable hour, and sometimes, yet not too often for discretion, Goring happened to be walking there too. All told, their meetings were not very numerous, nor very private. But every half-hour they spent in each other's company seemed to do the work of a month of intimacy.

July hastened to an end, but an autumn Session brought Goring up to town in November, and three months of absence found him and Mildred still at the same point. Sir Cyril Meres was already beginning to plan his wonderful *tableaux-vivants*, which, however, did not come off until February. The extraordinary imitative talent which his artistic career had been one long struggle to disguise, was for once to be allowed full play. The *tableaux* were to represent paintings by certain fellow-artists and friends; not actual pictures by them, but pictures which they might have painted, and the supposed authors were allowed a right of veto or criticism.

A stage of Renaissance design, which did not jar with the surrounding architecture, was erected in the depth of the portico at the end of the Hellenic room.

The human material at Meres's command was physically admirable. He had long been the chosen portrait-painter of wealth and fashion, and there was not a beauty in Society, with the biggest "S," who was not delighted to lend her charms for his purpose. The young men might grumble for form's sake, but at the bottom of their hearts they were equally sensible to the compliment of being asked to appear. It was when it came to the moulding of the material for artistic purposes, that the trouble began. The English have produced great actors, but in the bulk they have little natural aptitude for the stage; and what they have is discouraged by a social training which strains after the ideal composure, the few movements, the glassy eye of a waxwork. Only a small and chosen number, it is true, fully attain that ideal; but when we see them we recognize with a start, almost with a shudder, that it is there, the perfection of our deportment.

Cyril Meres was, however, an admirable stage-manager, exquisite in tact, in temper, and urbane patience. The results of his prolonged training were wonderful; yet again and again he found it impossible to carry out his idea without placing his cousin Mrs. Stewart at the vital point of his picture. She was certainly not the most physically beautiful woman there, but she was unrivalled by any other in the grace, the variety, the meaning of her gestures, the dramatic transformations of her countenance. She was Pandora, she was Hope, she was Lady Hammerton, she was the Vampire, and she was the Queen of Faerie.

There is jealousy on the amateur stage as well as on the professional, and ladies of social position, accustomed to see their beauty lauded in the newspapers, saw no reason why Mrs. Stewart should be thrust to the front of half of the pictures. Lady Langham, the "smart" Socialist, with whom George Goring had flirted last season, to Lady Augusta's real dismay, was the leading rival candidate for Mildred's rôles. But Lady Langham never guessed that Mrs. Stewart was the cause of George Goring's disappearance from the list of her admirers, and she still had hopes of his return.

The *tableaux* were a brilliant success. Ian was there on the first evening, so was Lady Augusta Goring. Lady Langham, peeping through the curtains, saw her, and swept the horizon—that is, the circle of black coats around the walls—in vain for George Goring. Then Lady Augusta became audible, saying that in the present state of affairs in the House it was quite impossible for Mr. Goring to leave it, even for dinner, on that evening or the next. Nevertheless, on the next evening, Lady Langham espied George Goring in the act of taking a vacant chair near the front, next to a social *protégée* of her own. She turned and mentioned the fact to a friend, who smiled meaningly and remarked, "In spite of Lady Augusta's whip!"

Mildred, passing, caught the information, the comment, the smile. During the rehearsals for the *tableaux*, she had heard people coupling the names of Goring and Lady Langham, not seriously, yet seriously enough for her. A winged shaft of jealousy pierced at once her heart and her pride. Was she allowing her whole inner life to be shaken, dissolved by the passing admiration of a flirt? Her intimate self had assurance that it was not so; but sometimes a colder wind, blowing she knew not whence, or the lash of a chance word, threw her into the attitude of a chance observer, one who sees, guesses, does not know.

Meantime George Goring had flung himself down in the only

vacant chair he could see, and careless of the brilliant company about him, careless even of the face of Aphrodite herself, smiling divinely, unconcerned with human affairs, from a far corner he waited for the curtain to go up. His neighbor spoke. She had met him at the Langhams last season. What a pity he had just missed Lady Langham's great *tableau*, "Helen before the Elders of Troy"! There was no one to be compared to Maud Langham, so beautiful, so clever! She would have made her fortune if she had gone on the stage. Goring gave the necessary assent.

The curtain went up, exhibiting a picture called "The Vampire." It was smaller than most and shown by a curious pale light. A fair young girl was lying in a deep sleep on a curtained bed, and hovering, crawling over her with a deadly, serpentine grace, was a white figure wrapped in a veiling garment that might have been a shroud. Out of white cerements showed a trail of yellow hair and a face alabaster white, save for the lips that were blood red—an intent face with a kind of terrible beauty, yet instinct with cruelty. One slender, bloodless hand was in the girl's hair, and, even without the title, it would have been plain that there was a deadly purpose in that creeping figure.

"Isn't it horrid?" whispered Goring's neighbor. "Fancy that Mrs. Stewart letting herself be made to look so dreadful!"

"Who?" asked Goring, horrified. He had not recognized Mildred.

"Why, the girl on the bed's Gertrude Waters, and the Vampire's a cousin of Sir Cyril Meres. A horrid little woman some people admire, but I shouldn't think any one would after this. I call it disgusting, don't you?"

"It's horrible!" gasped George; "it oughtn't to be allowed. What does that fellow Meres mean by inventing such deviltries? By Jove, I should like to thrash him!"

The neighbor stared. It was all very well to be horrified at Mrs. Stewart, but why this particular form of horror?

"Please call me when it's over," said Goring, putting his head down between his hands.

What an eccentric young man he was! But clever people often were eccentric.

In due course the *tableau* was over, and to the relief of one spectator at least, it was not encored. The next was some harmless domestic scene with people in short waists. George Goring looked in vain for Mildred among them, longing to see her, the real lovely her, and forget the horrible thing she had portrayed. Lady Langham was there, and his neighbor commended her tediously, convinced of pleasing.

There followed a large and very beautiful picture in the manner of a great English Pre-Raphaelite. This was called "Thomas the Rhymer, meeting with the Faerie Queen," but it did not follow the description of the ballad. The Faerie Queen, a figure of a Botticellian grace, was coming, with all her fellowship, out of a wonderful pinewood, while Thomas the Rhymer, handsome and young and lean and brown, his harp across his back, had just crossed a mountain-stream by a rough bridge. He appeared suddenly to have beheld her, pausing above him before descending the heathery bank that edged the wood; and looking in her face, to have entered at once into the land of Faerie. The pose, the figure, the face of the Faerie Queen were of the most exquisite charm and beauty, touched with a something of romance and mystery that no other woman there except Mildred could have lent it. The youth who personated Thomas the Rhymer was temporarily in love with Mrs. Stewart and acted his part with intense expression. Goring, shading his eyes with his hand, fixed them upon her as long as he dared; then glanced at the Rhymer and was angry. He turned to his chattering neighbor and asked:

"Who's the chap doing Thomas? Looks as if he wanted a wash."

"I don't know. Nobody particular, I should think. Wasn't it a pity they didn't have Lady Langham for the Faerie Queen? I do call it absurd the way Sir Cyril Meres has put that pert, insignificant cousin of his forward in quite half the pictures—and when he might have had Maud Langham."

Goring threw himself back in his chair and laughed his quite loud laugh.

"'A mad world, my masters,'" he quoted.

His neighbor took this for Mr. Goring's eccentric way of approving her sentiments. But what he really meant was: What a strange masquerade is the world! This neighbor of his, so ordinary, so desirous to please, would have shuddered at the notion of hinting to him the patent fact that Lady Augusta Goring was a tiring woman; while she pressed upon him laudations of a person to whom he was perfectly indifferent, mingled with insulting comments on the only woman in the world for him—the woman who was his world, without whom nothing was; on her whose very name, even on these silly, hostile lips, gave him a strong sensation, whether of pain or pleasure he could hardly tell.

After the performance he constrained himself to go the round of the ladies of his acquaintance who had been acting and compliment them cleverly and with good taste. Lady Langham of course seized the lion's share of his company and his compliments. He seemed to address only a few remarks of the same nature to Mrs. Stewart, but he had watched his opportunity and was able to say to her:

"I must leave in a quarter of an hour at latest. Please let me drive you back. You won't say no?"

There was a pleading note in the last phrase and his eyes met hers gravely, anxiously. It was evident that she must answer immediately, while their neighbors' attention was distracted from them. She was pale before under her stage make-up, and now she grew still paler.

"Thanks. I told Cousin Cyril I was tired and shouldn't stay long. I'll go and change at once."

Then Thomas the Rhymer was at her elbow again, bringing her something for which she had sent him.

The green-room, in which she resumed the old white lace evening-dress that she had worn to dine with her cousin, was strewn with the delicate underclothing, the sumptuous wraps and costly knick-knacks of wealthy women. She had felt ashamed, as she had undressed there, of her own poor little belongings among these; and ashamed to be so ashamed. As she had seen her garments overswept by the folds of the fair Socialist's white velvet mantle, lined with Arctic fox and clasped with diamonds, she had smiled ironically at the juxtaposition. Since circumstances and her own gifts had drawn her into the stream of the world, she had been more and more conscious, however unwillingly, of a longing for luxuries, for rich settings to her beauty, for some stage upon which her brilliant personality might shine uplifted, secure. For she seemed to herself sometimes like a tumbler at a fair, struggling in the crowd for a space in which to spread his carpet. Now—George Goring loved her. Let the others keep their furs and laces and gewgaws, their great fortunes or great names. Yet if it had been possible for her to take George Goring's love, he could have given her most of these things as well.

Wrapped in a gauzy white scarf, she seemed to float rather than walk down the stairs into the hall, where Thomas the Rhymer was lingering, in the hope of finding an excuse to escort her home. She was pale, with a clear, beautiful pallor, a strange smile was on her lips and her eyes shone like stars. The Queen of Faerie had looked less lovely, meeting him on the edge of the wood. She nodded him good-night and passed quickly on into the porch. With a boyish pang he saw her vanish, not into the darkness of night, but into the blond interior of a smart brougham. A young man, also smart—her husband, for aught he knew—paused on the step to give orders to the coachman, and followed her in. A moment he saw her dimly, in the glare of carriage-lamps, a white vision, half eclipsed by the black silhouette of the man at her side; then they glided away over the crunching gravel of the drive, into the fiery night of London.

"Do you really think it went off well?" she asked, as they passed through the gates into the street. George was taking off his hat and putting it down on the little shelf opposite. He leaned back and was silent a few seconds; then starting forward, laid his hand upon her knee.

"Don't let's waste time like that, Mildred," he said—and although he had never called her so before, it seemed natural that he should— "we haven't got much. You know, don't you, why I asked you to drive with me?"

She in her turn was silent a moment, then meeting his eyes:

"Yes," she said, quite simply and courageously.

"I thought you could hardly help seeing I loved you, however blind other people might be."

Her head was turned away again and she looked out of the window, as she answered in a voice that tried to be light:

"But it isn't of any consequence, is it? I suppose you're always in love with somebody or other."

"Is that what people told you about me?"—and it was new and wonderful to her to hear George Goring speak with this calmness and gravity—"You've not been long in the world, little girl, or you'd know how much to believe of what's said there."

"No," she answered, in turn becoming calm and deliberate. "When I come to think of it, people only say that women generally like you and that you flirt with them. I—I invented the rest."

"But, good Heavens! Why?" There was a note of pain and wonder in his voice.

She paused, and his hand moved under her cloak to be laid on the two slender hands clasped on her lap.

"I suppose I was jealous," she said.

He smiled.

MARGARET L. WOODS

"Absurd child! But I'm a bit of an ass that way myself. I was jealous of Thomas the Rhymer this evening."

"That brat!"

She laughed low, the sweet laugh that was like no one else's. It was past midnight and the streets were comparatively quiet and dark, but at that moment they were whirled into a glare of strong light. They looked in each other's eyes in silence, his hand tightening its hold upon hers. Then again they plunged into wavering dimness, and he resumed, gravely and calmly as before, but bending nearer her.

"If I weren't anxious to tell you the exact truth, to avoid exaggeration, I should say I fell in love with you the first time I met you. It seems to me now as though it had been so. And the second time—you remember it was one very hot day last July, when we both lunched with Meres—I hadn't the least doubt that if I had been free and you also, I should have left no stone unturned to get you for my wife."

Every word was sweet to her, yet she answered sombrely:

"But we are not free."

He, disregarding the answer, went on:

"You love me, as I love you?"

"As you love me, dearest; and from the first."

A minute's silence, while the hands held each other fast. Then low, triumphantly, he exclaimed: "Well?"

Her slim hands began to flutter a little in his as she answered all that that "Well" implied.

"It's impossible, dear. It's no use arguing about it. It's just waste of time—and we've only got this little time."

"To do what? To make love in? Dear, we've got all our lives if we please. We've both made a tremendous mistake, we've both got a chance now of going back on it, of setting our lives right again, making them better indeed than we ever dreamed of their being. We inflict some loss on other people—no loss comparable to our gain—we hurt them chiefly because of their bloated ideas of their claims on us. I know you've weighed things, have no prejudices. Rules, systems, are made for types and classes, not for us. You belong to no type, Mildred. I belong to no class."

She answered low, painfully:

"It's true I am unlike other people; that's the very reason, why—I—I'm not good to love." There was a low utterance that was music in her ears, yet she continued: "Then, dear friend, think of your career, ruined for me, by me. You might be happy for a while, then you'd regret it."

"That's where you're wrong. My career? A rotten little game, these House of Commons party politics, when you get into it! The big things go on outside them; there's all the world outside them. Anyhow, my career, as I planned it, is ruined already. The Ipswich gang have collared me; I can't call my tongue my own, Mildred. Think of that!"

She smiled faintly.

"Temporary, George! You'll soon have your head up—and your tongue out."

"Oh, from time to time, I presume, I shall always be the Horrid Vulgar Boy of those poor Barthops; I shall kick like a galvanized frog long after I'm dead. But—I wouldn't confess it to any one but you, dear—I'm not strong enough to stand against the everlasting pressure that's brought to bear upon me. You know what I mean, don't you?"

"Yes. You'll be no good if you let the originality be squeezed out of you. Don't allow it."

"Nothing can prevent it—unless the Faerie Queen will stretch out her dearest, sweetest hands to me and lead me, poor mortal, right away into the wide world, into some delightful country where there's plenty of love and no politics. I want love so much, Mildred; I've never had it, and no one has ever guessed how much I wanted it except you, dear—except you."

Yes, she had guessed. The queer childhood, so noisy yet so lonely, had been spoken of; the married life spoke for itself.

His arm was around her now, their faces drawn close together, and in the pale, faint light they looked each other deep in the eyes. Then their lips met in a long kiss.

"You see how it is," he whispered; "you can't help it. It's got to be. No one has power to prevent it."

But he spoke without knowledge, for there was one who had power to prevent it, one conquered, helpless, less than a ghost, who yet could lay an icy hand on the warm, high-beating heart of her subduer, and say: "Love and desire, the pride of life and the freedom of the world, are not for you. I forbid them to you—I—by a power stronger than the laws of God or man. True, you have no husband, you have no child, for those who seem to be yours are mine. You have taken them from me, and now you must keep them, whether you will or no. You have taken my life from me, and my life you must have, that and none other."

It was against this unknown and inflexible power that George Goring struggled with all the might of his love, and absolutely in vain.

Between him and Mildred there could be no lies, no subterfuges; only that one silence which to him, of all others, she dared not break.

She seemed to have been engaged in this struggle, at once so sweet and so bitter, for an eternity before she stood on her own doorstep, latch-key in hand.

"Good-night, Mr. Goring. So much obliged for the lift."

"Delighted, I'm sure. All right now? Good-night. Drop me at the House, Edwards."

He lifted his hat, stepped in and closed the carriage-door sharply behind him; and in a minute the brougham with its lights rolling almost noiselessly behind the big fast-trotting bay horse, had disappeared around a neighboring corner.

THE HOUSE WAS COLD AND dark, except for a candle which burned on an oak dresser in the narrow hall. As Mildred dragged herself up the stairs, she had a sensation of physical fatigue, almost bruisedness, as though she had come out of some actual bodily combat. Her room, fireless and cold, was solitary, for Ian's sleep had to be protected from disturbance. Nevertheless, having loosened her wraps, she threw herself on the bed and lay there long, her bare arms under her head. The sensation of chill, her own cold soft flesh against her face, seemed to brace her mind and body, to restore her powers of clear, calm judgment, so unlike the usual short-sighted, emotionalized judgments of youth. She had nothing of the ordinary woman's feeling of guilt towards her husband. The intimate bond between herself and George Goring did not seem in any relation the accidental one between her and Ian Stewart. She had never before faced the question, the possibility of a choice between the two. Now she weighed it with characteristic swiftness and decision. She reasoned that Ian had enjoyed a period of great happiness in his marriage with her, in spite of the singularity of its conditions; but that now, while Milly could never satisfy his fastidious nature, she herself had grown to be a hinderance, a dissonance in his life. Could she strike a blow which would sever him from her, he would suffer cruelly, no doubt; but it would send him back again to the student's life, the only life that could bring him honor, and in the long run satisfaction. And that life would not be lonely, because Tony, so completely his father's child, would be with him. As for herself and George Goring, she had no fear of the future. They two were strong enough to hew and build alone their own Palace of Delight. Her intuitive knowledge of the world informed her that, in the long run, society, if firmly disregarded, admits the claim of certain persons to go their own way—even rapidly admits it, though they be the merest bleating strays from the common fold, should they haply be possessed of rank or fortune. The way lay plain enough before Mildred, were it not for that Other. But she, the shadowy one, deep down in her limbo, laid a finger on the gate of that Earthly Paradise and held it, as inflexibly as any armed archangel, against the master key of her enemy's intelligence, the passionate assaults of her heart.

Mildred, however, was one who found it hard, if not impossible, to acquiesce in defeat. Two o'clock boomed from the watching towers of Westminster over the great city. She rose from her bed, cold as a marble figure on a monument, and went to the dressing-table to take off her few and simple ornaments. The mirror on it was the same from which that alien smile had peered twelve months ago, filling the sad soul of Milly with trembling fear and sinister foreboding. The white face that stole into its shadowy depths to-night, and looked Mildred in the eyes, was in a manner new to her also. It had a new seriousness, a new intensity, as of a woman whose vital energies, once spending themselves in mere corruscations, in mere action for action's sake, were now concentrated on one definite thought, one purpose, one emotion, which with an intense yet benign fire blended in perfect harmony the life of the soul and of the body.

For a moment the face in its gravity recalled to her the latest photograph of Milly, a tragic photograph she did not care to look at because it touched her with a pity, a remorse, which were after all quite useless. But the impression was false and momentary.

"No," she said, speaking to the glass, "it's not really like. Poor weak woman! I understand better now what you have suffered." Then almost repeating the words of her own cruel subconscious self—"But there's all the difference between the weak and the strong. I am the stronger, and the stronger must win; that's written, and it's no use struggling against the law of nature."

XXVIII

G eorge Goring was never so confident in himself as when he was fighting an apparently losing game; and the refusal of Mildred to come to him, a refusal based, as he supposed, on nothing but an insurmountable prejudice against doing what was not respectable, struck him as a stage in their relations rather than as the end of them. He did not attempt to see her until the close of the Easter Vacation. People began to couple their names, but lightly, without serious meaning, for Goring being popular with women, had a somewhat exaggerated reputation as a flirt. When a faithful cousin hinted things about him and Mrs. Stewart to Lady Augusta, she who believed herself to have seen a number of similar temporary enslavers, put the matter by, really glad that a harmless nobody should have succeeded to Maud Langham with her dangerous opinions.

Ian Stewart on his side was barely acquainted with Goring. Sir John Ireton and the newspapers informed him that George Goring was a flashy, untrustworthy politician; and the former added that he was a terrible nuisance to poor Lord Ipswich and Lady Augusta. That such a man could attract Mildred would never have occurred to him.

The fear of Milly's return, which she could not altogether banish, still at times checked and restrained Mildred. Could she but have secured Tims's assistance in keeping Milly away, she would have felt more confident of success. It was hopeless to appeal directly to the hypnotist, but her daring imagination began to conceive a situation in which mere good sense and humanity must compel Tims to forbid the return of Milly to a life made impossible for her. She had not seen Tims for many weeks, not since the Easter Vacation, which had already receded into a remote distance; so far had she journeyed since then along the path of her fate. Nor had she so much as wondered at not seeing Tims. But now her mind was turned to consider the latent power which that strange creature held over her life, her dearest interests; since how might not Milly comport herself with George?

Then it was that she realized how long it had been since Tims had crept up the stairs to her drawing-room; pausing probably in the middle of them to wipe away with hasty pocket-handkerchief some real or fancied trace of her foot on a carpet which she condemned as expensive.

Mildred had written her a note, but it was hardly posted when the door was flung open and Miss Timson was formally announced by the parlor-maid. Tony, who was looking at pictures with his mother, rose from her side, prepared to take a hop, skip, and jump and land with his arms around Tims's waist. But he stopped short and contemplated her with round-eyed solemnity. The ginger-colored man's wig had developed into a frizzy fringe and the rest of the coiffure of the hour. A large picture hat surmounted it, and her little person was clothed in a vivid heliotrope dress of the latest mode. It was a handsome dress, a handsome hat, a handsome wig, yet somehow the effect was jarring. Tony felt vaguely shocked. "Bless thee! Thou art translated!" he might have cried with Quince; but being a polite child, he said nothing, only put out a small hand sadly. Tims, however, unconscious of the slight chill cast by her appearance, kissed him in a perfunctory, patronizing way, as ladies do who are afraid of disarranging their veils. She greeted Mildred also with a parade of mundane elegance, and sat down deliberately on the sofa, spreading out her heliotrope skirts.

"You can run away just now, little man," she said to Tony. "I want to talk to your mother."

"How smart you are!" observed Mildred, seeing that comment of some kind would be welcome. "Been to Sir James Carus's big party at the Museum, I suppose. You're getting a personage, Tims."

"I dare say I shall look in later, but I shouldn't trouble to dress up for that, my girl. Clothes would be quite wasted there. But I think one should always try to look decent, don't you? One's men like it."

Mildred smiled.

"I suppose Ian would notice it if I positively wasn't decent. But, Tims, dear, does old Carus really criticise your frocks?"

For indeed the distinguished scientist, Miss Timson's chief, was the only man she could think of to whom Tims could possibly apply the possessive adjective. Tims bridled.

"Of course not; I was thinking of Mr. Fitzalan."

That she had for years been very kind to a lonely little man of that name who lived in the same block of chambers, Mildred knew, but— Heavens! Even Mildred's presence of mind failed her, and she stared. Meeting her amazed eye, Tims's borrowed smile suddenly broke its bounds and became her own familiar grin, only more so:

"We're engaged," she said.

"My dear Tims!" exclaimed Mildred, suppressing an inclination to burst out laughing. "What a surprise!"

"I quite thought you'd have been prepared for it," returned Tims. "A bit stupid of you not to guess it, don't you know, old girl. We've been courting long enough."

Mildred hastened to congratulate the strange bride and wish her happiness, with all that unusual grace which she knew how to employ in adorning the usual.

"I thought I should like you to be the first to know," said Tims, sentimentally, after a while; "because I was your bridesmaid, you see. It was the prettiest wedding I ever saw, and I should love to have a wedding like yours—all of us carrying lilies, you know."

"I remember there were green stains on my wedding-dress," returned Mildred, with forced gayety.

Tims, temporarily oblivious of all awkward circumstances, continued, still more sentimentally:

"Then I was there, as I've told you, when Ian's pop came to poor old M. Poor old girl! She was awfully spifligatingly happy, and I feel just the same now myself."

"Well, it wasn't I, anyhow, who felt 'awfully spifligatingly happy' on that occasion," replied Mildred, with a touch of asperity in her voice.

Tims, legitimately absorbed in her own feelings, did not notice it. She continued:

"I dare say the world will say Mr. Fitzalan had an eye on my money; and it's true I've done pretty well with my investments. But, bless you! he hadn't a notion of that. You see, I was brought up to be stingy, and I enjoy it. He thought of course I was a pauper, and proposed we should pauper along together. He was quite upset when he found I was an heiress. Wasn't it sweet of him?"

Mildred said it was.

"Flora Fitzalan!" breathed Tims, clasping her hands and smiling into space. "Isn't it a pretty name? It's always been my dream to have a pretty name." Then suddenly, as though in a flash seeing all those personal disadvantages which she usually contrived to ignore:

"Life's a queer lottery, Mil, my girl. We know what we are, we know not what we shall be, as old Billy says. Who'd ever have thought that a nice, quiet girl like Milly, marrying the lad of her heart and all that, would come to such awful grief; while look at me—a queer kind of girl you'd have laid your bottom dollar wouldn't have much luck, prospering like anything, well up in the Science business, and now, what's ever so much better, scrumptiously happy with a good sort of her own. Upon my word, Mil, I've half a mind to fetch old M. back to sympathize with me, for although you've said a peck of nice things, I don't believe you understand what I'm feeling the way the old girl would."

Mildred went a little pale and spoke quickly.

"You won't do that really, Tims? You won't be so cruel to—to every one?"

"I don't know. I don't see why you're always to be jolly and have everything your own way. Oh, Lord! When I think how happy old M. was when she was engaged, the same as I am, and then on her wedding-day—just the same as I shall be on mine."

Mildred straightened out the frill of a muslin cushion cover, her head bent.

"Just so. She had everything *her* own way that time. I gave her that happiness, it was all my doing. She's had it and she ought to be content. Don't be a fool, Tims—" she lifted her face and Tims was startled by its expression—"Can't you see how hard it is on me never to be allowed the happiness you've got and Milly's had? Don't you think I might care to know what love is like for myself? Don't you think I might happen to want—I tell you I'm a million times more alive than Milly—and I want—I want everything a million times more than she does."

Tims was astonished.

"But it's always struck me, don't you know, that Ian was a deal more in love with you than he ever was with poor old M."

"And you pretend to be in love and think that's enough! It's not enough; you must know it's not. It's like sitting at a Barmecide feast, very hungry, only the Barmecide's sitting opposite you eating all the time and talking about his food. I tell you it's maddening, perfectly maddening—" There was a fierce vehemence in her face, her voice, the clinch of her slender hands on the muslin frill. That strong vitality which before had seemed to carry her lightly as on wings, over all the rough places of life, had now not failed, but turned itself inwards, burning in an intense flame at once of pain and of rebellion against its own pain.

Tims in the midst of her happiness, felt vaguely scared. Mildred seeing it, recovered herself and plunged into the usual engagement talk. In a few minutes she was her old beguiling self—the self to whose charm Tims was as susceptible in her way as Thomas the Rhymer had been in his.

When she had left, and from time to time thereafter, Tims felt vaguely uncomfortable, remembering Mildred's outburst of vehement bitterness on the subject of love. It was so unlike her usual careless tone, which implied that it was men's business, or weakness, to be in love with women, and that only second-rate women fell in love themselves.

Mildred seemed altogether more serious than she used to be, and Milly herself could not have been more sympathetic over the engagement. Even Mr. Fitzalan, when Tims brought him to call on the Stewarts was not afraid of her, and found it possible to say a few words in reply to her remarks. Tims's ceremonious way of speaking of her betrothed, whom she never mentioned except as Mr. Fitzalan, made Ian reflect with sad humor on the number of offensively familiar forms of address which he himself had endured from her, and on the melancholy certainty that she had never spoken of him in his absence by any name more respectful than the plain unprefixed "Stewart." But he hoped that the excitement of her engagement had wiped out of her remembrance that afternoon when poor Milly had tried to return. For he did not like to think of that moment of weakness in which he had allowed Tims to divine so much of a state of mind which he could not unveil even to himself without a certain shame.

XXIX

The summer was reaching its height. The weather was perfect. Night after night hot London drawing-rooms were crowded to suffocation, awnings sprang mushroom-like from every West End pavement; the sound of music and the rolling of carriages made night, if not hideous, at least discordant to the unconsidered minority who went to bed as usual. Outside in the country, even in the suburbs, June came in glory, with woods in freshest livery of green, with fragrance of hawthorn and broom and gorse, buttercup meadows and gardens brimmed with roses. It seemed to George Goring and Mildred as though somehow this warmth, this gayety and richness of life in the earth had never been there before, but that Fate and Nature, of which their love was part, were leading them on in a great festal train to the inevitable consummation. The flame of life had never burned clearer or more steadily in Mildred, and every day she felt a growing confidence in having won so complete a possession of her whole bodily machinery that it would hardly be in the power of Milly to dethrone her. The sight of George Goring, the touch of his hand, the very touch of his garment, gave her a feeling of unconquerable life. It was impossible that she and George should part. All her sanguine and daring nature cried out to her that were she once his, Milly should not, could not, return. Tims, too, was there in reserve. Not that Tims would feel anything but horror at Mildred's conduct in leaving Ian and Tony; but the thing done, she would recognize the impossibility of allowing Milly to return to such a situation.

Ian, whose holidays were usually at the inevitable periods, was by some extraordinary collapse of that bloated thing, the Academic conscience, going away for a fortnight in June. He had been deputed to attend a centenary celebration at some German University, and a conference of savants to be held immediately after it, presented irresistible attractions.

One Sunday Tims and Mr. Fitzalan went to Hampton Court with the usual crowd of German, Italian, and French hair-dressers, waiters, cooks, and restaurant-keepers, besides native cockneys of all classes except the upper.

The noble old Palace welcomed this mass of very common humanity with such a pageant of beauty as never greeted the eyes of its royal builders. Centuries of sunshine seem to have melted into the rich reds and grays and cream-color of its walls, under which runs a quarter of a mile of flower-border, a glowing mass of color, yet as full of delicate and varied detail as the border of an illuminated missal. Everywhere this modern wealth and splendor of flowers is arranged, as jewels in a setting, within the architectural plan of the old garden. There the dark yews retain their intended proportion, the silver fountain rises where it was meant to rise, although it sprinkles new, unthought-of lilies. Behind it, on either side the stately vista of water, and beside it, in the straight alley, the trees in the freshness and fulness of their leafage, stand tall and green, less trim and solid it may be, but essentially as they were meant to stand when the garden grew long ago in the brain of a man. And out there beyond the terrace the Thames flows quietly, silverly on, seeming to shine with the memory of all the loveliness those gliding waters have reflected, since their ripples played with the long, tremulous image of Lechlade spire.

Seen from the cool, deep-windowed rooms of the Palace, where now the pictures hang and hundreds of plebeian feet tramp daily, the gardens gave forth a burning yet pleasant glow of heat and color in the full sunshine. Tims and Mr. Fitzalan, having eaten their frugal lunch early under the blossoming chestnut-trees in Bushey Park, went into the Picture Gallery in the Palace at an hour when it happened to be almost empty. The queer-looking woman not quite young, and the little, bald, narrow-chested, short-sighted man, would not have struck the passers-by as being a pair of lovers. A few sympathetic smiles, however, had been bestowed upon another couple seated in the deep window of one of the smaller rooms; a pretty young woman and an attractive man. The young man had disposed his hat and a newspaper in such a way as not to make it indecently obvious that he was holding her hand. It was she who called attention to the fact by hasty attempts to snatch it away when people came in.

"What do you do that for?" asked the young man. "There's not the slightest chance of any one we know coming along."

"But George—"

"Do try and adapt yourself to your *milieu*. These people are probably blaming me for not putting my arm around your waist."

"George! What an idiot you are!" She laughed a nervous laugh.

By this time the last party of fat, dark young women in rainbow hats, and narrow-shouldered, anæmic young men, had trooped away towards food. Goring waited till the sound of their footsteps had ceased.

He was holding Mildred's hand, but he had drawn it out from under the newspaper now, and the gay audacity of his look had changed to something at once more serious and more masterful.

"I don't like your seeming afraid, Mildred," he said. "It spoils my idea of you. I like to think of you as a high-spirited creature, conscious enough of your own worth to go your own way and despise the foolish comments of the crowd."

To hear herself so praised by him made the clear pink rise to Mildred's cheeks. How could she bear to fall below the level of his expectation, although the thing he expected of her had dangers of which he was ignorant?

"I'm glad you believe that of me," she said; "although it's not quite true. I cared a good deal about the opinion of the world before—before I knew you; only I was vain enough to think it would never treat me very badly."

"It won't," he replied, his audacious smile flashing out for a moment. "It'll come sneaking back to you before long; it can't keep away. Besides, I'm cynic enough to know my own advantages, Mildred. Society doesn't sulk forever with wealthy people, whatever they choose to do."

She answered low: "But I shouldn't care if it did, George. I want you—just to go right away with you."

A wonderful look of joy and tenderness came over his face. "Mildred! Can it really be you saying that?" he breathed. "Really you, Mildred?"

They looked each other in the eyes and were silent a minute; but while the hand next the window held hers, the other one stole out farther to clasp her. He was too much absorbed in that gaze to notice anything beyond it; but Mildred was suddenly aware of steps and a voice in the adjoining room. Tims and Mr. Fitzalan, in the course of a conscientious survey of all the pictures on the walls, had reached this point in their progress. The window-seat on which Goring and Mildred were sitting was visible through a doorway, and Tims had on her strongest glasses.

Since her engagement, Tims's old-maidish bringing up seemed to be bearing fruit for the first time.

"I think we'd better cough or do something," she said. "There's a couple in there going on disgracefully. I do think spooning in public such bad form."

"I dare say they think they're alone," returned the charitable Mr. Fitzalan, unable to see the delinquents because he was trying to put a loose lens back into his eye-glasses. Tims came to his assistance, talking loudly; and her voice was of a piercing quality. Mildred, leaning forward, saw Mr. Fitzalan and Tims, both struggling with eye-glasses. She slipped from George's encircling arm and stood in the doorway of the farther room, beckoning to him with a scared face. He got up and followed her.

"What's the matter?" he asked, more curious than anxious; for an encounter with Lady Augusta in person could only precipitate a crisis he was ready to welcome. Why should one simple, definite step from an old life to a new one, which his reason as much as his passion dictated, be so incredibly difficult to take?

Mildred hurried him away, explaining that she had seen some one she knew very well. He pointed out that it was of no real consequence. She could not tell him that if Tims suspected anything before the decisive step was taken, one of the safeguards under which she took it might fail.

They found no exit at the end of the suite of rooms, still less any place of concealment. Tims and Mr. Fitzalan came upon them discussing the genuineness of a picture in the last room but one. When Tims saw that it was Mildred, she made some of the most dreadful grimaces she had ever made in her life. Making them, she approached Mildred, who seeing there was no escape, turned around and greeted her with a welcoming smile.

"Were you—were you sitting on that window-seat?" asked Tims, fixing her with eyes that seemed bent on piercing to her very marrow.

Mildred smiled again, with a broader smile.

"I don't know about 'that window-seat.' I've sat on a good many window-seats, naturally, since I set forth on this pilgrimage. Is there anything particular about that one? I've never seen Hampton Court before, Mr. Fitzalan, so as some people I knew were coming to-day, I thought I'd come too. May I introduce Mr. Goring?"

So perfectly natural and easy was Mildred's manner, that Tims already half disbelieved her own eyes. They must have played her some trick; yet how could that be? She recalled the figures in the window-seat, as seen with all the peculiar, artificial distinctness conferred by strong glasses. The young man called Goring had smiled into the hidden face of his companion in a manner that Tims could not approve. She made up her mind that as soon as she had leisure she would call on Mildred and question her once more, and more straitly, concerning the mystery of that window-seat.

XXX

O n Monday and Tuesday an interesting experiment which she was conducting under Carus claimed Tims's whole attention, except for the evening hours, which were dedicated to Mr. Fitzalan. But she wrote to say that Mildred might expect her to tea on Wednesday. On Wednesday the post brought her a note from Mildred, dated Tuesday, midnight.

> DEAR TIMS,
>   I am afraid you will not find me to-morrow afternoon, as I am going out of town. But do go to tea with Tony, who is just back from the sea and looking bonny. He is such a darling! I always mind leaving him, although of course I am not his mother. Oh, dear, I am so sleepy, I hardly know what I am saying. Good-bye, Tims, dear. I am very glad you are so happy with that nice Mr. Fitzalan of yours.
>
> > Yours,
> > M. B. S.

So far the note, although bearing signs of haste, was in Mildred's usual clear handwriting; but there was a postscript scrawled crookedly across the inner sides of the sheet and prefixed by several flourishes:

> "Meet me at Paddington 4.30 train to-morrow. Meet me.
>
> > M.

Another flourish followed.

The note found Tims at the laboratory, which she had not intended leaving till half-past four. But the perplexing nature of the postscript, conflicting as it did with the body of the letter, made her the more inclined to obey its direction.

She arrived at Paddington in good time and soon caught sight of Mildred, although for the tenth part of a second she hesitated in identifying her; for Mildred seldom wore black, although she looked well in it. To-day she was dressed in a long, black silk wrap—which gathered about her slender figure by a ribbon, concealed her whole dress—and wore a long, black lace veil which might have baffled the eyes of a mere acquaintance. Tims could not fail to recognize that willowy figure, with its rare grace of motion, that amber hair, those turquoise-blue eyes that gleamed through the swathing veil with a restless brilliancy unusual even in them. With disordered dress and hat on one side, Tims hastened after Mildred.

"So here you are!" she exclaimed; "that's all right! I managed to come, you see, though it's been a bit of a rush."

Mildred looked around at her, astonished, possibly dismayed; but the veil acted as a mask.

"Well, this is a surprise, Tims! What on earth brought you here? Is anything the matter?"

"Just what I wanted to know. Why are you in black? Going to a funeral?"

"Good Heavens, no! The only funeral I mean to go to will be my own. But, Tims, I thought you were going to tea with Tony. Why have you come here?"

"Didn't you tell me to come in the postscript of your letter?"

Mildred was evidently puzzled.

"I don't remember anything about it," she said. "I was frightfully tired when I wrote to you—in fact, I went to sleep over the letter; but I can't imagine how I came to say that."

Tims was not altogether surprised. She had had an idea that Mildred was not answerable for that postscript, but Mildred herself had no clew to the mystery, never having been told of Milly's written communication of a year ago. She sickened at the possibility that in some moment of aberration she might have written words meant for another on the note to Tims.

Tims felt sure that Milly wished her to do something—but what?

"Where are you going?" she asked. "What are you going to do?"

"I'm going to stay with some friends who have a house on the river, and I'm going to do—what people always do on the river. Any other questions to ask, Tims?"

"Yes. I should like to know who your friends are."

Mildred laughed nervously.

"You won't be any the wiser if I tell you." And in the instant she reflected that what she said was true. "I am going to the Gorings'."

The difference between that and the exact truth was only the difference between the plural and the singular.

"Don't go, old girl," said Tims, earnestly. "Come back to Tony with me and wait till Ian comes home."

Mildred was very pale behind the heavy black lace of her veil and her heart beat hard; but she spoke with self-possession.

"Don't be absurd, Tims. Tony is perfectly well, and there's Mr. Goring who is to travel down with me. How can I possibly go back? You're worrying about Milly, I suppose. Well, I'm rather nervous about her myself. I always am when I go away alone. You don't mind my telling them to wire for you if I sleep too long, do you? And you'd come as quick as ever you could? Think how awkward it would be for Milly and for—for the Gorings."

"I'd come right enough," returned Tims, sombrely. "But if you feel like that, don't go."

"I don't feel like that," replied Mildred; "I never felt less like it, or I shouldn't go. Still, one should be prepared for anything that may happen. All the same, I very much doubt that you will ever see your poor friend Milly again, Tims. You must try to forgive me. Now do make haste and go to darling Tony—he's simply longing to have you. I see Mr. Goring has taken our places in the train, and I shall be left behind if I don't go. Good-bye, old Tims."

Mildred kissed Tims's heated, care-distorted face, and turned away to where Goring stood at the book-stall buying superfluous literature. Tims saw him lift his hat gravely to Mildred. It relieved her vaguely to notice that there seemed no warmth or familiarity about their greeting. She turned away towards the Metropolitan Railway, not feeling quite sure whether she had failed in an important mission or merely made a fool of herself.

She found Tony certainly looking bonny, and no more inclined to break his heart about his mother's departure than any other healthy, happy child under like circumstances. Indeed, it may be doubted whether a healthy, happy child, unknowing whence its beatitudes spring, does not in its deepest, most vital moment regard all grown-up people as necessary nuisances. No one came so delightfully near being another child as Mildred; but Tims was a capital playfellow too, a broad comedian of the kind appreciated on the nursery boards.

A rousing game with him and an evening at the theatre with Mr. Fitzalan, distracted Tims's thoughts from her anxieties. But at night she dreamed repeatedly and uneasily of Milly and Mildred as of two separate persons, and of Mr. Goring, whose vivid face seen in the full light of the window at Hampton Court, returned to her in sleep with a distinctness unobtainable in her waking memory.

MARGARET L. WOODS

On the following day her work with Sir James Carus was of absorbing interest, and she came home tired and preoccupied with it. Yet her dreams of the night before recurred in forms at once more confused and more poignant. At two o'clock in the morning she awoke, crying aloud: "I must get Milly back"; and her pillow was wet with tears. For the two following hours she must have been awake, because she heard all the quarters strike from a neighboring church-tower, yet they appeared like a prolonged nightmare. The emotional impression of some forgotten dream remained, and she passed them in an agony of grief for she knew not what, of remorse for having on a certain summer afternoon denied Milly's petition for her assistance, and of intense volition, resembling prayer, for Milly's return.

XXXI

The intense heat of early afternoon quivered on the steep woods which fell to the river opposite the house. The sunlit stream curved under them, moving clear and quiet over depths of brown, tangled water-growths, and along its fringe of gray and green reeds and grasses and creamy plumes of meadow-sweet. The house was not very large. It was square and white; an old wistaria, an old Gloire-de-Dijon, and a newer carmine cluster-rose contended for possession of its surface. Striped awnings were down over all the lower windows and some of the upper. A large lawn, close-shorn and velvety green, as only Thames-side lawns can be, stretched from the house to the river. It had no flower-beds on it, but a cedar here, an ilex there, dark and substantial on their own dark shadows, and trellises and pillars overrun by a flood of roses of every shade, from deep crimson to snow white. The lawn was surrounded by shrubberies and plantations, and beyond it there was nothing to be seen except the opposite woods and the river, and sometimes boats passing by with a measured sound of oars in the rowlocks, or the temporary commotion of a little steam-launch. It looked a respectable early Victorian house, but it had never been quite that, for it had been built by George Goring's father fifty years earlier, and he himself had spent much of his boyhood there.

Everything and every one seemed asleep, except a young man in flannels with a flapping hat hanging over his eyes, who stood at the end of a punt and pretended to fish. There was no one to look at him or at the house behind him, and if there had been observers, they would not have guessed that they were looking at the Garden of Eden and that he was Adam. Only last evening he and that fair Eve of his had stood by the river in the moonlight, where the shattering hawthorn-bloom made the air heavy with sweetness, and had spoken to each other of this their exquisite, undreamed-of happiness. There had been a Before, there would be an After, when they must stand on their defence against the world, must resist a thousand importunities, heart-breaking prayers, to return to the old, false, fruitless existence.

But just for these days they could be utterly alone in their paradise, undisturbed even by the thoughts of others, since no one knew they were there and together. Alas! they had been so only forty-eight hours, and already a cold little serpent of anxiety had crept in among their roses.

MARGARET L. WOODS

Before entrusting herself to him, Mildred had told him that, in spite of her apparent good health, she was occasionally subject to long trance-like fits, resembling sleep; should this happen, it would be useless to call an ordinary doctor, but that a Miss Timson, a well-known scientific woman and a friend of hers, must be summoned at once. He had taken Miss Timson's address and promised to do so; but Mildred had not seemed to look upon the fit as more than a remote contingency. Perhaps the excitement, the unconscious strain of the last few days had upset her nerves; for this morning she had lain in what he had taken for a natural sleep, until, finding her still sleeping profoundly at noon, he had remembered her words and telegraphed to Miss Timson. An answer to his telegram, saying that Miss Timson would come as soon as possible, lay crumpled up at the bottom of the punt.

The serpent was there, but Goring did not allow its peeping coils thoroughly to chill his roses. His temperament was too sanguine, he felt too completely steeped in happiness, the weather was too beautiful. Most likely Mildred would be all right to-morrow.

Meantime, up there in the shaded room, she who had been Mildred began to stir in her sleep. She opened her eyes and gazed through the square window, at the sunlit awning that overhung it, and at the green leaves and pale buds of the Gloire-de-Dijon rose. There was a hum of bees close by that seemed like the voice of the hot sunshine. It should have been a pleasant awakening, but Milly awoke from that long sleep of hers with a brooding sense of misfortune. The remembrance of the afternoon when she had so suddenly been snatched away returned to her, but it was not the revelation of Ian's passionate love for her supplanter that came back to her as the thing of most importance. Surely she must have known that long before, for now the pain seemed old and dulled from habit. It was the terrible strength with which the Evil Spirit had possessed her, seizing her channels of speech even while she was still there, hurling her from her seat without waiting for the passivity of sleep. No, her sense of misfortune was not altogether, or even mainly, connected with that last day of hers. Unlike Mildred, she had up till now been without any consciousness of things that had occurred during her quiescence, and she had now no vision; only a strong impression that something terrible had befallen Ian.

She looked around the bedroom, and it seemed to her very strange; something like an hotel room, yet at once too sumptuous and too shabby. There was a faded pink flock wall-paper with a gilt pattern upon it, the chairs were gilded and padded and covered with worn pink damask, the bed was gilded and hung with faded pink silk curtains. Everywhere there was pink and gilding, and everywhere it was old and faded and rubbed. A few early Victorian lithographs hung on the walls, portraits of ballet-dancers and noblemen with waists and whiskers. No one had tidied the room since the night before, and fine underclothing was flung carelessly about on chairs, a fussy petticoat here, the bodice of an evening dress there; everywhere just that touch of mingled daintiness and disorder which by this time Milly recognized only too well.

The bed was large, and some one else had evidently slept there besides herself, for the sheet and pillow were rumpled and there was a half-burnt candle and a man's watch-chain on the small table beside it. Wherever she was then, Ian was there too, so that she was at a loss to understand her own sinister foreboding.

She pulled at the bell-rope twice.

There were only three servants in the house; a housekeeper and two maids, who all dated from the days of Mrs. Maria Idle, ex-mistress of the late Lord Ipswich, dead herself now some six months. The housekeeper was asleep, the maids out of hearing. She opened the door and found a bathroom opposite her bedroom. It had a window which showed her a strip of lawn with flower-beds upon it, beyond that shrubberies and tall trees which shut out any farther view. A hoarse cuckoo was crying in the distance, and from the greenery came a twittering of birds and sometimes a few liquid pipings; but there was no sound of human life. The place seemed as empty as an enchanted palace in a fairy story.

Milly's toilet never took her very long. She put on a fresh, simple cotton dress, which seemed to have been worn the day before, and was just hesitating as to whether she should go down or wait for Ian to come, when Clarkson, the housekeeper, knocked at her door.

"I thought if you was awake, madam, you might like a bit of lunch," she said.

Milly refused, for this horrible feeling of depression and anxiety made her insensible to hunger. She looked at the housekeeper with a certain surprise, for Clarkson was as decorated and as much the worse for wear as the furniture of the bedroom. She was a large, fat woman, laced into a brown cashmere dress, with a cameo brooch on her ample bosom; her hair was unnaturally black, curled and dressed high on the top of her head, she had big gold earrings, and a wealth of powder on her large, red face.

"Can you tell me where I am likely to find Mr. Stewart?" asked Milly, politely.

The woman stared, and when she answered there was more than a shade of insolence in her coarse voice and smile.

"I'm sure I can't tell, madam. Mr. Stewart's not our gentleman here."

Milly, understanding the reply as little as the housekeeper had understood the question, yet felt that some impertinence was intended and turned away.

There was nothing for it but to explore on her own account. A staircase of the dull Victorian kind led down to a dark, cool hall. The front door was open. She walked to it and stood under a stumpy portico, looking out. The view was much the same as that seen from the bathroom, only that instead of grass and flower-beds there was a gravel sweep, and, just opposite the front door, a circle of grass with a tall monkey-puzzle tree in the centre. Except for the faded gorgeousness of the bedroom, the house looked like an ordinary country house, belonging to old people who did not care to move with the times. Why should she feel at every step a growing dread of what might meet her there?

She turned from the portico and opened, hesitatingly, the door of a room on the opposite side of the hall. It was a drawing-room, with traces of the same shabby gorgeousness that prevailed in the bedroom, but mitigated by a good deal of clean, faded chintz; and at one end was a brilliant full-length Millais portrait of Mrs. Maria Idle in blue silk and a crinoline. It was a long room, pleasant in the dim light; for although it had three windows, the farthest a French one and open, all were covered with awnings, coming low down and showing nothing of the outer world but a hand's breadth of turf and wandering bits of creeper. It was sweet with flowers, and on a consol table before a mirror stood a high vase from which waved and twined tall sprays and long streamers of cluster-roses, carmine and white. It was beautiful, yet Milly turned away from it almost with a shudder. She recognized the touch of the hand that must have set the roses there. And the nameless horror grew upon her.

Except for the flowers, there was little sign of occupation in the room. A large round rosewood table was set with blue glass vases on mats and some dozen photograph—albums and gift-books, dating from the sixties. But on a stool in a corner lay a newspaper; and the date on it gave her a shock. She had supposed herself to have been away about four months; she found she had been gone sixteen. There had been plenty of time for a misfortune to happen, and she felt convinced that it had happened. But what? If Ian or Tony were dead she would surely still be in mourning. Then on a little rosewood escritoire, such as ladies were wont to use when they had nothing to write, she spied an old leather writing-case with the initials M. B. F. upon it. It was one Aunt Beatrice had given her when she first went to Ascham, and it seemed to look on her pleasantly, like the face of an old friend. She found a few letters in the pockets, among them one from Ian written from Berlin a few days before, speaking of his speedy return and of Tony's amusing letter from the sea-side. She began to hope her feeling of anxiety and depression might be only the shadow of the fear and anguish which she had suffered on that horrible afternoon sixteen months ago. She must try not to think about it, must try to be bright for Ian's sake. Some one surely was with her at this queer place, since she was sharing a room with another person—probably a female friend of that Other's, who had such a crowd of them.

She drew the awning half-way up and stood on the step outside the French window. The lawn, the trees, the opposite hills were unknown to her, but the spirit of the river spoke to her familiarly, and she knew it for the Thames. A gardener in shirt-sleeves was filling a water-barrel by the river, under a hawthorn-tree, and the young man in the punt was putting up his fishing-tackle. As she looked, the strangeness of the scene passed away. She could not say where it was, but in some dream or vision she had certainly seen this lawn, that view, before; when the young man turned and came nearer she would know his face. And the dim, horrible thing that was waiting for her somewhere about the quiet house, the quiet garden, seemed to draw a step nearer, to lift its veil a little. Who was it that had stood not far from where the gardener was standing now, and seen the moon hanging large and golden over the mystery of the opposite woods? Whoever it was, some one's arm had been fast around her and there had been kisses—kisses.

It took but a few seconds for these half-revelations to drop into her mind, and before she had had time to reflect upon them, the young man in the punt looked up and saw her standing there on the step. He took off his floppy hat and waved it to her; then he put down his tackle, ran to the near end of the punt and jumped lightly ashore. He came up the green lawn, and her anxiety sent her down to meet him almost as eagerly as love would have done. The hat shaded all the upper part of his face, and at a distance, in the strong sunshine, the audacious chin, the red lower lip, caught her eye first and seemed to extinguish the rest of the face. And suddenly she disliked them. Who was the man, and how did she come to know him? But former experiences of strange awakenings had made her cautious, self-controlling, almost capable of hypocrisy.

"So you're awake!" shouted George, still a long way down the lawn. "Good! How are you? All right?"

She nodded "Yes," with a constrained smile.

In a minute they had met, he had turned her around, and with his arm under hers was leading her towards the house again.

"All right? Really all right?" he asked very softly, pressing her arm with his hand and stooping his head to bring his mouth on a level with her ear.

"Very nearly, at any rate," she answered, coldly, trying to draw away from him.

"What are you doing that for?" he asked. "Afraid of shocking the gardener, eh? What queer little dear little ways you've got! I suppose Undines are like that."

He drew her closer to him as he threw back his head and laughed a noisy laugh that jarred upon her nerves.

Milly began to feel indignant. It was just possible that a younger sister in Australia might have married and brought this extraordinary young man home to England, but his looks, his tone, were not fraternal; and she had never forgotten the Maxwell Davison episode. She walked on stiffly.

"Every one seems to be out," she observed, as calmly as she could.

He frowned.

"You mean those devils of servants haven't been looking after you?" he asked. "Yet I gave Clarkson her orders. Of course they're baggages, but I haven't had the heart to send them away from the old place, for who on earth would take them? I expect we aren't improving their chances, you and I, at this very moment; in spite of respecting the gardener's prejudices."

He chuckled, as at some occult joke of his own.

They stooped together under the half-raised awning of the French window, and entered the dim, flower-scented drawing-room side by side. The young man threw off his hat, and she saw the silky ripple of his nut-brown hair, his smooth forehead, his bright-glancing hazel eyes, all the happy pleasantness of his countenance. Before she had had time to reconsider her dislike of him, he had caught her in his arms and kissed her hair and face, whispering little words of love between the kisses. For one paralyzed moment Milly suffered these dreadful words, these horrible caresses. Then exerting the strength of frenzy, she pushed him from her and bounded to the other side of the room, entrenching herself behind the big rosewood table with its smug mats and vases and albums.

"You brute! you brute! you hateful cad!" she stammered with trembling lips; "how dare you touch me?"

George Goring stared at her with startled eyes.

"Mildred! Dearest! Good God! What's gone wrong?"

"Where's my husband?" she asked, in a voice sharp with anger and terror. "I want to go—I must leave this horrid place at once."

"Your husband?"

It was Goring's turn to feel himself plunged into the midst of a nightmare, and he grew almost as pale as Milly. How in Heaven's name was he going to manage her? She looked very ill and must of course be delirious. That would have been alarming in any case, and this particular form of delirium was excruciatingly painful.

"Yes, my husband—where is he? I shall tell him how you've dared to insult me. I must go. This is your house—I must leave it at once."

Goring did not attempt to come near her. He spoke very quietly.

"Try and remember, Mildred; Stewart is not here. He will not even be in England till to-morrow. You are alone with me. Hadn't you better go to bed again and—" he was about to say, "wait until Miss Timson comes," but as it was possible that the advent of the person she had wished him to summon might now irritate her, he substituted—"and keep quiet? I promise not to come near you if you don't wish to see me."

"I am alone here with you?" Milly repeated, slowly, and pressed her hand to her forehead. "Good God," she moaned to herself, "what can have happened?"

"Yes. For Heaven's sake, go and lie down. I expect the doctor can give you something to soothe your nerves and then perhaps you'll remember."

She made a gesture of fierce impatience.

"You think I'm mad, but I'm not. I have been mad and I am myself again; only I can't remember anything that's happened since I went out of my mind. I insist upon your telling me. Who are you? I never saw you before to my knowledge."

Her voice, her attitude were almost truculent as she faced him, her right hand dragging at the loose clasp of a big photograph album. Every word, every look, was agony to Goring, but he controlled himself by an effort.

"I am George Goring," he said, slowly, and paused with anxious eyes fixed upon her, hoping that the name might yet stir some answering string of tenderness in the broken lyre of her mind.

She too paused, as though tracking some far-off association with the name. Then:

"Ah! poor Lady Augusta's husband," she repeated, yet sterner than before in her anger. "My friend Lady Augusta's husband! And why am I here alone with you, Mr. Goring?"

"Because I am your lover, Mildred. Because I love you better than any one or any thing in the world; and yesterday you thought you loved me, you thought you could trust all your life to me."

She had known the answer already in her heart, but the fact stated plainly by another, became even more dreadful, more intolerable, than before. She uttered a low cry and covered her eyes with her hand.

"Mildred—dearest!" he breathed imploringly.

Then she raised her head and looked straight at him with flaming eyes, this fair, fragile creature transformed into a pitiless Fury. She forgot that indeed an Evil Spirit had dwelt within her; George Goring might be victim rather than culprit. In this hour of her anguish the identity of that body of hers, which through him was defiled, that honor of hers, yes and of Ian Stewart's, which through him was dragged in the dust, made her no longer able to keep clearly in mind the separateness of the Mildred Stewart of yesterday from herself.

"I tell you I was mad," she gasped; "and you—you vile, wicked man!— you took advantage of it to ruin my life—to ruin my husband's life! You must know Ian Stewart, a man whose shoes you are not fit to tie. Do you think any woman in her senses would leave him for you? Ah!—" she breathed a long, shuddering breath and her hand was clinched so hard upon the loose album clasp that it ran into her palm.

"Mildred!" cried George, staggered, stricken as though by some fiery rain.

"I ought to be sorry for your wife," she went on. "She is a splendid woman, she has done nothing to deserve that you should treat her so scandalously. But I can't—I can't"—a dry sob caught her voice—"be sorry for any one except myself and Ian. I always knew I wasn't good enough to be his wife, but I was so proud of it—so proud—and now—Oh, it's too horrible! I'm not fit to live."

George had sunk upon a chair and hidden his face in his hands.

"Don't say that," he muttered hoarsely, almost inaudibly. "It was my doing."

She broke out again.

"Of course it was. It's nothing to you, I suppose. You've broken my husband's heart and mine too; you've hopelessly disgraced us both and spoiled our lives; and all for the sake of a little amusement, a little low pleasure. We can't do anything, we can't punish you; but if curses were any use, oh, how I could curse you, Mr. Goring!"

The sobs rising in a storm choked her voice. She rushed from the room, closing the door behind her and leaving George Goring there, his head on his hands. He sat motionless, hearing nothing but the humming silence of the hot afternoon.

Milly, pressing back her tears, flew across the hall and up the stairs. The vague nightmare thing that had lurked for her in the shadows of the house, when she had descended them so quietly, had taken shape at last. She knew now the unspeakable secret of the pink and gold bedroom, the shabbily gorgeous bed, the posturing dancers, the simpering, tailored noblemen. The atmosphere of it, scented and close, despite the open window, seemed to take her by the throat. She dared not stop to think, lest this sick despair, this loathing of herself, should master her. To get home at once was her impulse, and she must do it before any one could interfere.

It was a matter of a few seconds to find a hat, gloves, a parasol. She noticed a purse in the pocket of her dress and counted the money in it. There was not much, but enough to take her home, since she felt sure the river shimmering over there was the Thames. She did not stay to change her thin shoes, but flitted down the stairs and out under the portico, as silent as a ghost. The drive curved through a shrubbery, and in a minute she was out of sight of the house. She hurried past the lodge, hesitating in which direction to turn, when a tradesman's cart drove past. She asked the young man who was driving it her way to the station, and he told her it was not very far, but that she could not catch the next train to town if she meant to walk. He was going in that direction himself and would give her a lift if she liked. She accepted the young man's offer; but if he made it in order to beguile the tedium of his way, he was disappointed.

The road was dusty and sunny, and this gave her a reason for opening her large parasol. She cowered under it, hiding herself from the women who rolled by in shiny carriages with high-stepping horses; not so much because she feared she might meet acquaintances, as from an instinctive desire to hide herself, a thing so shamed and everlastingly wretched, from every human eye. And so it happened that, when she was close to the station, she missed seeing and being seen by Tims, who was driving to Mr. Goring's house in a hired trap which he had sent to meet her.

XXXII

Milly took a ticket for Paddington and hurried to the train, which was waiting at the platform, choosing an empty compartment. Action had temporarily dulled the passion of her misery, her rage, her shuddering horror at herself. But alone in the train, it all returned upon her, only with a complete realization of circumstance which made it worse.

It had been her impulse to rush to her home, to her husband, as for refuge. Now she perceived that there was no refuge for her, no comfort in her despair, but rather another ordeal to be faced. She would have to tell her husband the truth, so far as she knew it. Good God! Why could she not shake off from her soul the degradation, the burning shame of this fair flesh of hers, and return to him with some other body, however homely, which should be hers and hers alone? She remembered that the man she loathed had said that Ian would not be back in England until to-morrow. She supposed the Evil Thing had counted on stealing home in time to meet him, and would have met him with an innocently smiling face.

A moment Milly triumphed in the thought that it was she herself who would meet Ian and reveal to him the treachery of the creature who had supplanted her in his heart. Then with a shudder she hid her face, remembering that it was, after all, her own dishonor and his which she must reveal. He would of course take her back, and if that could be the end, they might live down the thing together. But it would not be the end. "I am the stronger," that Evil Thing had said, and it was the stronger. At first step by step, now with swift advancing strides, it was robbing her of the months, the years, till soon, very soon, while in the world's eyes she seemed to live and thrive, she would be dead; dead, without a monument, without a tear, her very soul not free and in God's hands, but held somewhere in abeyance. And Ian? Through what degradation, to what public shame would he, the most refined and sensitive of men, be dragged! His child—her child and Ian's—would grow up like that poor wretched George Goring, breathing corruption, lies, dishonor, from his earliest years. And she, the wife, the mother, would seem to be guilty of all that, while she was really bound, helpless—dead.

The passion of her anger and despair stormed through her veins again with yet greater violence, but this time George Goring was forgotten and all its waves broke impotently against that adversary whose diabolical power she was so impotent to resist, who might return to-morrow, to-day for aught she knew.

She had been moving restlessly about the compartment, making vehement gestures in her desperation, but now a sudden, terrible, yet calming idea struck her to absolute quietness. There was a way, just one, to thwart this adversary; she could destroy the body into which it thought to return. At the same moment there arose in her soul two opposing waves of emotion—one of passionate self-pity to think that she, so weak and timid, should be driven to destroy herself; the other of triumph over her mortal foe delivered into her hands. She felt a kind of triumph too in the instantaneousness with which she was able to make up her mind that this was the only thing to be done—she, usually so full of mental and moral hesitation. Let it be done quickly—now, while the spur of excitement pricked her on. The Thing seemed to have a knowledge of her experiences which was not reciprocal. How it would laugh if it recollected in its uncanny way, that she had wanted to kill herself and it with her, that she had had it at her mercy and then had been too weak and cowardly to strike! Should she buy some poison when she reached Paddington? She knew nothing about poisons and their effects, except that carbolic caused terrible agony, and laudanum was not to be trusted unless you knew the dose. The train was slowing up and the lonely river gleamed silverly below. It beckoned to her, the river, upon whose stream she had spent so many young, happy days.

She got out at the little station and walked away from it with a quick, light step, as though hastening to keep some pleasurable appointment. After all the years of weak, bewildered subjection, of defeat and humiliation, her turn had come; she had found the answer to the Sphinx's riddle, the way to victory.

She knew the place where she found herself, for she had several times made one of a party rowing down from Oxford to London. But it was not one of the frequented parts of the river, being a quiet reach among solitary meadows. She remembered that there was a shabby little house standing by itself on the bank where boats could be hired, for they had put in there once to replace an oar, having lost one down a weir in the neighborhood. The weir had not been on the main stream, but they had come upon it in exploring a backwater. It could not be far off.

She walked quickly along the bank, turning over and over in her mind the same thoughts; the cruel wrong which now for so many years she had suffered, the final disgrace brought upon her and her husband, and she braced her courage to strike the blow that should revenge all. The act to which this fair-haired, once gentle woman was hurrying along the lonely river-bank, was not in its essence suicide; it was revenge, it was murder.

When she came to the shabby little house where the boats lay under an unlovely zinc-roofed shed, she wondered whether she might ask for ink and paper and write to some one. She longed to send one little word to Ian; but then what could she say? She could not have seen him and concealed the truth from him, but it was one of the advantages of her disappearance that he need never know the dishonor done him. And she knew he considered suicide a cowardly act. He was quite wrong there. It was an act of heroic courage to go out like this to meet death. It was so lonely; even lonelier than death must always be. She had the conviction that she was not doing wrong, but right. Hers was no common case. And for the first time she saw that there might be a reason for this doom which had befallen her. Men regard one sort of weakness as a sin to be struggled against, another as something harmless, even amiable, to be acquiesced in. But perhaps all weakness acquiesced in was a sin in the eyes of Eternal Wisdom, was at any rate to be left to the mercy of its own consequences. She looked back upon her life and saw herself never exerting her own judgment, always following in some one else's tracks, never fighting against her physical, mental, moral timidity. It was no doubt this weakness of hers that had laid her open to the mysterious curse which she was now, by a supreme effort of independent judgment and physical courage, resolved to throw off.

A stupid-looking man in a dirty cotton shirt got out the small boat she chose; stared a minute in surprise to see the style in which she, an Oxford girl born and bred, handled the sculls, and then went in again to continue sleeping off a pint of beer.

She pulled on mechanically, with a long, regular stroke, and one by one scenes, happy river-scenes out of past years, came back to her with wonderful vividness. Looking about her she saw an osier-bed dividing the stream, and beside it the opening into the willow-shaded backwater which she remembered. She turned the boat's head into it. Heavy clouds had rolled up and covered the sky, and there was a kind of twilight between the dark water and the netted boughs overhead. Very soon she heard the noise of a weir. Once such a sound had been pleasant in her ears; but now it turned her cold with fear. On one side

MARGARET L. WOODS

the backwater flowed sluggishly on around the osier-bed; on the other it hurried smoothly, silently away, to broaden suddenly before it swept in white foam over an open weir into a deep pool below. She trembled violently and the oars moved feebly in her hands, chill for all the warmth of the afternoon. Her boat was in the stream which led to the weir, but not yet fully caught by the current. A few more strokes and the thing would be done, she would be carried quickly on and over that dancing, sparkling edge into the deep pool below. Her courage failed, could not be screwed to the sticking-point; she hung on the oars, and the boat, as if answering to her thought, stopped, swung half around. As she held the boat with the oars and closed her eyes in an anguish of hesitation and terror, a strange convulsion shook her, such as she had felt once before, and a low cry, not her own, broke from her lips.

"No—no!" they uttered, hoarsely.

The Thing was there then, awake to its danger, and in another moment might snatch her from herself, return laughing at her cowardice, to that house by the river. She pressed her lips hard together, and silently, with all the strength of her hate and of her love, bent to the oars. The little boat shot forward into mid-stream, the current seized it and swept it rapidly on towards the dancing edge of water. She dropped the sculls and a hoarse shriek broke from her lips; but it was not she who shrieked, for in her heart was no fear, but triumph—triumph as of one who is at length avenged of her mortal enemy.

In the darkened drawing-room, the room so full of traces of all that had been exquisite in Mildred Stewart, Ian mourned alone. Presently the door opened a little, and a tall, slender, childish figure in a white smock, slipped in and closed it gently behind him. Tony stole up to his father and stood between his knees. He looked at Ian, silent, pale, large-eyed. That a grown-up person and a man should shed tears was strange, even portentous, to him.

"Won't Mummy come back, not ever?" asked the child at last, piteously, in a half whisper.

"No, never, Tony; Mummy won't ever come back. She's gone—gone for always."

The child looked in his father's eyes strangely, penetratingly.

"Which Mummy?" he asked.

THE END

A Note About the Author

Margaret L. Woods (1855–1945) was an English author known for her novels and poetry. As the daughter of a famed scholar, Woods and her sister, Mabel Birchenough, who was also a writer, received a quality education to nurture their writing career. In 1879, she married Henry George Woods, who later became the President of Trinity College in Oxford and was elected the Master of the Temple, a high honor. The couple had one child. Woods wrote for many different genres, including nonfiction, children's literature, fiction, and poetry. Her poem *Genuis Loci* is considered to be among the most influential and popular poems of her time.

A Note from the Publisher

Discover more of your favorite classics with Bookfinity™.

- Track your reading with custom book lists.
- Get great book recommendations for your personalized Reader Type.
- Add reviews for your favorite books.
- AND MUCH MORE!

Visit **bookfinity.com** and take the fun Reader Type quiz to get started.

Enjoy our classic and modern companion pairings!